MW00478003

Gangster Manqué: The Saga of Mayhem Jefferson

A Novel by C. Spencer Taylor

Gangster Manqué: The Saga of Mayhem Jefferson

© 2021 by **C. Spencer Taylor**

All rights reserved. No portion of this book may be reproduced, stored in a retrieval system, or transmitted in any form or by any means – electronic mechanical, photocopy, recording, scanning, or other – except for brief quotations in critical reviews or articles, without the prior written permission of the publisher.

Published by Blockhouse Publishing
blockhousepublishing@gmail.com

Publishing Adviser: AdvisedByAmber.com

Photographer: Mark Sullivan

Printed in the United States of America

ISBN-10: 978-0-9913006-0-0

Warning: This book contains profane language and dialogue and depictions of violent actions and episodes. This is a work of fiction not to be attributed to any particular event or person. All names, events, and happenings are fiction. This book is for mature audiences. It includes images and depictions of sociological themes often apparent in distressed communities. This is urban fiction with a reality some might consider risqué.

C. SPENCER TAYLOR was born and raised in Detroit, Michigan. A social scientist, he has always been a voracious reader and writer. His background and experiences inform the subtext of this urban parable and allows Taylor to improvise an allegory for some. One claims a utopian existence. Taylor proclaims an upsetting dystopian culture within the tapestry of America.

Dedication

To my mother, Mae Taylor. I live by the mantra you gave me and Al –

"We are not raising you for ourselves. We raise you both for society."

It was her love for children. Mae showed her love for young girls. She needed nothing to make those girls a baseball team or take them swimming. Her vision was that they were loved and valued.

Mae Taylor - Community Mother.

CONTENTS

ACKNOWLEDGEMENTS

This book has been in the making for the last century. Seriously. I want to apologize up front. In the streets, I've done countless interviews, and reviewed a variety of street intelligence, and I am thankful to everyone I have met along the way. It's evident that the third city is invisible to America but it has never been invisible to me. The lives, daily intersectional factors are visible within a sociological context. I simply cannot thank every person, neighborhood, school, business, and government institutions. To the holy men and women who represent organized religion - be they, Pastors, Imams, Priests, and Baba's. I thank everyone that has assisted me, prayed, or assembled and kept a spirit of goodwill. There are folks who have meant the difference in transforming me from the academic towers to the ground level of an aspiring authorship of a subtext that is based within a complicated maze of social science. The intersections, interrelationships and my own transcendental vision is telling a world that those who seem invisible are hardly invisible. The following are people who have contributed much directly to this ongoing tour de force.

My dear sister and friend, the late Professor Donna Bruton - my muse. She alone triggered my writing all around. Grateful forever. Dr. George Fleming. Dr. James and Mrs. Angie Brown Weathers, Mrs. Terrie Weathers Henderson and Dr. Maurice Henderson. Barristers, Brunetta Brandy and Gerald Evelyn. Community activist Ed Sanders, Joyce Dixon, Yusef B. Shakur, Bilal Nakoor, and Frank McGhee. To all the community leaders, block clubs, associations that are working daily for the good of their constituents well- being. The leadership of Northwest Activities Center, Ronald Roosevelt Lockett. Ethel Warren and the Warren Family. I could not name all of those that have contributed to the understanding of how Detroit families and communities work together.

1

Acknowledgements

Gratitude to both my family and extended families. Florene McGlo-thian-Taylor, Gene Spencer Taylor II, Shawn Taylor Moore, Leron Moore, Darlene Lynch, Andy Lynch, Virgil A. Taylor II, Braydon, Bryce, them Moore Boys. Tall young Nephew Cameron Brown-Taylor, niece Ashely Brown, Roz Everett and the Everett Clan - all of them. Grateful for all my nephews, adopted, adapted, along with my nieces too. The family is critical. Love to all those that are struggling every-day...Peacefully. My first family of President Clifton R. Wharton, Jr., First Lady Dolores Wharton and Professor Bruce Wharton.

My beloved Detroit Public School past. To Crossman Elementary, Roosevelt Elementary, Durfee Junior High, Central High. Much love. Thanks to all the educators and students from the old neighbor-hoods. Again, too many to name. Much love to the old classes of 63, 64,65,66 and 67 at Trailblazers Hall of Fame. The brilliant Babas, Umar Hassan, Wesley Anderson, Bro James, the late Otha Williams, and the late Horace Cartwright. So many to remember. Love them all. Yes there are influencers in this story. All of my stories include that village of the big CE. Betty Ware, Mike Hood, Rod Wallace, the Mo-reland Brothers, Saffords, Andrew Smith, Joetter Smith, Floyd Smith, John Pickett, Deb Jackson, The Hughes Sisters, The Tyler Family, Di-ane, Pat, June, Daddy Buddy and my second Mother, Ida Tyler. ALL the Central Teachers, Counselors, Clarence Tamoor, Mr. McGregor, theater guru Robert Riley, classmates, schoolmates Robert Boseman, Kenneth Carreathers, Melvin Bankston, Kevin Threatt, Sheila Hankins, Lois Hankins, Marcia McDonald and those who have passed too.

To Sparta, Gary Wilson, Steve Heinrich, Bill Blackwell - MSU for real real and my early days in East Lansing. All those in the Divine 9, Quinton Hedrick, the Midwest Shooting Club for providing backup security while I went too deep into the deep abyss of the third city. Especially my personal advisers who prayed and meditated for our projects that the world ignored despite the truth. Randall Nichols, Jordan Isaiah, Brandon Prince and Jordan Abrahams, Hollis, Will Nakian, Phil Lewis and all of my former students at all the places I dropped a visit. The fantastic techno players - especially cool Kyle Banks, emergency professional on all those technology questions. So-lo praise for the artful, descriptive and interpretation by the Michael "Mike" Griffin who took the portrait commission there. He did Mayhem Jefferson - the visual art piece from the actual story. Thanks to my technical advisor Mztisha Johnson and my old ally Dragana Millson, Thank you.

Love my Brother William Sparks and the lovely Valerie Safford Sparks, the ultimate promotional genius. My special force player La Mont Muhammad, along with Black Benny, Curious George, Debbie Death and my street mother, Black Margie. The whole MSUBA - Charles Smith, Sherman Eaton, Paris Ross, Lural Baltimore, Chief Marlon Lynch at MSU, Chief Anthony Holt, WSU, and Lillian Cunningham who explained the whole black woman police experience for real real.

Big shout, silent applause for my one and only Brother. Virgil Al Taylor, my consigliere, right hand, anchor of the Taylor Airship. You reflect a lifetime of moments that navigate success, happiness and Love. FOREVER.

My long list of scholars begins with Rich Lerner of Tufts, and the entire MSU sociology department. Professor Tom Dietz, a renowned environmental scholar has always supported our work. Likewise, Professor Linda Kalof who is a renowned scholar of animal studies. Whether fictional or non-fiction, discussion, and research of environmental issues have benefited from Tom Dietz. Likewise, Linda Kalof, brings both advocacy and activism to her scholarship that details the horrid culture of dog fighting and animal abuse Gratitude for all of my colleagues and citizens around the world who lend their expertise. My deepest appreciation of MSU History Professor Nwando Achebe. Her prolific scholarship in Africa is on the cutting edge. This incredible scholar brings leadership to our black female projects. Her scholarship is bringing a newfound understanding of Africa, African women, the nexus to African American culture. This is one of the finest scholars lending her assistance to out reaching communities within a truly world community. Thank you for all the knowledge and expertise shared. My gratitude to the Spartans Alicia Nails, Sharon Williams, Michelle Burkett, and Denise Mujahid who during their tenure as Black Aides contributed to the fellowship that empowered many MSU students during the Wharton era. I would be remiss if I did not thank all the former black aides, Chicano aides, Asian Pacific Aides during the 70s that propelled the national focus

Acknowledgements

on MSU for its early development of multiculturalism. Rodney Nelson, was one of our leaders and his work in urban communities continues to support constructive communities. Brother Daniel Mujahid is one of those inspirational keepers of the ancestral past. I appreciate and rely on his insights since the last century of the 70s, 80s, 90s, and into the new millennium...

The countless phone calls, nostalgia review about our family history always lead me to the best brother in the world. All of my undertakings have always had him as my co-pilot...Virgil (Al), my consigliere, life long partner, always down; Roz Everett and the Everett Clan. Old Henry Calhoun and Frank Netti. Professor Errol A. Henderson, nephews Virgil Allan Taylor, my sister Darlene Lynch, Randell Nichols, Jordan Abrahams, Brandon Prince. Jakkar Aimey... big thanks to my IT consultant Kyle Banks, he rocks. Mike Griffin – Big Thanks for the illustration of Mayhem Jefferson. The portrait is truly a work of authentic, acutely defined art. I love it...

Dr. Pamela R. Smith, without question ran a tight ship in our research, outreach and all for decades. Appreciate Courtney Minifee for editing, support and the Spanish interpretation for Gangster Manque'; Zakiya Minifee for consultancy on youth culture. My German Brother, Mike Taphouse, Love you and yours. Portia McGiles, the linguist that continually helps me with language. Baba Umar Hassan, Baba Bro James both are that old guard from early old days at Detroit Central along with brilliant military historian Wesley Anderson joined with the likes of homegirl JoAnn Harris and Baller Wesley Martin, they jolt great times in the city in the mid 60s. I was honored to have Barry Michael Cooper, author, filmmaker guide me during the past thirty plus years. Barry and I got together at the behest of the great icon Quincy Jones. He is, in my humble opinion, an insightful sage of black and world historical interactions. Grateful. To Wally Safford, part of Prince's crew and many more...Rock and Roll! Thanks Kenya Abbott, Jr.- one of my best students at MSU. An outrageously talented poet, author, and activist. Her family legacy is generationally powerful. Detroit Redd, as hip hop knows her, put me up with the professional wizardry of Ms. Amber Morson who brought our project to the forefront. She made it work. Grateful. A young one that is going places. Trust me...

The incomparable author Nettie Jones, her expertise in being an excellent author is well rooted in Detroits' early days and her understanding of the cultural landscape in both reading and writing has her landmark books defined as the newness of sexuality, gender and race. Thank you for always urging me to speak.

Sister Eleanor Bentley, her kindness and always a level head. A guardian angel. Blessed.

Finally, my deepest thanks and appreciation for Janice Rowley, one of many Muses in my life. Janice, a firebrand, superb editor, historian, proverbial consultant on public education. She rescued this project leading a team of street experts and third city denizens to make it work. An amazing woman who is the curator of The Gallery. The water in the oasis for me... Not surprised since her father, LeRoy Rowley, remains a major influence. The Rowley family is tops. Aunt Connie, a public health expert and her dear husband allowed their home to be one of my recovery places while in the field. The work and effort of "JRowley", as she is affectionately known by the thousands of Detroit Public School students, is a winner. Shout out to her niece, Tria who works at The White House. Thank you.

For anyone I missed please forgive me. I do appreciate.

INTRODUCTION

This is the parable of a young woman's evolution in the streets of Detroit. Mayhem Jefferson is the gangster who has to fight for street respect. Her journey is one of epic proportions for many urban females. Blood, death, and treachery rule the day as Mayhem counters the distant image of the one-dimensional "good girl." Professor Xavier Long tracks the winding road of Mayhem, who becomes a young aspiring hit woman. She comes from a criminal family described by Professor Long. This tale also includes characters like Pedwell "Peddy" Jefferson, head of the criminal family that is a far cry from traditional. This narrative tells the world of what poverty can become if left unattended.

An anomic tale of the normalization of ignorance and violence, this is what exists when all else has collapsed in urban America. An urban frontier reveals an array of mores, values and counterculture that followed the destruction of once-proud, working-class communities. It is here that Mayhem Jefferson defines the Negro tradition that awaits answers not yet found. This is a story about the people rarely seen beyond the distorted images in the media. Mayhem Jefferson is the tale of a young woman's struggles to fight against everybody, including those that failed to understand the hell of her daily life. Gangster Manqué is an experience taken from reality that is as much non-fiction as it is fiction.

1

ALIEN NATION IN MUTATION

1300 Beaubien
Detroit Police Headquarters
July 4, 2002

The voice is direct, strong and insistent.

"I am here representing Mayhem Jefferson. I want to see my client now." The interview room in the Homicide Division is ugly with faded, dingy, institutional gray walls. The lighting is bright with dirty concrete floors full of coffee stains and other unmentionable gross items. The detectives are standing outside the room in discussion about the young woman sitting at the table inside the room. The heavyset dark-skinned black woman is arguing about her client. The head of Homicide has a bewildered look, as the lawyer is demanding the release of her client.

"It was self defense. She was being raped by all three of them. It was a train. A dog ass gang rape." The Detectives are adamant about the cause of the trio's death. One detective is shaking his head, "I been at this for over eleven years in Homicide and I have never seen nothing like it." The Homicide Chief questions the medical report.

"It's not conclusive. She wouldn't let anyone touch her. No nurse, no social worker, no cops, no doctors, NOBODY!! So, we don't know if it was rape. She won't say nothing to my detectives."
The attorney is livid. She unleashes her true feelings on the whole division.

"You need to thank her. The Detroit Police can't do a damn thing. These rapists out here are preying on women, black women, Spanish women, Arab women, and white women because it's a sport in this city!" Suddenly, the assistant prosecutor walks up to the door of the interview room. Dressed in a black blazer with gray slacks, she sits down at the table with the young woman.

Looking at her with great authority, the prosecutor tells the young girl, "I need to know how this happened. I got three dead men with shotgun wounds." The young woman doesn't say a word. She is motionless, sitting straight up and looking into the eyes of the prosecutor as if she was transparent. Her hair is a spread of thick, reddish brown, curly locks sitting on her head like a crown that is flowing with an aura of cosmic sparkles. Her thick lips seemed to pout with an attitude that suggests a feeling of deep alienation and isolation from that criminal process in homicide. One detective who emerged from the room expressed frustration to the prosecutor with the silent treatment he had been subjected to from the young woman.

"The witness says at least three young girls were taken into that abandoned house at about noon. Lots of screams could be heard. The three men had guns openly showing when the girls went into the house. The witness was in shock when she heard what had happened in that old house."

Taking a sip of coffee, he sighed and continued to give his account of the crime scene.

"I was the first on the scene. The patrol car stopped that girl on the corner of Dexter and Richton. I couldn't believe my eyes. I knew two of the three dead were from the Niggas for Life crew. Those dangerous, killing types were laying dead in the front room. The next thing the witness says happened was that a girl ran across the street, buck naked, crying. Two other girls came out of the house. Then that young girl walked out with a big tote bag and she looked a little ruffled."

The prosecutor takes a call on her cell phone in the hallway. The young woman's attorney is waiting for the prosecutor to get off the phone. More police are gathering in the homicide division as word has gotten out about the dead on Courtland. Whispering, the detective tells the attorney she can talk to her client. The attorney sits down and looks at her client who is smiling a wicked grin. Before the two can talk, the prosecutor knocks on the door. Signaling to the lawyer to come out into the hall, she shows the attorney the crime scene pictures. There is an array of gruesome, hideous, up close shots of the three dead men.

Looking disgusted, the attorney tells the police, "Looks like some rapist got what they deserved." The prosecutor tells her that one of the victims admitted that the men were brutal, describing to the detectives how they were forced to do sexual acts. Smiling, the lawyer for the young woman questions the hold up on her client's release.

"So, what is the problem? It was rape. My client has nothing to say. I think she is still in shock."

The lead detective laughs out loud, "Shock? No, that would be the three dick less wonders she killed."

The prosecutor tells the defense attorney, "I got three severed penises, and one dead man with an up-close shotgun blast up his rectum. Now who did that?"
The lawyer shrugged her shoulders with an uncertain, puzzled look.

"Sorry guys. You don't have any charges against my client. We are leaving. If you want to interview my client, please call."
The prosecutor and the Chief of Homicide are standing in the outer office as the young woman begins to exit the interview room with her attorney.

The Homicide Chief, looking at the young woman with a curious probe asks, "What is your name young woman? Who are you?"
Looking thru the detective, she walks right into his face.

Looking at her super large hands, he feels uncomfortable as she offered, "I am Mayhem Jefferson."

Chapter 1: Alien Nation in Mutation

July 24, 2009

On this hot summer day, the aroma from Floyd Lee's restaurant fills the block. Professor Xavier Long is getting out of his black Ford diesel truck on Mack Avenue. Dr. Long is the Thurgood Marshall Professor of Social Justice at the Detroit College of Urban Ecological Studies based in the heart of downtown Detroit. He is also a Senior Fellow at Frederick Douglass College. Dressed in a beige linen suit, his baldhead reflects the hot sunlight. Floyd Lee's place serves as an oasis for Xavier. During the last several months, his academic meetings seem to be more frequent while the streets, often the subject of his research, seem to be more violent. It had been a fruitful morning that began with several retired professors meeting in East Pyramid, Michigan.

East Pyramid is a small hamlet community between Detroit and Ann Arbor. History says that the community of mixed racial heritage was a source of major support for those traveling through the Underground Railroad during the Civil War. Many of the residents are lifers who are fourth generation, "free black families," as they like to point out. Ironically, Frederick Douglass College was a private school based in East Pyramid. Xavier was always amazed by the feats of that freed slave. Naming a college after Douglass near the Underground Railroad was a decision full of historical implications that most folks didn't realize. Xavier was aware of all of the history that was special and good about colored folks. Frederick Douglass College was a secret of sorts, directly connected to the labor and civil rights movements. The school's leadership had provided assistance and space for meetings of great historical importance. Many civil rights leaders, not only in America but elsewhere, had visited the campus. Perhaps the most famous visit was that of the famed sociologist and activist, W.E.B. Du Bois. Even Dr. DuBois counted on the rich support from the college. Brailsford Fielder, founder Jeremiah Fielder's grandson, had been a close ally of the distinguished scholar. In many ways, the college was really a Think Tank for many of the great social justice activists including Benjamin Mays, A. Phillip Randolph, and Mary McLeod Bethune. The likes of serious Negro businesses found

Douglass College a place to brainstorm. Even New York City's Madame Sinclair of the "The Numbers" business vacationed in the colored resort of Idlewild after stopping off at Douglass College. The late Paul Roberson visited many times. Xavier Long had close relations with the college his entire life since his mother's brother, Virgil Thomas had, at one time, been a board member. The college has been based there since 1923.

The college is renowned for its tradition of African American leadership that had been rooted in the civil rights movement. While small and private, it is well known, in these parts, that there is a strong connection to the big city of Detroit. Theodore Brown, considered both an old head and a legendary sociologist, shared a number of interviews regarding the first colored men who worked in the foundry at the River Rouge Ford Plant in the late 1920's. Xavier marveled at how much historical information the old heads had in their possession. It was especially eye opening for Xavier to have the black historian, Horatio L. Riley, reveal stories about the early days of elite groups of doctors, attorneys, educators, policemen, and colored professional women movements.

Floyd Lee, 87, looked a vibrant 60, and his secret was well known.

"I don't eat that damn pig. I cook it and I sell it. My wife, Lucille made me drop lots of weight after that big scare in '69. I stopped eating that swine in the early 70's. I laid off dat damn whiskey water and took up wine. My oldest girl is a doctor. She's a smart girl, indeed."

Xavier loves Floyd Lees. It allows him to reconnect with the Detroit he knew so well as a younger man. The city that seemed to be disappearing as each day passed. The restaurant is divided into two sections; a large dining area with pictures of Detroit's jazz days and the smaller section called the "sandwich room." The music is definitely the reason Xavier enjoys and gobbles up the essence of this black cultural space and place. The photos that adorn the walls are pictorial stories of how great life used to be. It is the visual presentation of street culture and its royalty. There is even a huge picture of Prophet Jones draped in a white mink coat.

Chapter 1: Alien Nation in Mutation

Xavier remembers his grandmother and Aunt Maralia and their arguments about sissies and preachers. Caught in a trance of nostalgia, suddenly a figure arrives at the red and white-checkered tablecloth. The smell of chicken frying captured his imagination.

The voice suggests, "Excuse me Mr. Professor. Today is Wednesday. The special today is chicken wings with soul-getti. If I am correct, you owe me and the good gentlemen of the Black Oak Chess Club lunch for your bet about that new school policy introduced by that cock-eyed, boot-licking toady. I told ya Doc. So did ole Solomon, Petey and even Mrs. Venus. The Exploiters sent that fool and he is up to NO GOOD. So, pay up young man!"
Old Man River is a retired autoworker and a mentor to Xavier. Professor Long reminds young men during his travels that he has met many mentors during his years of research. River is a wise man, someone that Long appreciates. Old Man River loves books.

That is how Xavier met the street scholar. While he is retired from Chrysler since 1978, it was his shoeshine job at Blues that enabled him to meet Xavier Long. Blues is legendary. It is the best shoeshine spot in the city. For Long, Blues is another place to find black men, old and young, in a harmonious atmosphere spiked with life lessons.

River, a tall gray-haired man of some years, is a voracious reader. In their first encounter, Xavier's book bag was the focus of River's curiosity. In recent years, Blues has become part of the old vs. young opinion bowl. Old Man River reads his books between shoeshines. Blues is safe, so safe it has a small clientele of Caucasians in the early morning that includes police, lawyers, business types and of course, the old black guard; retired black men who have the royal order of attire and grooming.

Across the street from the shoe shine parlor is Brother Akbar, the elder Black Muslim barber. Xavier has said, many times, that there is a wealth of knowledge on Mack Avenue. He continues to believe that the area has a host of places that many of his colleagues, in the Ivory Tower, will never experience since they don't understand their value at all. As Xavier hugs Old Man River, he notices that his tall, rail thin body seemed to be getting smaller. It bothers Xavier because it makes him think that yet another great mentor is slowly slipping away.

Acknowledging that lunch is his payment, the tables are arranged together by a young man with a head full of twisted braids pulled back into a ponytail. Ms. Venus is the owner of Venus Hair, a small salon next door to Floyd Lees. On this day, Ms. Venus is listening as River lectures about the state of affairs in the good city of Detroit. A large picture of Arkansas Mud Tea is placed on the table as the Black Oak Chess Club begins to be seated. There are twelve members of the chess club, including Old Man River.

As the first round of New Orleans fish sausage is set on the table, River sighs in disgust, "I'm telling you, Detroit is in real trouble. These people in this city are not getting this old carpetbagger. That fool is bankrupting all these here schools. Floyd Lee raised all his kids, and at least half his grandchildren in Detroit Public Schools. His children are successful. They is the ants of this community. We got a city full of grasshoppers and the damn destructive locusts. Grasshoppers is lazy. They wait til the snow is here and that's why they get frozen. Waiting til the last minute to do what they should have done last summer."

The words were stinging to Xavier's ears. He didn't like the insect analysis. He understood the anger and mistrust as well as the truth of what his old mentor said and what he meant. Dr. Long was reminded of the skulls piled high in the outer villages of the Rwandan landscape after the holocaust that left a world looking but not helping until thousands of innocent people, including little children, died in the whirlpool of ignorance and violence. While the ant analogy was accurate, America did not seem to comprehend the legacy of hard work left in its wake. The real scary thing for Xavier was the precise description of the deadly locusts. Old Man River was like John The Baptist in the wilderness. Warning the world, like a prophet, River asserted that the new policies in the city, especially the absence of a strong public education doctrine, would give rise to a nationalism of ignorant, uneducated denizens from the new D-Troit, or the Third City.

2

THE DARK PAST

London, England
3 months later

Xavier looked at the rain on the runway at Heathrow Airport. He thought about how England seemed to have clouds and rain all the time. It was the last departure from a foreign airport on a trip that had taken him to more than one foreign country. Long was thinking about the irony of how he would have preferred to be leaving from Israel instead of Great Britain. The Israeli's security was intimidating and comforting at the same time, if you understood that nothing was getting past their elite security system. The British were pretentiously fussy despite the fact that they had yet to find any relief from the memory of the notorious Shoe Bomber.

Dr. Long's group of graduate students had spent over a month studying youth who participated in the Intifada against the government of Israel. Long was proud that he was a part of a leadership institute that was responsible for bringing a multi-cultural team of college students, faculty, high school teachers, and students to foreign countries all over the globe. Xavier was listening to a conversation Detroit Public School teacher Marion Tubman was having with a student.

Tubman, a petite woman, directed a small cadre of excellent high school students who were participants in a leadership institute that required them to travel to a foreign country. This group of students had already been admitted into college. Ms. Tubman lectured about the historical issues of the communes in Israel and the Madrassas in the Middle East. Marion Tubman came from a well to do, upper middle-class family. Her participation in the journey abroad was pivotal in breaking down the wall of negativity laid on the public schools and the people from urban places. Marion Tubman looked not much older than her students. While in her early thirties, she still displayed the athletic body of a world-class hurdler. Her short brown hair had several strands of gray. Her piercing brown eyes seemed to hypnotize her students whenever she decided she needed their complete undivided attention. Tubman, a former track star in high school and college, led the way to demand that Detroit youth be allowed to participate in an out of the country experience. Political winds were high with resistance in the ghetto schools and by some involved with the project. Xavier had studied Detroit in his on-going research on youth violence, gangs and global cities. Detroit was hardly accepted as anything but "that place from hell." It was Professor Long's political power that had made it possible for several of Ms. Tubman's special students from Detroit to participate in this project.

One young girl was of special interest to Xavier. This student observed the airport with the same wide-eyes she had observed everything else on the excursion. Long smiled at the lively conversation in the terminal between Marion and Revemba Masekela; a graduate student from the College of Urban Ecological Studies. Masekela was a loyal and dedicated student of Long's. Her father was a South African who had married her mother, Debra Jackson, during their undergraduate studies. The conversation covered how the team was feeling about Great Britain and the other stops they made over the last month. Tubman was popular and well respected by the student body at her Washington Carver High School in Detroit. One of the students named Revemba was a slim built young woman who had grown close to Marion. Revemba was raised by her grandparents, while her mother pursued medical school at Meharry Medical College in Tennessee. Marion, a well-traveled person, had bonded with Revemba early and the young girl, under her mentorship, had become part of the overall following of young girls in Detroit. That following was part of the Detroit African-American Woman Development Project, which both Masekela and Tubman participated.

Revemba was not the only favorite of Xavier's. There was also another young lady that he had grown quite fond of. The young girl was named Eboni Johnson and Dr. Long had requested that Marion

Tubman work with her. A retired postal worker and her husband had adopted Eboni. As a favor to a social worker, Xavier had been involved in a serious sexual abuse case that resulted in Eboni being taken from her birth family. Unknown to anyone, Eboni Johnson was the biological daughter of a ruthless criminal named Pedwell "Peddy" Jefferson. Pedwell had named his children the vilest names he could think of in his constant and all out assault on society. He had six sons and two daughters. One of the girls was named Mayhem and the other was Desecration. The ugly stories of this family were horrifying and led to the decision by the social worker to remove the young girl from the home. Now, the young Eboni was one of the lucky students, along with Ms. Masekela, to have Ms. Tubman as a Teacher. Ms. Tubman was surprised to hear Eboni telling the group that this trip was something she would have never thought about a year earlier.

"This trip is something I would have never had if it wasn't for Ms. Tubman and Revee. No way." The airport is busy. There are a number of flight delays because of the increased fog on such a rainy day. Long loved Great Britain and especially enjoyed watching the Brits carry their traditional raincoats, boots and umbrellas. Marion Tubman smiled at the expression on Xavier's face. Xavier was listening to his iPod remembering how he met Desecration, now Eboni Johnson, when she was but a child. He was seated away from the crowd but Marion knew he had to be listening to Coltrane since the sound of that horn always brought him peace. Professor Long could not get enough of that Coltrane groove, not even with his special custom headphones. Xavier treasured music.

He agreed with his old mentor who used to remind him, "Music has the ability to calm the soul."
Finally relaxed, Xavier couldn't help but to remember little Des Jefferson.

Sitting in a trance of sorts, Xavier recalls the horror he found that dark day he met Des. The call from the social worker at Roosevelt Elementary was ugly and scary. Carmen Embry was a young, energetic social worker that called Xavier that morning. Xavier remembered the moment exactly; right down to the coat he was wearing. It was as if he had stepped off of a time travel machine. He found himself surrounded by the sound of a desperate cry and an angry, barely audible voice.

"Dr. Long, I need your advice, we have an emergency. Could you come to Roosevelt right away? There is a baby girl who is in danger and I don't really know what to do." Whatever it was, something made him rush over to Roosevelt as he thought about his grandmother and her wise words, "God will show you the way. There ain't no need to think about nothing."

When he arrived at Roosevelt, Eboni was laughing and playing and Dr. Long couldn't help but to thank God that she had been rescued from that messed up family. Marion Tubman had taught other members of the Jefferson clan and she, along with Carmen, went full tilt to save each of the children of Peddy Jefferson. That day was still blazed into his memory. The school itself was historical. Both the school and the neighborhood were once the strong hold of a thriving Jewish community. Roosevelt Elementary was one of three schools in what was known as the Central High School complex. In the 1950's, it was truly a magnificent site. The complex was a replica of the University of Oxford in England. Crabapple trees, manicured lawns, bushes, walkways; each building represented an investment in children, youth and families at its best. Roosevelt had two greenhouses, two auditoriums, and was so well kept that Xavier remembered the pride he felt earlier in his childhood as a student who attended Roosevelt. After a few moments, Dr. Long found Carmen in the nurses' office with a little lithe body. The baby girl was crying while the nurse tried to comfort her. The baby girl's back was covered with cigarette burns and worse still – there was the report that there had been a sexual penetration of her.

"Doc, the plane is boarding."

Dr. Long was caught up thinking about the Jefferson family.

He thought, "How could anyone call that group of people a family?" Pedwell was something lower than a snake and his family should have been called a criminal enterprise. Xavier couldn't shake the memory of Peddy's other daughter, Mayhem. She was the one that didn't get away that day. She was the one that fell through the proverbial "cracks." Looking at Eboni was like watching a movie featuring his grandmother comforting him during one of the many challenges he faced as a child. It was as if his grandmother were in the airport with him at that very moment.

Eboni had a beautiful smile and an aura of love emitted from her face. She was walking between Marion and Revemba feeling safe and secure. It was like her life, as Des Jefferson never happened. Xavier went to business class while the others kidded him about being bourgeoisie. Marion, wearing her 1984 Olympic team jacket, was proud of the women she had guided over the past years in the Detroit African-American Woman Development Project. The trip had been a good one but now it was time to continue the war in Detroit. Israel, Ghana, South Africa and Great Britain had been foreign travel enough. Yet, Detroit was one place that the world really didn't seem to understand and now, it seemed, no one really cared.

Marion and Xavier were both less than thrilled with the recent experiment by *Time* Magazine. The front page of *Time* had a caption of the city being the last civilized city in the world. Marion considered the reporters inept at best. As an educator, her sense of teaching kids seemed lost. Tubman was a proud woman. Her father had been a pioneer in education. He was the first African American man hired by the same district as an instrumental music teacher. She was witnessing the decline of public education – and she knew it. Xavier had listened as Revemba discussed the embarrassing school board with Marion. School board members, teachers, and administrators – it was like a huge ball of confusion.

Jimmy Ruffin, the brother of the infamous lead singer of the iconic Temptations, was now playing on Xavier's iPod. He chuckled at the fact that his musical tastes were so wide ranging. While in London, the group had gone to a club and, completely by accident, was treated to a performance by Ruffin who was singing his signature Motown classic, "*What Becomes of the Brokenhearted.*" Xavier was clearer than most that the young people in the group were experiencing a treat that was being lost on them. Most of the students didn't know who David Ruffin was, even if they did know the Temps. Like always, Xavier championed the Motown era.

"Funny," he thought to himself, "the brokenhearted was really about the Jefferson children suffering at the hands of that awful Peddy Jefferson."

While they sat in different sections of the plane, both Xavier and Marion could not shake the depressing feeling of returning to what was once a great city. Xavier Long had just co-authored an essay on Urbicide. The essay by Xavier J. Long and Nina P. Wise, explained that Urbicide was the destruction of a city's character and reputation by outside sources. As the group settled in their seats, Marion walked up to the business section. She wanted Xavier to see a picture taken in the slave castles with the students from Detroit. The blonde flight attendant was staring at Eboni's hair as the two chocolate females walked up to section 4B. Eboni's hair was neatly twisted into little twisted braids. Perhaps the flight attendant was taken aback by the bright orange tee shirt with a little stick figure, and a caption that read, "Happy cuz I'm Nappy."

Arriving at the seat, they found Dr. Long's big baldhead lying on the neck pillow with his Dr. Dre headphones covering his earring-clad ears. His eyes were closed, while his seatmate had not gotten over the Goliath sitting next to him. Eboni laughed as Xavier opened his eyes suddenly having felt Marion placing the pictures in his lap. As the headphones fell onto his neck, the seatmate was startled hearing the loud blaring lyrics of the late Notorious B.I.G., "*Pink Gators...My Detroit Players.*"

Marion and Xavier communicate at times, without saying a single word. As he looked at the photographs, his big eyes screamed seeing the Detroit youth in front of the washed white walls of the fortress on the coastline of Ghana. The photos themselves were powerful. Four Detroit high school students clad in modern day hip-hop gear posing in caves still full of the voices and spirits of their ancestors. You could almost hear the sounds of ghosts crying. For Xavier Long, it was a great deal more than a photograph. He saw the faces of the young people – like Eboni in more of an ongoing video on the screen in his head. He saw images of the Motherland, slaves, the Klan, his beloved Detroit, the 1943 race riots, the 1967 insurrection, the horrible heroin invasion, Mayor Coleman A. Young, and all those

Japanese imports. Xavier couldn't help but think about the Detroit that now included Pedwell Jefferson's children.

It was a seven-hour flight from London to Detroit. After napping for nearly an hour, Xavier wakes up and decides to look at his email on the computer. The MacBook Pro is his connection to the streets while away from East Pyramid in Detroit. Music is the lifeline for Xav. He had to have his music. The Mac kept his precious musical treasure of over 4,000 recordings made up of mostly jazz, Motown, rhythm and blues, and classical music. Tyquan had sent some new music to Doc in an email. The ongoing joke between Xavier and Tyquan was Long's love of Motown music and his resistance to even listening to hip-hop. Tyquan Miller, a former gang warrior, had sent the music of Dwele and Raheem DeVaughn. Xavier really digs the old school crooners including the likes of Sam Cooke and Marvin Gaye and he wonders if these "young boys" have what it takes to carry the torch of singing and composing real music. No doubt along with *XXL, Vibe, Ebony,* and *Source* magazines, Xavier is up on the "old" and "new" colored folks.

Most of the emails are boring with the exception of a note from Jason Hampton, a recently retired Alexander State University police detective. Captain Hampton had been the only police officer that Xavier could genuinely count on while doing research in the city. Hampton was also very helpful to Xavier during the county investigation that included the Grand Jury investigation of Dr. Long that took place in the late 80's. Jason, a veteran of the Vietnam War, was considered one of the best detectives in the state. Internal bickering about the difference between "real" city police vs. the college graduate, well-trained university police was historical and, at the time, Hampton was often at the center of the discussion.

Alexander State was a strong research university. While highly respected as an institution of higher learning and situated in an urban center, it remained a white only institution in Detroit. The blacks over the years that attended Alexander State understood the double standard. Hampton, an alumnus of Alexander State University, was a moderately built, African American who was a native of Detroit. He was an outstanding martial artist and had bonded with Professor Long from an early age. It was Hampton's intelligence and understanding of the various gangs and gangsters that allowed Xavier first hand knowledge that black organized crime had always existed, evolving into what is terrorizing most black colonies in America today.

The email was coded saying, "Keithland has hired Pedwell Jefferson's company in the dispute with the A-Rabbs."

Xavier immediately thought, "That is not good for Detroit. That is extra bad for anyone in the path of the notorious Peddy and sons."

Long wondered, "What did that mean for Mayhem?"
Marion, Carmen and Revemba all had tried valiantly to bring the young female thug into the circle of their black woman development project. Revemba had even tried, in vain, to change her name both legally and psychologically. That damn name! Xavier never understood that name and the sound of it always bothered him.

MAY-HEM...Mayhem Jefferson, Assault Jefferson, Homicide Jefferson, Contempt Jefferson, Felonious Jefferson, Hate Jefferson, Rape Jefferson, and the girl formerly known as Desecration who is now Eboni Johnson. All those names.

Xav thought about the words of the old head when he said, "Peddy Jefferson is the devil. The man is an evil low life and should be put out of his misery."
It was so senseless to Xavier. How could the mother let that fool name her babies those names? Xavier searched to find anyone that could explain the madness. His good friend, Brenda Silberstein, a superstar litigator, who represented some of the city's biggest cases, often joked with Xavier about the messed-up names that sounded like food labels.

"People are crazy, you know ghetto crazy," she would tell him. Who ever heard of naming your child Mayhem, Homicide, Rape or Assault? Brenda was baffled by the name choices for children. Silberstein, a feared and respected attorney, offers a rapid-fire analysis.

"Doc, don't ask me what this means. I just represent clients. My clients have names that black folks just invent I guess?"

Chapter 2: The Dark Past

Brenda was a Detroit resident who was also well known in the black community for her fundraising talent. Her name tricked outsiders who always looked for a Jewish Brenda Silberstein. She had been teased all her life but her father and mother, both black, explained it was just a name, a good name so she quickly learned not to react to folks just because of their name. When Xavier first heard about Homicide, Rape, and those other hideous names, he was baffled also. That paled compared to naming your daughter Mayhem. The problem with Peddy was much deeper and more troubling than Dr. Long first thought. Everything changed once he started to review the Jefferson family background. It had been ten years since Xavier first met Mayhem. Suddenly, the music playing in Xavier's head was that of *Karma* by Pharaoh Sanders.

The sultry and powerful voice of Leon Thomas was singing, "the Master has but one demand, peace and happiness for every man."

Long was visibly angry seeing the real-life impact of gangsterism. It didn't matter if it was Billy The Kid, Al Capone or Peddy Jefferson. America loved to be entertained by hoodlums. Xavier thought of Pedwell in a variety of ways but none of them were good. What in the hell was this monster called Pedwell? What did he do to that woman, his wife, to allow him license to abuse his own family as if he were God himself? The first time Xavier met the young skinny black girl was in the principal's office at Roosevelt Elementary. Long had no idea who anyone in the office was. Ms. Embry quickly explained to Xavier that there had been sexual and physical abuse of the young child. Knowing that Xavier knew Peddy Jefferson, it was her understanding that this little brown baby was Jefferson's child.

Carmen Embry introduced Mayhem Jefferson. Mayhem represented that she was the mother of Des Jefferson. Xavier looked at Mayhem, not realizing that this young girl was part of the notorious criminal family. Professor Long was well acquainted with Homicide, Assault, and Felonious-those treacherous young Jefferson boys. Dr. Long wondered if Sergeant Hampton knew there was a female in the dangerous species of that Jefferson clan? He could feel the danger. Xavier would later recount how a sense of danger emitted from Mayhem's being. Mayhem looked young at first glance but upon closer analysis, she looked like she had already lived a hundred years. Mayhem's fist was clinched and she had her other hand inside the pocket of her tight blue jeans. She leveled a death voodoo stare on Carmen, Xavier, and the nurse, that was chilling to say the least.

Although Mayhem was young chronologically, she spoke as if she was some sort of ageless soul.

"What is dis bout? Leave her lone. I'm taking her home."
The nurse, a stout middle-aged white woman, pushed Mayhem to the side. The nurse informed everyone in the room that a crime had been committed against the little girl.
"You will do no such thing."

A detective from the Detroit Police department, along with someone from protective services will be coming soon. Ms. Embry is the Social Worker and Dr. Long agrees that this little girl is in grave danger.

"Who are you anyway young lady?"
Mayhem was dressed in tight blue jeans and a dark blue turtleneck sweater.

Her skinny figure seemed to grow much larger as she rebuked the nurse, "I am her sister. My moms sent me. Y'all ain't doing shit. We're going home – me and my lil' sister."
Mayhem pushed the nurse back away from her sister. Her strength surprised the nurse. One swift move and the nurse had been sent hurling to the ground. Xavier went to help the nurse from the floor. Carmen raised her hand in front of Mayhem.

"Young lady, we are trying to help your sister. This is a serious matter. Nurse Wilson is trying to save your little sister."
Mayhem screamed, "Bitch, I know she fucked up. I know how she got fucked up. What y'all gonna do? My daddy will smoke all y'all. My daddy is a beast!"
The room seemed to freeze with a sense of hopelessness.

A tall man walked in and asked, "Young lady, are you her mother?"
Mayhem turned toward the voice in an almost robotic motion. A beam from her eyes could have burned a hole through the man. Her

slim hand was wrapped around her sister. Mayhem pointed her other hand towards the man. Xavier can still feel the intensity of a decade ago. His memory of that moment still has the same blazing horror that it took on that day.

Mayhem made a defensive and offensive move in the same motion. The flashback is in 3 D in Xavier's mind. What is not clear is that Xavier also hears the faint voice of what sounds like a pilot in the background. The pilots voice was announcing that the plane had crossed into the United States and Detroit was only a couple hours away.

It bothered Xavier deeply that Peddy had never come close to being stopped - not now nor those many years ago.

Doc thought, "they should have disconnected his dick or better yet, destroyed his reproductive organs or hell, just plain destroyed the evil bastard all together."

That day Mayhem was trying to rescue her sister, she was the only mother in that damn family.

"No one could save poor Jerenda," thought Xavier.

It was as if Jerenda was some kind of muted sex slave. Peddy pumped babies out of Jerenda. She never went to any of the schools to see about her children. In fact, those Jefferson children barely attended school at all according to the records Xavier had reviewed over the years during his gang research.

Detroit Public Schools had tried to meet the challenge of the mercenary parental units. They were labeled the Merc's in Dr. Long's Detroit Gang Research Project. Social worker Carmen Embry explained back then that the schools could not handle the parents who were the enemies of the system. Xavier had documented the new parental units in all of their glorious ignorance. Worse still to Xavier was how they had "updated" the playing field for teaching children. It was Pedwell who taught his boys to fuck the teachers.

Xavier pondered that dreadful day at Roosevelt. The man who attempted to intervene was the principal. Thomas Majors was the son of one of the first black principals in the system. A proud young man at that time, he was forever changed when Mayhem pulled a small pistol out. While she was arrested following the conflict, the hatred she had already developed towards authority erased part of the historical past of all educators in the entire Detroit system. Majors had been shaken to the bone. So much so that Carol Embry shared with Xavier later that Majors met her and others from his administration that dark day at the local bar hours after the ordeal. The teachers hangout back then was a small bar called Sparky's. Carol explained to Long how that single incident had an immensely negative impact on the entire faculty.

"Well, we knew that something was wrong with that child because she was so dirty and unkempt all the time. Her teachers loved that little baby girl. They tried earnestly to provide some relief by bringing her clothes and sending her to the nurse's station regularly."

Xavier remembered that the emotional cry was coming through the phone. Carmen really needed to talk. The intensity and horror of the incident led Long to suggest that they meet at his favorite place. Sadie's Mississippi Fish House was on Dexter. Sadie's was the generational stronghold for old temple cooking. It was one of those places that made whatever better, whenever. Dr. Long entered the Fish House. Sadie Jenkins was the semi-retired owner. She had two daughters, Cathy and Stephanie "Stevie" Jenkins, who she was training to take over the reins of this black Detroit institution. It was during these times that Carmen felt comfortable enough to release the fears and frustrations of her involvement with the new parents who seemed the same kind of destructive and hateful parents that Pedwell represented so well.

"When that child's father came to school, he was scary. Tommy Majors father, Thomas Sr., was the principal. Tommy said that his father actually remembered Peddy from many years ago when he was still teaching, a number of years before he became an assistant principal. Xav, Mr. Majors, Sr. said he could never forget his visit to the Jefferson's home, over on Pingree and Twelfth years ago."
Long knew about the home life of Pedwell Jefferson from social workers reports and the extensive court records of abuse and violence against his own family. Back then domestic violence was no big deal. Xavier thought back to when he was a graduate student and he re-

membered his great professor, Zolton Ferency who taught him about the policy that he had entitled, the 'Rule of Thumb'. The policy, Professor Ferency explained, meant that a man could resort to beating his wife with any kind of object as long as it was not thicker than the size of his thumb. The Professor labeled the violent policy as misogynist, brutal, and sexist. But this policy was a real sign of the times; the same time period that the Frankenstein-like Peddy Jefferson unleashed himself and his spawn onto the streets of Detroit.

Carol began to recount the story of how shaken and scared Tommy Majors was after Tommy shared the incident with his retired father. The look of horror on the old mans face would have led an onlooker to believe he was in full cardiac arrest. Carmen, listening intensely, concurred that this predatory species known as Peddy was a monster that everyone should fear if folks like Tommy were spooked.

"Tommy is an army veteran and his father was one of the most respected educators in the country. This shit sounds like we have a psychopath in our schools. What in the hell can we do?"
Those words echoed in Xavier's head as he thought about Eboni. He also shuttered at the thought that the most powerful criminal organization Detroit had seen since the Purple Gang was merging with the likes of Pedwell Jefferson. Nothing in Detroit seemed the same to Xavier. Not even his beloved hangout, Sadie's. The new thing at Sadie's was while the old jukebox still played, there was a new digital jukebox that had been introduced by Sadie's hip hopping grandchildren. Instead of the Temps, the sultry sound of Rihanna was heard blaring from the speakers.

3

METRO DETROIT AIRPORT

Xavier loved returning from abroad, yet, Detroit news seemed to always be conflicted, violent and depressing. Despite that fact, the landing was a happy homecoming for the group from Detroit. Waiting at the entry of the luggage area was Tyquan Miller. He was happy, smiling and anxious to see Professor Long. Miller is solidly built, a mocha colored handsome young man. His eyes are always searching the landscape for anything remotely wrong or even the slightest bit suspicious. Unofficially, Tyquan was Long's personal bodyguard and adopted son. The safe return of the high school students was a victory. Eboni Johnson walked with confidence as her parents, Bill and Wilma Johnson, beamed with pride as their adopted daughter waved along with Revemba, and Marion.

Tyquan, with his glistering, perfect, bald-head, wore a bright orange and navy *Peace* hoody, along with small white gold earrings. It gave him a look of mystique. The *Peace* hoody was important to Xavier Long. It was symbolic of a truce among young gang members in Detroit. Xavier's younger brother, who was a former Naval Intelligence Officer, was the leader of the enormously important Peace Initiative. If the Pedwell Jefferson clan was the epitome of the criminal family, the Long family was the antithesis. Xavier was one of five boys and four sisters. His parents were part of the traditional Negro professional class with his mother, a retired teacher and his father, Solomon Long, a retired judge. Saul Long, the youngest son, had been involved with youth after Xavier made a personal plea to his siblings to help the cause of young folks. Saul's military career was highly distinguished including serving two presidents as an intelligence advisor. Judge Long served in the Army as a military judge. All of his sons served in the armed forces with the exception of Xavier. The twins, Paul and Phillip, were West Pointe graduates later serving in the Marines. David Long flew jets in the Air Force, and currently is an instructor at the prestigious Top Gun training school. David is the only Long sibling not living in Michigan. The women were split, as Xavier always said, between the educators and the warriors. The oldest sisters were both educators. Althea taught science and math in high school while Grace taught music at the Detroit Music Conservatory. The female warriors were Lynette, who was a prison warden and Constance, who was a federal judge.

The homecoming was going smoothly until a dark cloud appeared over the luggage area. Tyquan, with his hawk vision, saw what he knew was trouble. Worse, the front of the airport shook and rattled from the loud bass of Pac's, *I See Death Around the Corner*, booming from a blacked windowed custom Denali. The curbside suddenly began to look like the Dark Side was actually rising. Tyquan knew the whole dark convoy was made up of the death merchants. Sensing something was wrong, Xavier walked towards Marion Tubman. Their eyes were talking but there was not a word being uttered between them. It seemed everyone with Marion began holding her hand tightly as the entire group encircled Eboni. The booming bass made Bill Johnson cringe as he held his ears. An Alexander County Deputy pulled his wrap around shooting glasses off to stare at the convoy.

Wondering to himself, "Who in the world could this be pulling in front of the terminal like they are Secret Service for President Obama?"

A tall, lanky figure emerged from the first car. There was a total of six BADD ASS black vehicles. The deputy barked, or as they say in the street, he wolfed at the tall man in front of the Denali.

"Move your car. No parking. Can you read?"

Laughter could be heard from the Denali along with pulsating beats and the bass blasting. The tall man was dressed in a long black leather coat with shiny black cowboy boots with silver spurs. His hair was long and straight and it was lying on his shoulder. The deputy walks a little closer in disbelief since the tall man acts as if he doesn't hear a word. Another deputy follows. He is the Captain and he is rushing fast to catch up with his deputy.

The tall man is Homicide Jefferson. His expensive black shirt is double-breasted, Western style with expensive silver buttons that match his spurs. A beautiful turquoise string tie holder of thin black leather with silver tips swings loosely. As the captain reached his deputy, Gucci Mane's *Bricks* seemed to explode from a surround sound set of loud speakers. There was an endless sea of black figures emerging from the convoy of Escalades, Porsche Cayennes, Mercedes Benzes and BMWs. It was as if some black wizard had blown black powder over the terminal entry. The men were there to meet the coming of Keithland James, his main bodyguard Big Tiny, and the infamous Pedwell Jefferson. The Jefferson clan was showing off at the same time that Eboni would be returning to America. A circle of love, led by strong willed Marion Tubman, tightly encircled the young girl. Tyquan moved in front of Marion as his eyes seemed to talk to Tubman. The message they silently shared was clear. Nothing but nothing was going to see, touch or feel this baby girl.

The deputy looked and felt like his stomach was about to explode as Homicide announced, "Officer, we here to pick up my daddy, Aightt? Just a few minutes, das all we need, k"?

The captain pulled the dazed deputy back while explaining in a low voice with great concern, "Deputy, this is not Traffic. This is Major Crimes! The Detroit Police, the State Police and the Feds are aware of this bunch. Those are some bad players. All you gotta do is just observe."

As the deputy pulls back, a sudden jolt comes out of the terminal. Leading the way to the black SUV is Big Tiny clearing the way for his boss, Keithland James. Walking and smiling is the tenebrific Pedwell 'Peddy" Jefferson. He has no idea that his youngest daughter is so close.

Dr. Long is meditating while silently talking to God. His prayers are answered as always. Not very academic, nonetheless he is standing in the middle of baggage claim next to the holy man. The good Reverend Dr. Nehemiah Jeremiah Stillwater smiles at Xavier. His voice is calming. He is looking straight ahead as he denounces all evil in defense of all God's children. Stillwater was a guest on the trip along with a small choir from his church. The church had hired him as the Youth Minister. Long had a special bond with the young minister. In Xavier's mind, Stillwater's prayers and presence at this dark time manifested as an answer from God himself. There was something comforting, something that words could not explain. It reminded Xavier of his Grandmother Adrean's connection with the Spirit.

The convoy pulled off after the show time atmosphere of clowns dancing and the jewelry parade of the Jefferson Boys - Homicide, Felonious, Hate, Rape, Contempt and Assault. Peddy was smelling himself and he was delighted in his new status of protecting the street Niggah of Niggahs. The only one missing was his lone daughter, Mayhem. Xavier was so relieved when the entourage pulled off that he sighed. The young minister smiled as the atmosphere lightened almost immediately.

"Dr. Long. God is always here. Eboni is God's child. She has no other father or mother."

4

DEAD DOGS AND FOOLS

The police cruiser had its lights on as the officers arrived at 2349 Cove. An elderly couple was standing in front of the abandoned apartment. They were flailing their arms about in an attempt to wave the police down. George and Helen Goss lived across the street from the apartment building. Helen Goss, 83, was a beautiful grayish blue haired woman. Her skin looks weathered yet it still appears tight. Her beloved George owned the Big G grocery store on the corner of 12th Street and Lawrence. The couple was visibly upset, pointing towards the large building.

"Officers, they took my dog, Rufus. They dog fighting in there all the time. At night, you can hear the screams and all that barking." The police are not really concerned. They look around as they walk towards the front entry.

The officer with a large flashlight walks towards the couple and explains, "Look, it's all kinds of needles and bottles in there. Nobody in his or her right mind would go in there. Are you sure your dog was taken? Did you see anyone actually take the dog?" One officer is a young Latino male. He is visibly annoyed as he looks at his partner who is a young white female.

As he places his flashlight on the seat, he opens the driver side door and tells the couple, "If we see anything, we will let you know. Leave us your phone number. I think you should return to your house."

George Goss asked, "Is Sgt. Bannon on duty?"

The female officer nods her head with disgust, "He is around. I can call him. What is your name again?"

At the rear of the building, a van pulls up with three hooded figures getting out with dogs in tow. The van is old and loud music is blasting away. Four cars follow the van and eventually park in the rear of the building. The elderly couple is walking fast. There seems to be a growing crowd at the building. The old man is shaking his head as he tells his wife that Sgt. Bannon will come. As her husband unlocked the front door, Helen started crying. As she watched the young men with the baggy jeans and vicious dogs enter the apartment, she got even more upset. A small group of homeless men were sitting on the porch of the abandoned yellow brick four-family flat next door to the apartment. It was the local homeless hangout. One of the men, with a dirty short beard, hollered across the street to old man Goss.

"Hey, they took your dog, lady. They gonna use it for fun. Better get the police back here. It's bout to start. Them niggahs will eat that dog with the quickness."
A red Toyota Camry pulled up in front of the house next to the four-family flat. A young woman dressed in a blue denim pantsuit speaks to the men sitting on the porch. She is Rochelle Atkins. She shares a house with her wayward, dope addict brothers and a cousin they call "DJ" who is an alcoholic. Carrying a big bag of KFC chicken, she motions to the bearded man to come to the car.

"Hey, got chicken, mashed pota-toes and gravy and some apple pies." The man smiles and gets excited.

"You did the yard real good. Is Sugarfoot watching my dogs?"
Rochelle feeds homeless folks everyday like clockwork. Her girlfriend Freda is a nurse and she helps Rochelle unload her trunk that is full of food. Freda is a roommate in the modest bungalow. The house looks weird; just like the Goss house across the street. Weird is the appropriate description because there are only a few homes remaining on the block. It looks like the plague just missed a few homes, leaving behind the near total destruction of a once prosperous middle-class family block. There are only twelve houses on Cove now. Ten years ago, there were about thirty-three. At one point, the street was full of houses. Even the flats were filled with families. Then the plague hit.

Rochelle's mother had been a teacher while her father was an autoworker. Rochelle was the director of a community center. Married to Jake Buntin, her life took a turn for the worse three years ago when Jake was murdered by the dope selling organization called the Keithland James organization. This group was known in the streets as the Detroit Original Gangsters, also known as the DOGS. Jake Buntin had a corner store where he sold candy, pop, chips and burgers. Known as Jakes Party Corner, it was a place where school kids felt safe and everybody knew Big Jake was not having any nonsense in or around his store. He had been a Black Panther who had served in the Army during Viet Nam. He was foolishly fearless and decided to take on the Keithland crew not giving any thought to the fact that lots of young boys were down with Keithland and took pride in pumping him up. The older guys pretended to be big brothers but all they did was keep the young boys crazy with propaganda about the Godfather - Keithland. The truth was that Keithland James came from a family of criminals. His reputation extended well beyond Detroit since he had taken out all other contenders for selling dope.

Keithland James had a reputation for being ruthless and double-crossing and to make matters worse, Keithland decided to partner with the serious organized crime boss named Joseph Corelli.

Jake Buntin believed in Black Power and he advocated for a black power economic base. Buntin hated heroin, cocaine, and any other illegal drug. He and his organization, the Community Black Watch, would not allow illicit narcotics commerce. Jake put this rule in full effect. He single handedly chased out the original dope pushers, which included the mob of Corelli. When Keithland tried to buyout Jake's folks, he found out that the big Panther was not having it. The problem was that Keithland and his crew had taken over every corner down Dexter, Linwood, Grand River and all the main arteries of the city. He had taken over Detroit and turned it into "D-Troit" or the "Bad Lands." Big Jake protected the community. He wasn't scared of anything. Yet, one late evening, Jake was murdered by a war party from the Keithland young boys. Murdering Jake sent a message to the entire black community.

The message declared, "I am your God."

Helen Goss went out on her porch and began calling out to Rochelle. While yelling out loudly, a black Viper pulled directly behind Rochelle's car. The tall young woman opened the Viper door.

Chapter 4: Dead Dogs and Fools

The sound of Trina asserting, *"I'm the baddest Bitch"* was playing loudly as if it were her own personal soundtrack. Dressed in all black, she looked like a model for the magazine *Guns and Ammo*. She carried a black automatic pistol with white pearl grips stuck in a narrow waistband. Her ankle boots were a perfect fit with the white suede West

Pointe cadet jacket lying on her wide shoulders. Smiling had never been Mayhem's image. But Rochelle was her rare compadre. As Mayhem walked towards the house, her short cut hair laid on her head with uncanny neatness. Helen's voice was alarming until a scream boomed from the backyard of Rochelle's house.

"They got Jingles. Help! Help! Ms. Rochelle, they got yo Jingles."

The loud growling and blood yelling of an animal in severe pain was excruciating to anyone with ears. Helen Goss was jumping up and down on her porch. George went and got his shotgun. Rochelle dropped her bags and ran to the backyard. There was a circle of pit bulls devouring something on the ground with brutal swiftness. Sugarfoot, a petite young boy, was trying to fight off the pack of wild dogs. A skinny young girl was fighting Sugarfoot along with two husky tattooed men with big white t-shirts. Both t-shirts had large black letters that read DOG on both the front and the back. The men, with guns drawn, began beating Sugarfoot while he attempted, in vain, to get the dog from the mouths of the snarling predators. Blood is spurting everywhere as Mayhem seems to appear instantly, like magic. Without uttering a word, and with a pistol in each hand, she fires rapidly into the pack of dogs. BOOM BOOM BOOM BOOM BOOM. The wild pack yelps as one of the pit bulls lunges towards Mayhem. Rochelle grasps her dog Jingles and yells at Freda to get Rufus.

"That's Rufus. Get him Fred. That's Rufus."

The mouth of the charging pit bull is blown to pieces. Mayhem falls to the ground. The tattooed men turned their guns towards Mayhem as she lie on the ground. Before anyone could say anything, another louder boom exploded in the face of the men with tattoos. A powerful blast from a sawed off shotgun came from the motorcycle posted on the backyard alley side. The smell of gunpowder filled the air. The big bike was the custom kind. The figure sitting on the bike wore a dark blue helmet. The person wearing the helmet was intently pumping the sawed-off Beretta shotgun. Laughter came from the helmet. The laugh was a wicked laugh that warned everybody to take cover.

"Step the fuck off. Yo nigga. Drop yo shit or the next blast is gonna be yo bitch ass" The tattooed man looked at his partner. Blood was gushing from his neck in the same place the head used to be. With a look of utter terror, the tattooed man dropped his gun. The dogs, now dying, were still yelping and moaning. Mayhem picked herself up from the ground. She was smiling.

Looking at her partner on the motorcycle, she nodded in approval and said, "Good looking big girl. These here fools is foul."

There is a crowd of young gangsters who have snarls plastered across their faces. Each of them was holding a dog on a leash. As more young boys walk down the alley, guns are drawn. Numerically, the vast majority of the crowd is made up of young men wearing white t-shirts. Most of the young men have tattoos. Suddenly, the person wearing the helmet removes it from their head. A young but thick woman has blazing blue eyes and, as she removes the helmet, she shakes out her long blond and bronze ponytail. Everybody is staring at the young woman on the big bike. In one hand, she holds a shotgun while she places her helmet on the center of the bike. Her blue bike matches her blue leather jacket and pants. The leather ensemble fits her like somebody spray-painted it on her big, well-developed ass.

Dogs are barking and some are howling. Tempers are hot. Two of the Latino boys begin cursing at Mayhem along with a group of six Hmong boys holding their pistols at their sides as they glare at Mayhem and her comrade on the motorcycle. Rochelle and Freda quickly run into her backdoor right when one of the tattooed fellas shoots at Mayhem. The alley becomes one big fury of orange and blue sparks flying with gun smoke rising to the sky. The racketing loud noise draws the old woman Helen from her porch. She begins to walk up to the front door of Rochelle's burgundy brick house.

Chapter 4: Dead Dogs and Fools

With her coat wide open, she began to cry. George, unquestionably loyal, stood right next to her with his big shotgun in hand. "George, it's shooting back there. God don't let nothin' happen to Rufus."

The rampage accelerates in the backyard as shooters from the alley took cover with their weapons taking aim at Mayhem. Picking up his other gun, the big tattooed figure is rushing Mayhem with two pistols firing. Without ducking or moving, and with no sweat at all, Mayhem begins popping off deadly rapid fire into her next dead t-shirt. As the shooting sounds off, the skinny girl yells to Mayhem from the side of the four family home next to Rochelles house. Her voice trembles yet it is authoritative.

"Bitch, dis here Blackheart boys. You best hold up bitch!"
The crew can hear something big in the alley. As they look out, they have guns blazing. The skinny girl runs towards Mayhem with a pistol in her hand. There are two people on a motorcycle. The person who was riding shotgun began to fire violently on the young girl. The hit misses most of the skinny girl yet the blast gets a piece of her lower right knee and she screams out in pain. Then, the whole alley explodes with Hmong and Latino crews lighting up everything in sight. It's like the OK Corral.

Amazingly, that loud sound is actually a big black Hummer with a black steel brush guard and beaming searchlights fully lit as the smell of gunpowder smoke fills the alley. A group of young girls are in the Hummer firing AK-47's and MP-5's. The girls are attempting to kill everything in sight that is trying to shoot Mayhem. Suddenly, the massacre ends. There are dead dogs everywhere. There are also bodies lying all over the alley. There are dead Hmong boys and dead Latino boys. The crew responsible for the massacre was made up of the girls that roll with Mayhem Jefferson. Mayhem smiles as she nods to the four young girls who do not appear to be moved by the results of their "little" battle. The motorcycle rider is Mayhem's top girl enforcer. The visit to her friend Rochelle could have told the dog fighting folks a known fact, that Mayhem Jefferson had seceded from the Jefferson clan. She had her own thing. It was called FMI or FEMALE MURDER INCORPORATED. Mayhem gave a smile to the motorcycling Big Girl, and a "Fuck you to her monster ass Daddy."

5

COMING OUT OF THE STREETSIDE ECONOMY

The headlines read, "Nine Dead at Dog fighting site" in the *Detroit Times*. The radio shows were all crazy with editorials about street violence. Over at Envenom, the noonday crowd is glued to News 1 as local anchors detail the latest massacre. Envenom is the hot nightclub owned by Keithland James. While the city is dealing with a significant loss of revenue, his club is booming. The club serves as a hangout for bigger than life Ballers. The scene in this club included one large room of adult entertainment unlike any other club scene in Detroit. The draw for all the sexy tittie dancers is well known. While the horrors of Detroit are constant, many men from all over the region go to Envenoms. Security is everywhere so there are no robberies and no carjackings. The club is completely crime free. If any fool were to start even a small fight, they would find themselves smashed. Big Tiny was the Enforcer. He shadows Keithland and is known as the Terminator. The club has a five star restaurant that serves a host of characters - politicians, preachers, pimps, lawyers and even a few white mob guys. The fact is that this club served members of organized black crime. J. Edgar Hoover denied the Costra Nostra even existed. The nation, confused because of its own blindness, and the insistence on casting black folk as *niggardly black criminals and sharecroppers*, should have awakened before Keithland took over the world by spreading his worldwide criminal rule.

Music is everywhere. There is jazz in the small room where the old heads hang out. The much larger hip-hop crowd is a result of hundreds of young soldiers that work for the Nigga of Niggahs - Keithland. Hip hop producers eat, play and party at Envenom because Keithland has three sons, all young G's who have their own record company and video studio. The news about the shooting hit the club and Keithlands sons were obviously upset and they are arguing about the shootings.

"Man, dem our boys. Dat lesbo bitch killed my boys. Big Tiny, somebody got to do something. Dem Blackheart Boys is our niggahs. Dat ho bitch shot all of dem boys. She killed dey dogs too. Me, Katown, and Krispy, we all hate dat bitch. I don't care bout her brothers or dat muthafucking Peddy," yelled Kenni James.

The mood is solemn. The sound of *Backstabbers* by the O'Jays can be heard playing in the background. The powerful Blackheart Boys are under the regime the Detroit Original Gangstas.

The bartender smiles and advised, "Peddy can't control that little girl. You know that she did dat all on her own."
Mayhem is like a man, maybe worse. She got dat big boxing bitch who works out over at Peppers Boxing Club. Dat girl is something else. Word has it that she done went into business for herself. In his private office, Keithland is talking with Pedwell about the incident with Blackheart.

"Peddy, word is your girl fucked up a dogfight last night. Iz dis you? Lots of niggahs are dead! Wassup?"

Keithland is a short, well-developed, muscular guy that reminds you of a young Mike Tyson. His hair is faded and the sides are long while the top is relaxed. He is fanatical about both his hair and his fingernails. Keithland pampers himself, which was something he learned from his grandfather, an old dope man from the days of Black Frank Netti. Keithland often looks at Pedwell with disgust because he thinks he is an arch misogynist and a dogmatic leader. Pedwells' desk is neat. There is a large computer monitor that sits on a smoked glass desk cover with three red phones. A reporter over hears Keithland saying that the dog fighting has been linked to a criminal organization called DOG. As if he weren't pissed enough, in walks James Perry, the attorney for all of Keithland's legitimate businesses and real estate. Perry, a fair skinned, heavyset man who walks with a limp, is uncomfortable when he sees Pedwell lying across the black leather couch in the office. Peddy is smiling as he announces that he has everything under control.

"Baby girl is just hot headed. Whatever it is, I got it. K, you know the boys and me will fix it. She is always trying to be badder than her brothers."

James Perry is amazed that Pedwell can be so articulate whenever he pleases. He has known about Pedwell for years. The stories are endless since Peddy was once rumored to have been a Black Muslim. The other story is that Pedwell is the son of Lawton Peabody Jefferson. While there is truth of the legacy, something happened that landed Peddy on the wrong side of the tracks. Lawton Peabody Jefferson was from the oldest and most beaugoise black money family in Detroit. Everybody wants to know how Pedwell could have possibly fallen from grace. It is a fact that the Jefferson clan disowned Pedwell years ago. There was Richard Jefferson, a surgeon, who is Pedwell's older brother. Stories suggest that Pedwell is half white. Others say he is actually the product of the old man messing around with the help. Peddy has always given Perry the creeps. Whenever Peddy was lying on the couch, he always seemed to look right into your being. It was always spooky. Peddy sits up as the lawyer looks at Keithland and begins to talk in a low, mono voice.

"I just got a call from a source that says Rickey Ricardo Braddock turned over some books from your warehouse. He is under the Feds protection Keithland. This is serious. He can tell about that other thing with all the Councilmen and those contracts with Corelli." Pedwell blurts out suddenly, "Ricky Ricardo is a snitch?"

Keithland pushes a black button on the side of his desk. Big Tiny walks in with two men behind him. Keithland pulls off his suit jacket. He stands up and walks to the long black marble bar that is situated behind his desk. Opening a bottle of cognac, he pours the liquor into a cognac sniffer. The smell of old, high-end cognac is a familiar scent to the self-pampered gangster. Staring at Perry, he speaks to his enforcer in a stern voice. His eyes seem to darken as he mentions Rick Braddock.

"Tiny. That muthafucking Ricky Ricardo is singing to the Feds. I got to have him. Put it out there. We need dat niggah stanking dead. Whatever it costs."
Peddy becomes visibly crazed at the mention of money for the hits.

"K man, me and my boys will smoke the whole city if the bank is that good!"

James Perry is nervous and begins clearing his throat.

"I am leaving. We want to be very far away from this conversation Keithland. This situation is not like anything we've faced before. You cannot be connected to anything remotely close to the harm of a federal witness."

Keithland tells Pedwell the rules. He is firm in both tone and instruction.

"Peddy, if you niggahs do it, I will make you a partner on all the dope houses that you do for us. This task is a no brainer for you. If you git one of your friends from Chicago, St. Louis, or Philly to take care of it, that would be fine with me. I really don't care. Tiny knows what I want. Perry, what they got besides Rick?"

James Perry wonders why all the thugs over in the warehouse could not have seen this coming. Making sure he doesn't upset Tiny, he cautiously asked how this happened?

"Hey Tiny, wasn't Rick doing well with all the warehouse business? He was wired with some deputies from Alexander County and that Lt. Williamson, the white boy, was always at the gambling parties with all the black girls?"

"Don't know. Rick used to be straight. He was making real good bank. I heard something bout that girl Walena, about when she used to dance. Somebody said she started working at the church with some other ex dancers. I'm calling over there so I can speak with Gwenny."

Tiny can't wait so he calls over to the warehouse to talk with Gwenny. Gwenny G is Keithland's younger sister. She runs the warehouse, keeps tabs on the thieves, stays up on the gambling parties and lives with Marlo Jackson. Marlo is the head of a crew that used to be known as the NFL or Niggahs For Life before they went to work for DOG.

Peddy leaps up and runs out of Envenom to his boys who are waiting for him in the parking lot.

"Call your sister. I need to talk with her about last night. Homi, did you know that bitch ass sister of yours killed the whole damn dogfight of the Blackheart crew?   That crazy bitch is making me look bad. K got trouble. We gonna hit this snitching bitch Ricky Ricardo before somebody gits him."

Inside the black Jaguar, Homicide, the oldest son, is smoking a giant blunt. Homicide is laughing about his sister's deeds from the night before.

"Mayhem smoked dem silly niggahs. That girl hit dem Chinese muthafucka's too. Con says she is really bad now."

In the rear seat is Hate Jefferson, who is single-minded. He is focused on one subject – the contract to perform the hit.

"Ricky Ricardo was a cold soldier fo dem dog niggahs. What made him switch over to dat snitching shit?"

Hate is the brother who lifts weights and looks like Mr. Universe. He is both amused by and proud of his sister. He doesn't agree with his father and says so.

"Mayhem just letting it lay. Dat Bitch is all beast. She is a gangster. No doubt about it. I heard she been beating niggahs down for old ass Ruby Redd. Daddy, you need to recognize. She ain't no little girl bitch. She can hurt a niggah. Dat girl ain't scared of shit."

Hate is dressed in a neat Addias sweat suit with a patch from the State University of Michigan. He is sitting next to his other brother Contempt who everybody calls Con. Contempt is the only brother that Mayhem trusts. His hair is long like Homicides but it looks more kept, almost as coiffed as the looks of a woman. Contempt is soft spoken yet he is a proven killer. He listens but makes no comment as his father goes on and on about how Mayhem is causing him grief. Contempt often sends gifts to the Johnson's for his baby sister, disguising himself as a distant cousin of hers who does not live in Michigan. Con loves his sisters. Mayhem bonded with him because he was the lone brother who refused to participate in the forced sex that Pedwell instructed his sons to perform on their sister. Con was also the brother that refused to treat their mother like a servant, or worse a slave. The ungodly beatings by his father did not deter Con's refusal to mistreat his mother. When Contempt got older and able to make his own money, he paid for piano lessons for himself and Mayhem. They both took lessons from an elderly music teacher on

Blaine. Music lessons and books were the things that set Peddy off. Jerenda knew, as most mothers did, that her children wanted to be loved. Even her kids were children with regular desires. Peddy beat her and perversely made their lives a living hell.

The Jaguar rolled down Mack Avenue. Peddy figured he would catch his daughter at Ruby Redds Club. Con was sitting with Hate but he quietly texted Mayhem, unbeknownst to his brother.

"Peddy is coming over to Redd's. He is mad bout last night."

Mayhem was at Redds enjoying war stories. Ruby Redd was the Queen of the underground or ruler of the underworld in Detroit. Back in the day, Richard "Big Dickie" Redd was her father and her grandmother was the original dealmaker for all the street hustlers back in the day.

As they pulled into the rear of the parking lot, Peddy tells his sons, "Take off your shit. Ruby got them Lesbian bitches watching. She will fuck you up trying to carry in there."

The sons laughed. Ruby has a loyal staff and her security is super tight. While Peddy is still a deadly man, he begrudgingly honors and respects Ruby's turf. Pedwell walked into the club with his boys. Once inside, they met up with two, large gun-toting women. A petite woman named Lil Bit was in charge. Lil Bit was not happy to see the likes of the Jefferson Clan. She grabbed her walkie-talkie and called Ruby's office.

"Ru, tell Ms. May that her father is looking for her. We ain't letting his ass loose. He got those three boys of his with him."

Lit Bit was wearing black leather pants and a small compact Glock 45 is neatly concealed in her waistband. She has so little hair that she is almost bald. Her large earrings give her the look of an African pirate of sorts. While she is small in size, Bit has an aura that is reminiscent of the old adage about athletes; Bit moved small but played large.

Peddy does not like the club. In part, because he hates when women are in control and he has great contempt for women in positions of authority.This is a club that is strikingly similar to the adult entertainment clubs designed with men in mind. Ruby Redd's club caters exclusively to women - lots and lots of women. Not all of them are black and not all of them are from Detroit. As the men wait for Mayhem, there are several male dancers walking into the club. Peddy frowns while he whispers to Homicide. Hate and Con begin walking away from the vile comments that they knew were coming soon.

"Look at these bitch ass niggahs. Man, look at that little big dick muthafucka over there. Dancers? Look at that sissy ass bitch wit dat little cloth covering his big dick. Now you know dats some faggot shit. These here niggahs want a man, not a fe-male. All dese here boys are fucking each other. I know fags when I see'em."

Unknown to his brothers, Contempt changed his name to Conquest a few years ago. If Peddy had heard the new name, he probably would have thought his son was a fag. Con often thought that his father might really be gay. Why else would he blabber about gay men in such a disgusting way, like he had something to hide. Con and Mayhem would sneak perfume from their mother before she got crazy depressed about her younger brother dying from dope. Peddy had something to do with her brother's death and Jerenda had always known that Peddy was also the one who killed her favorite Aunt Irene over some dope. Even though Mayhem hated her father, she loved her brother Contempt dearly. The worst thing in her young life had been watching Peddy torture her mother. Her mother was like a trained animal. Peddy would sometimes beat her and Mayhem. Peddy was a constant threat to his own little baby girl. All of her brothers were used to the beatings. Jerenda just gave up especially when Peddy started to teach the boys to curse her. The boys would just kayo the grandfather. Peddy then took his boys to graduate school by teaching them to expose themselves to women and the lesson started with Jerenda and her family.

Mayhem didn't care what Con was. It didn't matter that he was kind of like a woman or something like a girl. Con was the most confident in the entire messed up family. Sometimes Con would think about his sexuality, how he felt different about the world. Homicide was like the dangerous leader in the family. Pedwell loved to make the children fight each other. Mayhem learned early that as the first-born girl, she became the "junior" mother. Even when she was really young, she would take the ass beatings meant for Jerenda. Only Contempt would stand up for her. Only Contempt would fight with Homicide, Assault, Felonious and Rape. Contempt learned some fighting moves from this Chinese boy named Victor Kim. Victor was really bad and he knew judo real good. Victor and Contempt went to elementary school together. Victor wasn't scared of Homicide or any of the Jefferson boys. When Victor showed Contempt some moves, it made Con a better fighter. Peddy was jealous because sometimes he used to let his nasty old boys, Calhoun, Calloway and Big Willie, do nasty things to his kids. Contempt would take whatever freak shit he had to in order to stop them dog ass niggahs from doing it to Mayhem. Peddy did not like that shit. The brothers could see that Contempt was stronger and badder than them. Peddy got so mad he would call Victor and his folks some "Chinese mutha-fuckas with slanted eyes." He ultimately decided that Victor could not play with Con anymore.

"Little Chinese Japanese muthafucka wit all dat fancy ass karate. I'll shoot his Chinese ass."

Contempt became a different type of gangster. He resisted all of the madness that Peddy taught him and his siblings. Con loved his Uncle Ronnie on his mothers' side. There was a rumor that Ronnie was a bona fide sissy. Ronnie Tinsley worked at Motown as a sound engineer. He was so good that even after Motown left Detroit, he was able to get a gig with the Detroit Symphony Orchestra as a soundman. It was Uncle Ronnie that bought Con books and he was also the one who introduced Con to Piano lessons. He took Mayhem to the church where he was the choir director. Mayhem loved gospel music. Uncle Ronnie took his niece and nephew to see some gospel concerts. Peddy hated his brother in law and, like the Devil himself, gospel music made his skin crawl. On a serious note, while talk of God and good made most people behave appropriately, all the happy talk made Pedwell Jefferson act ugly. Their late grandmother said that Peddy couldn't listen to the Angels sing. She would laugh as Mahaila Jackson records or the old radio show with Martha 'Jean' The Queen gospel hour played at noon everyday, and that kept Peddy from the Tinsley homestead. The devil known as Peddy did not like to hear the songs of the church.

Chapter 5: Coming Out of the Streetside Economy

Alberta Tinsley was an old autoworker and her deceased husband had been an autoworker too. Jerenda Tinsley met Peddy when she was thirteen years old. He knew she was fast and that she was lying about her age. Pedwell was acting like he was a Black Muslim back then. Ms. Alberta reminded everyone that Peddy was actually nothing less than a pedophile.

"Jerenda wasn't barely thirteen years old when that man kidnapped her. A grown ass man, taking up with a fast ass little hussy. I couldn't do much with her. My husband was drunk all the time. We had other children but she was always running around up on 12th Street where all the girls that sell themselves hangout."
When Mayhem appeared, she just looked at the men.

"Wassup? Why y'all here?" Noticing Contempt, she smiles and winks as they hug each other with joy.

"Girl, you been a bad ass girl. Laying down all dem killing dogs," he laughs. Standing in the hall, the smell of fried chicken haunts everyone. It is the cuisine of New Orleans. Gumbo Supreme and chicken wings, New Orleans style. Smelling the aroma makes Peddy hungry. Looking at Mayhem makes him angry because she looks good, real good. The boys are waiting for him to put her in her place. Homicide is annoyed that his sister is feeling strong. He has deep-seated resentment against a woman feeling like she can stand on her own two. He doesn't like the bond that Mayhem and Contempt share. It wasn't that long ago that Contempt had beaten Rape down. Mayhem came home from school questioning her parents about the family's true identity. Mayhem screamed at her mother wondering why she allowed Peddy to name the children all those loathsome names.

Pedwell laughed and asked her, "What in the world are you crying about? Lookee here little bitch, you are fucked up jest like yo fucked up mammy. I can name y'all anything I want to. Who told you it wasn't French-African? I know, I named all of y'all."

Contempt told Peddy that he and Mayhem heard a teacher at the school telling the principal that their names were the result of a deeply disturbed and abusive father. Homicide was in a state of disbelief when Mayhem told the family that she was regularly attending a church that Ms. Martha had taken her to in the summer. Homicide had to pull Contempt off of Rape for trying to stick Mayhem. Mayhem seemed to lose touch with reality after she went to that church. Rape was the brother that seemed to enjoy all kinds of nasty things. Rape was the brother who would stick his brother when Pedwell told him it was "bitch time."

"Fuck or git fucked" was the battle cry of Peddy and his three-dog ass running boys, Big Dick Willie, Calhoun and Calloway. They were the culprits that had their way with Mayhem. Homicide and Rape were allowed to do nasty things with the three dogs.

"Then the shit got seriously fucked up" according to Homicide. Peddy would never forget the day Mayhem flipped out. Pedwell had beaten his wife severely and all the sudden out of nowhere BOOM BAM BAM. Mayhem pulled out a sawed-off shotgun. It was a badass Beretta shotgun. She shot her father and her brothers Rape and Homicide. Good thing the thugs had on some heavy-duty bulletproof vests or they would have been history. It was a sobering moment and from that day on, nobody put a hand on Mayhem. Maybe the bigger blow was that Contempt helped his sister find three dog night with Big Dick Willie, Calhoun and Calloway. It was a gruesome hit. Nobody knew that it was Pedwell's own son and daughter who paid for the hit on the nasty men that had violated them when they were little children. Nobody in the Jefferson clan said it.

Homicide would often look at Mayhem and Contempt and think about, "how the two muthafucka's ain't like me and my other brothers."

Ruby Redd walked into the hall. As she smiles at Mayhem, she points the family to the big red door with the big shiny R in little white lights.

"Ms. Mayhem, y'all go on in the Red Room. You and your folks can have some Gumbo. Mista Peddy looks hungry."
Homicide feels helpless and naked without his gat.

Rolling his eyes and smirking at Mayhem, Peddy thinks to himself, "This lesbian bitch thinks she is better than me."

He hates Ruby. He hates the way his daughter and this young female seem to be calling the shots. "Bitch ain't the shot caller. Dats for real!!"

The Red Room is just that; red, wall-to-wall with furniture, cold and shiny chrome bars and luxurious, soft bar chairs. A huge red topped pool table and a red jukebox plays, Let's Get It On by Marvin Gaye. Ruby Redd is a dark-skinned woman with a complexion that is clean and glows making her look like the Queen Ruby of the Red Castle. The club is for women. Nothing remotely suggests that men are welcome. Scores of well developed, raw boy toys of all shapes and sizes parade the hall. Peddy suddenly remembers exactly how much he hates the club filled with thong wearing, dick bagged, faggot dancers. Peddy has difficulty ignoring the aroma from the feast. He is dressed in a regal hook up. It's a custom-made denim jacket with a full air brushed picture of himself on the back. His signature black and blue alligator cowboy boots grab everyones attention. Peddy begins to lecture Mayhem on "family values."

"Baby girl, wassup? Last night yo decision to smoke the whole Blackheart posse was not a good thing. In fact, the whole thing is not good at all."

Mayhem is not listening to anything Peddy is putting down. Before she can say a word, seven young girls enter the Red Room. The leader of the group of girls is the Big Girl. Homicide can't control his eyes as he looks at the statuesque squad of females. Peddy is pissed.

"Who in the hell do these girls think they are?"

What is most noticeable is that the girls are armed, carrying their big expensive Louis Vuitton tote bags. Hate can see the barrels of the guns protruding from more than one bag. Mayhem and Lil Bit enter the room as Ruby looks on. Ruby is dressed in a tight red cigarette skirt with a revealing red and white top. Her hair is cut in layers with silver gray streaks. Her red and silver wire glasses are tinted a soft red. Her perfect white teeth make her look as if she could be the twin sister of Tina Turner. The females with Mayhem are all lined up behind the table as the Jefferson boys shake the Louisiana hot sauce over the entire bowl of whole chicken wings. Marvin Gaye's, *What's going on* is purring with smoothness as if he were in the room. The speakers are expensive and Ruby is gliding across the floor while announcing that Mayhem is always welcome at the club.

"Mr. Peddy, dis here girl of yours is becoming quite a player. She is always welcome here cuz she is a young woman in charge!!"
Standing in front of the wall of star pictures, Mayhem smiles at Peddy. She enjoys the fact that she is messin' with his crazy ass. There is a huge picture of fine ass Marvin Gaye in a white suit holding Ruby Redd real close to him. Teddy Pendergrass, Aretha "Queen" Franklin, David Ruffin, Florence Ballad, Mary Wilson, Diana Ross, Levi Stubbs; the whole wall is filled with pictures of Ruby and many of her favorite entertainers.

Mayhem finally says, "Daddy, last night was really not that bad. In fact, for the most part, that was my good side. Dem Chinese bitches and the Chile Boys, all of dem was fucking wit my friend."
Peddy is enraged and cannot control his temper. He stands quickly, holding a large drumstick, revealing his diamond-encrusted rings on multiple fingers. Big Girl begins starring at Peddy so tough, he felt the side of his face burning. All of a sudden and without a word, she raises a black MP-5 from her Louis V. Hate grabs at his waist but misses his gat. The boys are handicapped with nothing in their hands but their dicks.

Contempt is worried and speaks softly to his dear sister, "May-hem, its cool. Tell your girl to chill. We jest trying to enjoy sum gumbo May-hem."
Sensing the moment with rising tension, Ruby laughs.

"Look here. Everybody best relax. This room is blood red already."
Mayhem looks at Ruby and smiles.

Walking right up to her father she explains, "Y'all may as well leave Daddy, Homi, and Hate. I am doing me, ok? I got my own thang. I am out. Peddy, last night was my business. Dhem boys asked fo it. I wasn't fucking wit nobody. Dats it. I ain't part of y'all thang. I really never was. Ain't having it. Dis is me. Dis is my thang and you gotta respect dat."

Peddy can't believe his ears and neither can Hate or Homicide. Not much is said after Mayhem declared her independence.

Peddy sits down. Con is worried since he knows that Peddy does not take well to female power. Signaling to his sons, Peddy indicates he is no longer hungry. It becomes quiet at the table since Mayhem is leaving the room with her girls.

Whispering to Big Girl, "Watch Peddy, he is pissed."
She feels real good and strong, like a true gangster. Mayhem has her own crew. They are her family not some knucklehead niggahs. She hadn't felt this good since her and Con smoked the three dogs that night. Homicide is much more upset than Peddy. Mayhem was really feeling like she was the original gangster. Homicide strongly believed that women, "fe-males" as he liked to say, were simply bitches and hoes. Homicide was the one person that cheered for Peddy. It was his leadership, his distorted sense of righteousness that resulted in him doing perverted things to his brothers and sisters. If it weren't for Mayhem, Homicide would have done nasty dick things to his baby sister. Pedwell even had his sons doing the kinky nasty things to their own mother. Once there was a detective talking with a caseworker who had called protective services to help Jerenda Jefferson after she had been beaten. The detective told another detective his feelings about Pedwell Jefferson. Mayhem never forgot what the detective said.

"This breed is alien. These children don't have a chance in the world to be anything but damned. This bastard makes his boys fuck their own family including their own mother and sister."
Sitting in Ruby's big red leather throne like chair in the office, Mayhem was thinking about how she had made the boys respect her juice. Homicide had always challenged her as a female. Sometimes he would orchestrate his sister's torture using his brothers as the assailants. As Mayhem sat in the big throne, her memories were frozen to the day at the playground when two boys fought with her on the monkey bars.

The little skinny black girl was on the monkey bars as two larger and older boys walked up and announced, "Git off bitch. Dis here is our bars. Git off now! Git off the playground you ugly ass little bitch."

The boys laughed as they pushed the girl to the ground. There was a smaller girl who began to cry as the skinny older girl jumped up from the ground charging the two boys. Her clothes were dirty and baggy like a worn potato sack. Her intensity was noticed by an older girl who pointed to a distant group of youngsters on the far end of the athletic complex.

"Dose girls is wit dem Dog boys. Dat girl is the younger sister of Homi Jefferson and those other Jefferson brothers. That bitch is bad. She might be little and young, but her and her girls are BAD. Dats dem on dose bad ass scooters over dhere."

Mayhem can still hear the music as she remembers that moment of embarrassment. A convoy of more than twelve Honda scooters cut across the complex towards the playground.

Speakers on the scooters blared lyrics by Tupac, "My mind state preoccupied with homicide."
The youngsters all wore red and black Nike and Reebok sweat suits with black helmets with black visors. The scene looked and sounded like a music video on BET. As they arrived at the monkey bars, the little skinny girl was swinging and hollering at the two boys that had manhandled her moments earlier. The boys were laughing as one of them hit the little girl directly in her mouth as hard as he could. Her mouth exploded with blood and her teeth were falling out. The first scooter stopped. The youngster took off his helmet and began shaking his head in disgust.

A small crowd was standing and admiring the sleekness of the crew. The young boy got off the scooter and bent over as if he was going to assist the damaged and crying young girl. Another young boy flew off his scooter with a small baseball bat. The bat was swung with an adult like viciousness that took the first boy by surprise. The girl was lying there barely able to move. The young boy bent over her and laughed in her face.

"Mayhem, yous a weak little bitch. You ain't never gonna be a gangster because you will always be a weak ass fe-male. Daddy knows you is weak too."
The young Contempt swung his bat with a vengeance. Both boys were trying to escape the full pressing attack. Bones were cracking

while voices could be heard howling in pain. One young boy fell to the ground trying unsuccessfully to protect his head. Within minutes, the convoy had pulled off. Everyone was gone except young Contempt. Crying, Mayhem slowly got up looking at her brother. She was barely able to open her ruptured mouth.

"I am a G. I am a gangster. It was two niggahs."

Mayhem was a hundred percent G. She was true to the game. Gangster supreme she be!!! The music of Harold Melvin and the Blue notes was blowing in the background. You could hear the soulful voice of Teddy Pendergrass leading the fitting song for the moment, 'Be for Real.'

6

TRUTH B TOLD

Sgt. Peter Bannon sat in the living room with Helen and George Goss. Bannon was a tall, wiry man with graying hair and a mustache. He was not far from retirement. The old couch was faded burgundy, velvet-like material. There was a fireplace with a number of pictures on the mantel. Bannon thought about how the photos told a story about a proud colored family. The pictures of Reverend Dr. Martin Luther King, Jr., President John F. Kennedy and his brother Robert Kennedy were all in one big frame. Right next to the historic iconic picture is the larger picture of President Barack Obama smiling. The whole mantel has family pictures including a new family picture of President Obama, his wife Michelle, and their two daughters. Staring at the pictures, Bannon can't help but to think about the early days when the Detroit Police Officers Association had pictures of Mayor Coleman A. Young with a drawn in Hitler mustache in their union hall. That was 1974 and now there is a black president. His partner, Roy McFarley hated Coleman Young, as did most of the white police officers at that time. For McFarley, a black city councilman would have been a stretch. As if that weren't bad enough, now there is a Black President of the United States of America.

Bannon's interview with the Goss's was an attempt to piece together and understand the violent battle that happened the night of the dogfight.

Bannon listened as Helen tried to explain, "I just want my dog back. Sgt. Bannon, we didn't see anything. We heard a lot of popping that sounded like firecrackers. I was trying to get back there. George didn't want to look in the alley. He says those empty buildings have all sorts of things in them including places for dog fighting. Our Rufus was back there. I want my Rufus back."

Bannon was really working hard to pinpoint the exact moment when things went crazy. He couldn't find anyone to tell him

51

what had happened or what had left death all over the alley that night. Helen Goss was thankful for what she called, "that nice bad girl." Bannon was puzzled as he listened to the Goss' describe the black car and the young black girl.

"She's a nice girl. We have seen her before up at the store. She visits Rochelle a lot. She always waves to Rufus and me when we are taking our walks. That day, she drove up, got out of that little fast black car and that is when all the noise and popping happened." George Goss hesitated before he let on about his thoughts on Mayhem.

"Sarge, I think she is a dangerous little girl. I have seen her with that bad guy - that gangster. She was with those bad guys you know. The ones who seem to be controlled by the fancy dressing bad guy that was on Channel One accused of killing an informer or something. Pe-ddy something."

As if he had heard the name of Frank Bruno or Jimmy 'Flat Nose" Hoffman, Bannon blurted out the name, "Peddy Jefferson? Do you mean the Detroit Original Gangsters' D-O-G? The young girl was with Pedwell? Are you sure? The tall, black skinny girl was with Peddy Jefferson? She was the one getting out of the black car?"

Sgt. Bannon was visibly excited. That name was something Detroit Police knew all too well. Bannon seemed to fly to his unmarked black Queen Victoria sedan. His cell phone rang and his partner, Detective Roy Mac Farley was asking him what kind of sandwich he wanted.

Bannon yells, "Roy, the shooters may be part of Peddy Jefferson's gang. Does he have a daughter?"

The cruiser drives off fast while the conversation continues, "Bannon, do you want the special today? The corned beef and cabbage smell good. The old man says you can't eat potato bread anymore. Can you have mustard?"

The voice continues, "Peddy Jefferson? I don't think he has no girls. Been awhile since I worked on his cases."

Bannon was driving fast and arrived at Murphy's on Vernon within twelve minutes. The stout, half bald McFarley comes out the front door holding two large bags. His ruffled shirt with an ugly beer stained tie makes him look like a police detective from the 1950's.

He is breathing hard as he informs Bannon, "That social worker over there with Mary Ellen worked with that case when they took a child from that creature. A nice-looking colored girl. You know, she is some fancy training person. I would call her or Mary Ellen at social services."

Sgt. Bannon and Detective McFarley are familiar with the Jefferson clan. But Mayhem has remained a secret, in large part, because most of the known crime that this clan committed had been at the hands of Peddy and his sons. Another reason Mayhem has remained unknown is because neither of these men could ever imagine a female of this kind. The problem was the blinding sexism of both men. Mayhem has killed before recent times. The truth is that she is actually an excellent assassin. She is well trained and has crazy discipline. While her mother and others didn't approve, she learned to kill early in her life simply having survived the upbringing of her diabolical father. The mantra of "kill or be killed" was what she had always known. Now, she is grown in the third city, where there are no children, no teenagers and certainly, no innocence. The phone calls to the social services department make one thing clear. Mayhem Jefferson is the daughter of Pedwell and Jerenda Jefferson.

The detective and homicide units are comparing notes. The mayor's office and the Police Chief's office want to know what happened with the dog-fighting massacre. Sgt. Bannon has been designated the lead detective of the team with Lt. Gale Rowe who is the head of Homicide. Lt. Rowe is considered a rising star. Her academic background includes a degree from the University of Detroit in biology and chemistry. She also has a law degree from the University of Michigan. She is currently a doctoral student in Forensic Anthropology at Michigan State University. Her studies are under the direction of the famed cultural anthropologist, Professor Margaret Marshall. The men in homicide have had it rough under Rowe's leadership. Rowe has the uncanny ability to balance real hardcore science with the facts of real street experiences. A good friend of the Long family,

Xavier has advocated for her since her early days at the University of Detroit.

Bannon opened the meeting with a voice full of trepidation, "Well, all we know is that we have nine people and thirteen dogs all DEAD and all of it is gang affiliated. What we know for sure is that it's an operation that is under the umbrella of the Keithland James crew."

Dressed in a worn black fatigue jacket with burnt brown Red Wing work boots, an orange and black wool lumberjack shirt with loose fitting worn Carhart jeans, Lt. Rowe gives strict orders.

"The scene is now under the multi-jurisdiction of the Federal task force which I am the co-leader."

Bannon is annoyed. His eyes and the eyes of Detective MacFarley portray a sense of rage and embarrassment. MacFarley thinks that the whole city is under the leadership of egghead, college trained police. Looking at each other in amazement, neither of them can believe what they are now seeing and hearing. Standing at the highly technical wide screen, Lt. Rowe begins to share intelligence about the shooting site.

"This we know. A young woman led this shooting. We have information that suggests she is related, in some way, to the notorious Pedwell Jefferson. We have recovered evidence of a custom motorcycle that belongs to one, Rene Mankiller. All of this evidence was brought to our attention from our task force member, Scientific Command One."

Bannon bolts from his seat into the face of Rowe.

"What in the name of Mary is going on?"

Catching his temper he tries, in vain, to hide his outrage.

He continued his questions, "You are telling us that while we are all out gathering information, somebody already has all of this evidence?"

Lt. Rowe smiles. She understands how old school police and police tactics are a part of a dying breed. Her badge is looped around her neck on a medium nickel chain. Wearing a black fitted baseball cap with an old English D wrapped perfectly around her head, she commands the attention of all in the meeting.

Gangster Manqué: The Saga of Mayhem Jefferson

"This incident interrupted an international and federal case on gun smuggling. The Hmong and Latino gangs are much bigger players than the local tribal conflict. That is all we can say. Bannon, you and the detectives will know more as the charges come out. At this point, I can only tell you that we are reviewing all associations of Keithland James. This girl crew is new and it is all females. They are all young and black. They represent something we haven't seen. The woman on the bike is part Native American, Cherokee I've heard. Mayhem Jefferson is something we are just discovering."

Roy is looking livid as the meeting breaks. It seems he can't understand anything. He doesn't like Rowe and he is upset with at least three new detectives in the unit. All of them are college graduates - real graduates. While McFarley had a college degree, it had been a long haul for him and the older cops. They all went to Miltoast College. Miltoast gave cops a free ride. It was a secret kept inside the rank and file of the old guard. The new college graduates came from all over. Grand Valley State, Eastern Michigan, Western Michigan, the University of Detroit, Mercy College, Alexander State University; you name it. One of the young women is from Michigan State University and the other two came from the College of Urban Development.

Brains, all smarts, both Bannon and McFarley were part of the white resistance better known as the Detroit Police Political Action Group (D-PPAG). These men were the last of the old guard like their fathers, uncles, brothers, and cousins - the real good ole boys. They represented an assortment of troublemaking darkies that had made inroads.

Worse, it had been that damn Mayor Coleman A. Young who advocated for putting blacks and women in leadership roles. The Detroit Police Action Group had lawyers that filed lawsuits and they went after 'Hizzoner' with everything they had. They controlled the ranks of patrol, but in the long run, Mayor Young had changed the look and color of the Detroit Police. Now, in the new day, its mayor and common council were always over-represented by the "dark folks," as Mac would assert every chance that presented itself.

Chapter 6: Truth B Told

The detectives leave the meeting in a fuss. Its a big crowd of the old officers, some retired, that frequented O'Malleys Beer Garden downtown, directly across the street from district court. Joining the old guard were several homicide unit members. Strange as it seemed, there were several blacks, Latinos, and Asians at the overall gathering. Sgt. Linda Glass, a seasoned homicide investigator, laughed as the younger officers discussed the old controversial S.T.R.E.S.S. unit and the riots. Glass, whose father was an undercover officer in the unit, discussed her feelings as a young black girl growing up on the Westside of the city.

"My old man believed in STRESS. He loved the undercover unit. My mother hated it. They were getting guys all the time."

One of the new homicide detectives interrupted, "Well, that dog fighting and shooting reminds us that we need to do something to stop all the unsolved shootings we have had."

Another detective remarked, "The chief didn't share much with us. I think they believe we are like the cowboys and old guys."
The reference to cowboys is about the robbery unit that behaves as though they are policing in the days of Wyatt Earp. Another homicide detective is Sgt. Vince Davis who is an eighteen-year veteran of the force. His words are about an incident that took place during the riot of 1967. He agreed that the Cowboys made policing bad.

"Cowboys is crazy. It's not the first time the department has had some extremists. My grandfather was a commander when the riot took place. He went to his grave with some unholy memories of what DPD did to blacks. The Algiers Motel incident was so infamous that a book was written that detailed the murders of all those young black men."Looking sad, the tall young blond shook his head as he detailed what happened at the Algiers. As the men drank, Roy looked at the composition of the new Detroit Police. His father had also been a cop. He fought in the Korean War. His uncles had all been cops. He had disdain for how minorities had become not only police but now they seemed to run the whole department. While the "nigger" label had different translations, he was looking at the new Detroit Police and how they didn't look anything like the Irish, Jewish or Italians from decades ago. Anyway, none of this meant anything and it certainly would not give them any leads to arrest anyone for the dog slaughter.

Vince Davis said he had a file on Mayhem that he worked with Sgt. Glass. The intelligence unit shared some interesting facts related to Mayhem. Although there was a good deal of intelligence, much of the information had been misinterpreted by many members of the multi-jurisdictional task forces. Weak was the sharing of information and strong were the assumptions, the sexism, the racism and the overall outdated means of communicating within the old department. Vince Davis, sitting at the bar, told Sgt.

Bannon that his memories of Mayhem Jefferson were scary. He remembered what he felt when he first heard what she did as a young street dealer of around sixteen years.

"I was in Narcotics and we just could not believe how this little, skinny, 16-year- old girl had handled a rival from the corner of Elmhurst and Parkway. It was Linda Glass working that side of Elmhurst with two crews from the 10th Precinct. The Dexter Boys were trying to take over her corner. She couldn't have weighed much more than one hundred pounds. The boys were the treacherous Brown Brothers. The biggest brother must have weighed 250 pounds or more. He actually picked her up over his head. She was kicking and fighting as he slammed her into a metal mail box like she was a rag doll."

Linda Glass remembered the moment. Laughing, she seemed to catch herself in one of those rare moments in the street. A young girl was wrapping herself around that bull neck of Mach Brown. With full contact, she just jumped up from the ground like a jumping jack. Her eyes looked crazed. She fought like her life depended on every blow she delivered.

"I had the video camera and caught it all. She had those little braids covered in that Black skull cap that made her look like a boy. She choked Mach and bit a chunk of flesh out of the side of his neck. Man, he started hollerin' and screamin' and all kinds of blood gushed out of his wound. She spat the bloody flesh out as if it was poison."

Sipping his beer, he shook his head, reliving the moment. Linda Glass had reviewed the juvenile records of Mayhem and her brothers. The overall attitude of the old guard was that policing juveniles was not really critical to real police work. A young girl was too easy.

She would be put off on the old police matrons who didn't carry guns. Glass knew that her father, despite being an African American, understood that "woman plus black" meant the full force of the white resistance within DPD. Vince Davis was an average officer. He was nothing like his Gestapo father or his uncles. While Lt. Glass moved up over the years, she knew that resistance still existed in some of the old guard and their off springs. She offered her memory of that first encounter with Mayhem. Her crew that day represented the United Nations, as labeled by their boss, the infamous Inspector Dack Hollawell. Hollawell had been the enforcer for the white resistance in the old days. The fact that young Vince Davis, Linda Glass, Chinese-American Keith Cheng, Angela Garcia of Cuban-American decent, and Polish- American Oswald Pulaski were under his wing, he decided that Detroit had become the United Nations training arm. It was not the film of the battle between the Brown Brothers with Mayhem that made the task force pay attention. It was the discovery of the two brothers hours later found in the trunk of their brand-new silver Mercedes Benz sedan.

Vince Davis and Linda Glass were the first at the scene. Behind the Shrimp Shack on Richton and Dexter, the brothers were bound with their feet wrapped in black electrical wire and their mouths gagged. The bullet-riddled corpses had been stuffed into the trunk. Everyone in the neighborhood stood like the statue made up of the three monkeys, See No Evil, Say No Evil and Hear No Evil. To that motto, Inspector Dack Hollowell remarked to his fresh young crew in narcotics, "This here is what the monkeys do to their own. This is what you get when you let'em run free. You get all out-MONKEY MADNESS in the jungles of our city. All you minority types need to leave now and let the United Nations send in the peacekeeping troops."

7

FEMALE RISING

The club began to rock as Mayhem and her girls were holding court. Little Bit sent a waitress over to tell Mayhem that she had guests waiting for her at the back door. Since Peddy and the boys had left, Mayhem was feeling good and respected. Little Bit pointed towards the backdoor entrance.

She yelled, "There are two Puerto Rican girls that say they are down with some guy you know. Some girls named Jamilia and Rita Q are out here and them girls got some beautiful fly ponytails."
Mayhem is glad to see the girls. She greets them with hugs.

"Wassup? Y'all lookin' good. How is business?"
The two young Puerto Ricans represent the organization of Latino gangs that have consolidated into an organization that is now called the Spanish Fly. Jamilia is from New York and Rita Q is the enforcement chief from the island itself. Mayhem comments about how colorful and spiffy their attire is whenever she works with Spanish Fly. Mayhem loves their airbrushed sweatshirts with their pictures looking exactly like them. The red and white DKNY shoes are custom crafted by a young Cuban graffiti artist named PenMan. Jamilia sits down at the desk by the back door.

Ruby Redds has heavy-duty girls standing all over the entrance and back door. While Mayhem listened to Jamilia, it became crystal clear that Rita was impressed with the firearms displayed by the mannish looking women. She knows that Mayhem is a weapon of mass destruction. Ms. Jefferson ain't scared of nothing and she can even the score real quick. Just three months ago, Rita had hired Mayhem and her crew of female predators to wipeout the competition in Newark. That hit made Rita a believer since the gang that Mayhem removed had big guns and everybody knew they were some serious gangsters. What was amazing was that the gang was known as Lone Star Wolf.

Chapter 7: Female Rising

LSW, as they were known, were some serious cowboys from Maco, Texas, near the northwest Mexican border. LSW was comprised of some former border patrol officers and former law enforcement, as well as former armed forces that were mostly whites that had superior firepower in their possession. LSW had a reputation for killing their opposition using both military precision and strategies. Who could stand up to the tough military types? The media reported it was the Mexican Cartel that had destroyed the powerful LSW. It was one of the most brutal hits seen by anyone in years. Mayhem and Rene played the nasty ass Cowboys-LSW boys. They set them sex hungry boys up at the fake tittie bar. Got it on video to show all the big willies how a female can make it work.

The video captured the boldness of LSW. The Newark scene was urban and the Cowboys came into the tittie bar like they owned it. One of the Cowboys laughed about Newark specifically explaining their superiority. The big cowboy hats and the slick western style pistols made them look like they were starring in some modern-day Wild West sideshow. The thick cigars, colorful cowboy clothes and the big custom-made badges had been their personal trademarks. Standing at the bar, wearing a brown and tan cowboy leather jacket with the long fringes hanging from his sleeves, the thick blond mustached face smiled as he watched Big Girl come out with cowgirl boots and a short sexy mini skirt revealing her large breasts hanging low in a matching bra. On top of the stage, the music played the old school tune, Cowboys and Girls by the Intruders. Rene, despite her thick yet toned thighs, was as agile as a cat. Her bronze ponytail hung down her back resting on her perfect ass. The long orange feathers on a headband revealed the actual Native American flavor of Rene. Flirting with the Cowboys, Rene revealed her sexiness that was balanced with her other side simply known as Big Girl. She danced slowly and inviting along with two other beautiful young women.

The first girl was a radiant smiling Asian, whose yellow tight-fitting tights with a medium breast protruding made the fat cowboy wearing a blue suede shirt with matching cowboy boots comment, "This little bitch is from China. She even got a sword. Hell, this Injun girl got an arrow and a bow."

As the music played, another cowboy laughed and began to dance. He was one of the leaders. They called him Hoss since he reminded everyone of the legendary character off the cowboy themed show Bonanza. Hoss was wearing two pistols with a long horsewhip on his neck. Hoss, a man of the wild, wild, west, was a tough, whiskey-drinking cowboy with an attitude. Standing at the bar, he passed gas while belching. The bartender walked to the other end of the bar. The smell is ungodly and the scent seems to worsen as it lingers in the middle of the mist of cigar smoke.

Hoss bellowed with arrogance, "Hey bitch. You too good to smell my shit? Fucking China girl over here."
The Asian dancer smiled. Actually, she was holding her breath, pretending like the deep stanky odor would eventually dissolve. The attractive Asian moves about with a sword in her hand. The bartender was furious.

She glared at Hoss, thinking to herself, "this pig muthafucka is just like my no-good ass daddy."

The last dancer on the stage was the petite figure of an African American girl dressed smartly in a short military jacket with fishnet stockings. Her large eyes stared into the crowd of about twelve cowboys deep who were situated all around the bar. The bartender poured drinks and turned up a new tune. A loud hiphop tune, heavily bass laden, suddenly made the cowboys agitated, perhaps even angry. Jay Z's and UKG's Big Pimpin bounced off the stage.

Big Hoss, still drinking beer and sweating profusely, begins to holler, "We don't listen to that nigger ass rap music!"
Before the other twelve can laugh again at the music, it suddenly changed from Pimpin to the old James Brown promise of the Big Payback. As the chorus sang "the big payback," the lights went real dark. The music changed again. The spirit of a grim reaper had entered the bar.

The bartender, suddenly and without warning, pulled out the small deadly HK-55 assault rifle and let loose. Like a synthesizer used in an opera, the Asian girl used the sword with a kind of precise swiftness that ended with big Hoss decapitated. Gunfire sprayed all twelve helpless Cowboys around the bar. Big Girl took aim with her bow and arrow. She sent an arrow flying into the back of the badass cowboy with the brown fringe jacket. Swords, arrows and bullets ripped into the LSW crew. As the music played, an old classic soothes the moment with Walter Jackson's, It's All Over Now. It was, in fact, all over in a matter of seconds. The bartender, with her wrap around shooter glasses, stepped out from behind the bar ordering the crew to move out. It was dead silent as Mayhem took off her white bartender jacket and laughed.

"Shut that video off. These cowboy muthfucka's done finished their rodeo."

As Jamilia and Rita Q knew well, Mayhem Jefferson had perfected what many in the street didn't know. Mayhem and her band of deadly women proved that evening in Newark, New Jersey that equality, equity and street enlightenment included the dark female species.

The women from the Spanish Fly wanted to explain to Mayhem what they needed. Rita Q is a woman who doesn't beat around the bush.

"Mayhem, I need your muscle. We got some business here in Detroit. We need you to make sure we don't get caught up with some young boys whose papa's is real heavy."

Big Girl closes the door on the Red Room. Jamilia is drinking a rum and coke. She lets Rita explain the details. A red and black tattoo on the left inner arm is such an authentic illustration of a dragon that it almost looked alive. Mayhem watches as Big Girl is huddled with Little Bit at the bar. Little Bit is telling Big Girl the news about the big contract out on Rickey Ricardo.

"Rene, y'all know dat dog ass daddy of Mayhems' is after Rickey. Dat sad fella done started talking to the Feds."

Pulling her ponytail back for a little refresher, she frowns and says exactly what's on her mind, "Sounds serious. Peddy didn't say much. Mayhem got him spinnin' so it's out there for whoever tags this silly ass!"

As Big Girl probes more, Mayhem is listening to the Puerto Rican women. Mayhem doesn't drink alcohol or smoke dope. She is sipping her favorite non-alcoholic drink. It's a concoction of Canada

Dry ginger ale and lime juice with three red cherries. Feeling well respected, she is eager to make more money. Rita continues with her request.

"Well, we need to hide this girl and her babies. She left one of the big Willies from Mexico. Her brothers are over in New York. They say they need her safe. I'm saying, you should be the one to protect her cuz nobody knows how you hangin'."

Mayhem smiles as she turns to Tweeny the bartender and asks, "How bout some of dat sweet hot sauce with dem wings and give my people here sum of dat Kogie salad."

Tweeny is an older woman who did twenty years for killing an abusive boyfriend. She is bartender, personal chef to Ruby, and health expert for all the street girls. A tall woman with a head full of reddish braids, her youthful look belies a street insider of over thirty years. Tweeny loves Mayhem and tends to heap special love on the young thug. A Kogie salad was once the prime attraction at Carl's Chop House; yet another once thriving business that is defunct, dead, no moe. Tweeny learned to make the salad of boiled eggs, turkey, boiled shrimp, and chicken breast during her early release work program at Carl's. A huge bed of lettuce with Swiss cheese and the special Tweeny sauce, the salad and the sweet potato fries are among the favorites of all the young girls. As the conversation continues, the DJ plays Mayhems' old jam from back in the day. She always loved Flashlight by George Clinton and P-Funk and it echoes in her head. Suddenly, Mayhems' look is one of total disbelief.

Jamilia just smiles with the words every young G waits for, "My people said after you blasted them Cowboy muthafucka's, we needed YOU, not yo daddy."

These days, Mayhem was more deadly than Peddy, she thought to herself. Tyquan was the only one who understood that, even as a girl, she was an amazing assassin. Tyquan, with his fine ass, always told Mayhem she could hold it down. Now she has major players coming to the D to bring a girl on. As Cube said, "Today is a good day." Rita likes the Kogie. She is not sure if she wants a little more of that sauce or is it salad dressing?

"We gonna bring in some big paper from overseas. The international border is cool. We got some A-rabbs who need yo kinda weight. The international boarders are really tight right now. You are right here in Detroit so we can use the boarders between yo city and Canada to handle our business. You know how it be! So we got two or three jobs all at the same time? Y'all know some old Italian named Messalina?"

Big Girl is listening to Little Bit with one eye on her girl Mayhem.

She begins to think, "I wonder how many fellas out in the street are going for the contract? Peddy is the kind of man that will kill everybody for this contract."

Little Bit shakes her head. She knows that everything is different. Nobody ever used females for nothing like this.

Little Bit just smiles as she tells Big Girl, "Girl, times dun changed. All we used to git was "sell ya body" or "hold dis bag or gat." Now she is making her own noise. Mayhem got folks looking at her now. She out here representin'. Maybe having a gangster family is straight."

Big Girl knows that Peddy was not overjoyed with his daughter being recognized as a real one.

Ruby Redd re-entered the room telling Mayhem, "Messalina, the original gangster is supposedly in Detroit. Joseph "Stiletto" Messalina was the enforcer for the Bruno Family. My daddy did business with them."

Drinking a tall glass of iced tea, she continued to ask why she wanted to know about Messalina, "Ms. Mayhem, mafia seriously an old man. Old like back in the day. The kind of old like Purple Gang old."

Looking puzzled, Mayhem asked, "Wassup wit you and him?"
Rita Q interrupts attempting to elaborate on the reason for asking about the mobster.

In her Puerto Rican accented, rapid-fire tongue she yelled, "We hear that somebody is his grandson. Folks say this grandson is not a true G – that he just thinks he is."

Mayhem says she doesn't know any Bruno or Messalina personally. She knows that the mafia exists and that her father, on occasion, had worked for them.

"What's this grandsons' name?"

Rita offered, "They say his name is Roc-ko. He supposedly got a crew out of GPointe."

Mayhem's face is frowned up.

She slowly says, "We know a little white boy called Rocco or something. I know he cool. He is a little fella. He dresses real clever and he knows my brothers cuz he likes to gamble over at the club. Sometimes he be wit dem twin white boys Ounce and Bounce."

G-Pointe? Now the joke is on the Puerto Ricans. G is for Grosse Pointe. It's like the place all the lily-white people, or all those that have, live. Now this is hilarious to Ruby and Tweeny.

They laugh out loud, "Grosse Pointe has gangsters? You have got to be kidding?" Little Bit explained that it might not be that funny.

"Young fella goes both ways. Ruby, he be here looking at dicks lots of nights. As a matter of fact, I think he plays with Three Balls Tommy."

Three Balls Tommy is a well-known hustler. He is also a homosexual drug operator. The name makes the claim that he does not have a penis. Supposedly, he has just three testicles. In certain street circles, Tommy is regarded as a pervert of sorts since he preys on little boys as young as elementary school age. Ruby Redd is an old ancient temple abider. While she likes her money, she accepts the gay life, but does not extend such liberties to underage youth. Three Balls Tommy is not welcomed in her place of business if he is on the prowl for food. Legal doesn't cut it with Ruby. Even a young person celebrating her coming of age is off limits. Special parties are not unusual and sometimes the crowd might be younger than the legal drinking age. If the money is cool, Ruby shuts down all liquor flow and allows a special rent for anyone. Anyone except those who break the ancient rule her daddy and granddaddy imposed at the inception of the club.

Chapter 7: Female Rising

Mayhem wants to know exactly what the problem is with this Rocco boy. Rita hunched her shoulders and looked at Jamilia.

"Well, the A-rab says that these Rocco people control all the action in Detroit. Nothing can come in or leave out without their ok."

Mayhem smiled coyly, "Ain't nothing like dat. Shit ain't laying like dat no more." As the women talk, it's a short meeting. The visitors leave with an agreement that gives them the services they need for organizing their operations into Detroit. As soon as their guests leave, Big Girl motions for Mayhem to come to the table. The music is hip hopping now. It's Lil Wayne doing his thing as he talks about a woman police officer. One of the crew laughs as they are celebrating their new status.

She shouts to the slim DJ, "play dat fine ass bitch Trina. We feelin' like dat kind of love."

Big Girl smiles and leans over to whisper into Mayhems' ear. Her ponytail is hanging down her muscular back as she slowly tells her girl about the big contract on Ricky Ricardo. Mayhem's eyes seem to glow brighter as Big Girl explained the situation. Drinking her ginger ale concoction, Mayhem looks as if she is going into a deep trance. She begins thinking about her independence, her power, and her future. As the conversation wraps up, Big Girl Rene gets deeper into her Native American groove.

Looking directly at Mayhem, Big Girl yells, "Its you. This is yo time. I know Peddy is going for the contract on Rickey. Dat niggah Keithland will reward the shit out of anybody cuz dis is money and more."

The party is on and Mayhem celebrates like never before. She had already made up her mind. She was taking the contract on Rickey Ricardo. Rickey had been cool with her all her life. Mayhem went to school with Rick's sister, Ranita. It was just business, just like Pedwell would say. Rationalizing the reality of the streets, she thought about when her and the boys were younger. Peddy had told the whole brood of Jefferson's, including those who were with his crew that little kids were just like big people.

Peddy declared, before Mayhem was eight years old, "If somebody has something you like, you should take it from them." Peddy taught his children at an early age that the world was theirs for the taking. His voice echoed in her ears, "git or git got." Mayhem liked the club. She especially enjoyed the cute boys running around, luring all the women. There were all kinds of wo-men in the club who always had, "dollars in exchange for dicks" as Ruby would say. Some really fat women had a table inside the big party room. They were screaming loud and showing off all their money. Mayhem recognized one extremely large woman as a social worker she had to speak to one of those times when Peddy had chased everybody out of the house. Mayhem was around thirteen. She couldn't recall the woman's' name. One of the young male dancers named Sweet Meat was on the table in front of the social worker. There was also a short guy with beaming white teeth.

Teeth didn't really matter to any of the women. Sweet Meat was well built and his muscles were defined in such a manner that his thighs were thick like Adonis. Sweet Meat was so muscular that even his dark mahogany ankles were well developed.

The big social worker kept saying, "Lawdy, lawdy have mercy on my soul."

She was jumping up and down and her yellow and orange striped sack dress appeared filled with air like a giant balloon. Her hair was flying all around like it was a head of orange fire.Mayhem and Big Girl were mesmerized, as Sweet Meat seemed to turn into a snake. He got down on his stomach and made some movement as if he were on the jungle floor searching for prey. When he got up, there were dollar bills showering over his body like heavy rain. It was even more puzzling to see a couple of men folk at the table next to the screaming social workers. The three men were equally excited and it was clear that they were thrilled to observe the attached python covered in a leopard print dick cover on Sweet Meat. While Sweet Meat was short, his endowment was rather long and large. While he was dancing on his back, he raised his buttocks and balanced himself with his coconut colored shaped head.

Chapter 7: Female Rising

The room was rocking with the pulsating music mixed by none other than DJ Sex-E who is an icon in the underground mixing of both old school and new school hip hop. The song was part "Erotic City" by Prince and "Its your Thing" by the Isley Brothers. The two songs eventually transition into the hip-hop medley of Throw that Dick by Two Live Crew featuring Luke Skywalker.

"Look at dat big fat bitch Rene. I knows dat bitch from middle school."

Big Girl smiles. Her attire is picture perfect as she lets some younger girls pose with her. Mayhem, admired by several of the young girls, is dressed in a white leather jacket and pants with some sexy knee-high white boots.

One of the young girls asked Big Girl, "Ain't dat Mayhem Jefferson? She is the sister of Conquest and dem other Jefferson boys dat be smoking muthafucka's. Dem niggahs is the shit fo real!!"

8

EAST PYRAMID, MICHIGAN

The campus of Frederick Douglass College sits on the shore of the Grande Torro River. This serene small hamlet of a city is definitely a college town. While Detroit Urban Ecological University was based in Detroit, it was Dr. Long's challenge as a senior fellow at Frederick Douglass College to bridge the two institutions to work specifically on the looming challenges concerning the continual demise of Detroit. Professor Long had already tapped Marion Tubman to spearhead a much-needed effort to transform public education in Detroit. To many, it seemed radical to have an urban institution leading the revival of the City of Detroit. But not to Xavier. He had a network of family, friends, fraternity brothers, members of all the Black Greek organizations, grass root organizations, faith-based institutions and countless concerned folks from the academy that he knew could impact Detroit for the better.

The idea was to have the Detroit Urban Ecological University lead all the public universities in the state and each of them would be under the brilliant leadership of Governor William Newman. It was Newman who wanted an atmosphere that would allow Michigan citizens higher education from diverse fields of studies. Xavier Long came to Frederick Douglass after teaching overseas in Asia and Africa. In the new school of justice, he has a following of students from all over the United States. His commitment to Detroit and other urban populations is critical in his scholarship. Long has always been an advocate of social justice. He is extremely concerned about urban youth and public education. The movement towards charter schools is of great concern to Xavier. More pressing is the continued and consistent rise of school dropouts.In a conversation that led to Tyquan returning to school, Dr. Long underscored what the late Mayor Coleman Young had stated so well.

"No city in the world can afford to lose a million people and survive." Xavier had explained to Tyquan that education was critical to social mobility.

"Knowledge is vital to making strong and stable communities" was not just a cliché to Dr. Long. Tyquan, who had been a star athlete, did graduate from Martin Luther King, Jr. High School. Tyquan had not felt or believed that education was critical.

"I know enough and street knowledge is more important Doc."

That was the firing point for Xavier who organized his family members and Marian Tubman to gang up on the young brother. Over the years, Tyquan had no place to hide from the all-out assault of Dr. Xavier Long.

Xavier is in his office. Tyquan walks in and greets the secretary. Tyquan is bald. His small earrings give him that Moorish look that he tries to display ever since going to New York to see Othello with Dr. Long. It was that trip that changed Tyquan forever. A meeting with the old heads that weekend brought about a spiritual awakening. A moving lecture by Bishop John Hurst Adams at Xavier's family headquarters on Convent Avenue turned young Tyquan into a serious seeker of higher education. Bishop John Hurst Adams, of the A.M.E. Church was an icon. Tyquan had questioned education and God.

"If God knows all, how come he lets Detroit crumble like this?"

Dr. Long has stirring conversations and intense debates with various Long family members, all of whom have a special relationship with the young warrior, Tyquan.

Judge Long was frustrated with Tyquan, telling his music teacher daughter, "That young man has something in him that allows Xavier to love him like a son. On the other hand, he really believes in the justice of the street. I can't get him to let go of the streets enough to see true justice. He's a good kid. A real tough, real good kid."

Tyquan found the good judge and Xav's family good, real straight, but Judge Long was old, real old. The one bonding factor with Professor Long and T-Quan, as he was known in the streets, was their two-way exchange of what street life meant in its present form. Tyquan was the teacher on why, it seemed, young black men loved violence. It was Tyquan that introduced Xavier to the young thug woman named Mayhem. Mayhem knew of Dr. Xavier Long from years ago when officials removed her little baby sister from their dark and twisted family. Xavier taught Tyquan everything and took him everywhere including to the continent of Africa last year. Trust, faith, and a deep admiration connected the old school scholar with the street respected warrior or soldier as Tyquan referred to himself many times. The soldier label didn't do well with the Long men folks. Saul especially resented any mention of street people as soldiers. He felt those people trampled on his beloved armed services experience. For all the hoopla, including severe charges of being bourgeoisie, Saul could not handle it when young gangsters and thugs referred to themselves as soldiers. Xavier, the only non-military male in his family, understood in theory how Tyquan considered "soldier" an appropriate label for himself and others like him.

The big news was that Tyquan was graduating from Detroit Community College after only a year and a half. His Associate degree was in Para-legal and Criminal Justice. Tyquan had progressed at a rapid pace in the programs with Judge Long overseeing his direction with a host of support and assistance from his professional children. Tyquan was graduating with high honors, which meant a great deal to him.

"Man, I can't believe I am graduating with high honors. I mean I am going to Frederick Douglass College in the fall. I got mad skills like computer love, reading, writing and some math. Now I am going to do it all at Frederick Douglass College and later, I'm going to Graduate school at Detroit Urban Ecological University."

Sitting in the office smiling and thanking his mentor makes Xavier think about the project over at Youthville that Saul started years ago. Tyquan became the superstar student which led to a few more b-boys entering college with T-Quan as their "model of success." Looking at Tyquan, Xavier reflected on the blessing, "Man", he thought deeply of his grandmother who had passed two years ago. It had been a long road with the young man whose own crew championed him to stay on the bright side instead of the dark side. Professor Long thought about all the years that had passed since he first met Tyquan as a teenage ruffian. He had cold eyes that seemed to shout, "Death to the world." At that time, Tyquan trusted no one and nothing. He hated everything, not unlike his environs. Back then, he only wanted to hear Tupac's Runnin, Dyin to Live, he only wore hip-hop attire, and he settled all of his disputes with violence. Now, the young man was beaming as he talked about a lecture by a preacher who once held the authorities at bay. He had intervened for the infamous Black Panthers, who were hiding in this church for safety. It was the fire from the lecture declaring to young black men that there was a better path than the streets or prisons. He was looking back and visualizing the tall, half bald, light-skinned Bishop Adams with his thick white beard and head of hair. Looking out into the audience as he pointed to his mentee, Xavier Long and Rev. Dr. Nehemiah Stillwater kneeled at the biblical scholar altar. And, of course, from right there in Harlem was the gang leader, Azuma, with his legions of black warriors who were known in the Harlem streets as the Black Lions. All of these people and organizations made an impression on black youth that was important and necessary.

Young Tyquan Miller was moving up and taking his position in Detroit. Tyquan was no longer feared. Now, he was respected by many. It was the neighborhood boys, the cousins of Mayhem Jefferson, who regarded Tyquan Miller as "Hero" not the dreaded DOGS or other counterproductive gangs and crews. Smiling to himself, Tyquan was wondering if one day he might be like Doc. As he was sitting in the office looking out the window down at the river, he began to understand the words the old wise man said to him a couple years ago. It was right after somebody had fed a pigeon an Alka Seltzer pill. Everybody hanging out in front of the Coney Island on Davison was laughing at the gross bloody remains. Old Man River came out of the restaurant and confronted the crowd for being both cruel and ignorant. When one of the young gangsters got loud, Old Man River firmly denounced the gangster without blinking. Old Man River was chastising Big Girl, Mayhem, and the boys with the Davison crew explaining that, these days, ignorance was more than abundant.

Tyquan never said anything when Mr. River spoke. He understood that Dr. Long loved Old Man River as much as he had loved his own grandfather. As the old man's laser focused tongue ripped the transgressor apart, his message sounded so familiar.

"Out here killing sea gulls. Makes you wonder what is going on? All these fast-food places right here and not one decent grocery market. You folks got no skills. Just sitting out here with nothing of value. Can any of you read? Can any of you write? No!!! You are just wasting away - just like the neighborhood."

It was Tyquans' responsibility to protect the elder statesman so he didn't mind beaming the crew with a look that said clearly, "Do not disrespect this man. Say nothing." Tyquan felt good about the fact that the old man always gave him books that were full of lots of wise sayings. Even in the midst of his rage, Old Man River would kick historical facts to the young knuckleheads.

There was another "old head" that Tyquan had gained mad respect for. He was a retired teacher named LeRoy Estelle.

"Young man, you must stand for something good. Gambling, sexing, fighting and worse, making babies and not being there is a part of what is killing our communities."
It was etched in Tyquans' psyche.

Mr. Estelle says it all the time, "You must make a positive contribution of some kind Tyquan."
Both LeRoy Estelle and Mr. Joseph "Old Man" River came to DCC when Tyquan graduated. As Tyquan closed his eyes, he could still see the big smiles from his favorite old heads. River hair was snow-white, while Mr. Estelle was always well groomed with a salt and pepper short haircut. Tyquan remembered the love he always felt from Mr. River and Mr. Estelle, especially when he clenched them around their shoulders. River and Estelle had given Tyquan a big package. Inside, Tyquan had a bible, an Oxford Dictionary and a Special Edition of *The Fire Next Time* by the Master, James Baldwin. Tyquan Miller was about to embark on a journey as a full-time student at Frederick Douglass. He knew that his role shined and even the tough street-smart Mayhem Jefferson and her folks admired that guy, Ty-Quan Quincy Miller.

9

THE FORMATIVE YEARS

Washington-Carver High School is hosting the Girls City Basketball Championships. Marian Tubman, who teaches history, is also the Athletic Director. A former high school and college track star, Tubman believes strongly in the student aspect of the term student-athlete. Washington Carver High is named after the pioneering scientist George Washington Carver. Known as the Sabers, the basketball team is undefeated with a perfect record of twelve wins and zero defeats. The team is led by the high school All-American point guard Zina Althea Gibson. Mayhem went to elementary school with Zina. They had a bond that, despite all of the wicked Pedwell's deeds, remained cool. There seemed to be no confusion for either young girl since one became famous and the other infamous. The championship is against Hillgate High, a cross-town rival. The two schools have a fierce and long competitive history. Everyone seemed to be in attendance at the cold winter night game.

It had only been one day since Mayhem learned about the contract on Rickey Ricardo. Big Girl was a big sports fan and an avid boxer. Her love for boxing came from her grandfather who managed and trained the young Walker Smith and Joe Louis Barrows in their early days at King Solomon Recreational Center. Big Girl had a brother, Ray, who trained under his famous grandfather. Asa "Sarge" Kilabrew, nicknamed because he was a sergeant during World War II, had a promising career in the ring cut short after a piece of fragmented bullet was left lodged near his spine from the war. Sarge Kilabrew was a loyal worker at Ford Motor Company.

His life was boxing but, "Ford paid the rent," was all he used to say. Big Girls' mother married Sarge's son not long after they met at Alexander State University. Ray Kilabrew met the young dark Ojibwa at ASU. She was on an academic scholarship from her reservation in the upper half of Michigan. Ray had served two tours as a

74

Green Beret in Viet Nam. Sarge was proud of his sons' duty in the army following his patriot road of duty to his nation. The beautiful young Ojibwa quickly explained to Ray how much she hated the continuous distortion of and about her people.

"I am from the Ojibwa tribe. I am not an Indian. Indians are from India. Christopher Columbus made a mistake thinking that he had landed in the East. Indians are from India but my people are from the Great Lakes region."

After a short time, the two young students graduated and got married. The young couple soon found good jobs in Detroit and life was good. Unfortunately, for the family of Ray Kilabrew and Grace "Morning Sun" Mankiller, their lives changed forever when Grace was killed in an automobile accident. Ray was left with two babies and died soon after of a broken heart. The two young babies, a boy and girl, were left under the wing of Sarge Kilabrew. Ray, Jr. and his sister, Rene "Morning River," were left to be raised by their grandparents, Sarge and his wife Lucille. Both children were loved and raised in the church. Lucille was a quiet woman from Swamp Haven, Florida. She claimed to come from the black Seminoles. The black Seminoles were legendary since they were a community of the Seminole Indian tribe and a host of different runaway African slaves. Ms. Lucille, like an African Griot, was often overheard, telling her grandchildren that their Native American status was bona fide. She explained that their beautiful mother was an Ojibwa but their bloodline also included her black Seminoles. Rene, as a young girl, was both proud and fascinated to have a combination of tribal blood. While she was a Sunday school teacher, Lucille would share great war stories about how the black Seminoles were the most invincible of warriors. She hinted, for years, that her black Seminoles were mixed with a regal tribe from an island off the great continent of Africa.

Lucille explained to her grandchildren that they were descendants of a great warrior tribe known as the G'Psai's. They lived on the island of Jechri, and it was home of the G'Psai's. They were the warriors who were great hunters and protectors of the continent. Big Girl loved those stories. She also loved the images of boxing champions from Detroit. Sarge worshipped Walker Smith who was also known as Sugar Ray Robinson. The fact was that Sarge named his beloved first-born son Ray after the greatest boxer of all time - Sugar Ray Robinson. Growing up in the gym and watching all the "Cat Daddies" with their big Buicks and pimp types with their Cadillac's, had a lasting impression on young Rene. Lucille scolded her husband for keeping the children in that "musty old gym."

"That gym is no place for a young Christian girl."

Rene earned the name "Big Girl" in that gym. At times, it seemed that Sarge forgot that he had a granddaughter. She wanted to box so he trained her like he trained young Ray Junior. He taught her stances, punches, proper defense, and conditioning. While boxing was fun, Lucille forbade any actual physical boxing matches for her granddaughter. Sarge loved his baby boxer and never forgot that she was a young lady. Just as his Lucille demanded. She loved sports and she was very athletic. She enjoyed softball, track, volleyball, and she also went out for the junior high basketball team.

On an early day at Dunbar Junior High, the basketball team showcased a young, fast scoring machine named Zina or "Z." A young woman who was fresh out of college coached "Z" and her teammates. The team had another skinny girl with a big attitude at the other guard position. Rounding out the super talented junior high team was the tall thick girl with the beautiful ponytail. MJeff was the other guard known in the streets as Mayhem Jefferson and the thick girl was young Rene Mankiller. This team of young girls played as if they were in college. Everything seemed great until the stands heard a battle cry that was foreign, dark and ugly. At that game, the audience was horrified to hear the profanity and brutal vulgarity in the orders that were coming from the young guards' father.

Peddy Jefferson took great pride in showing up for his daughters' game dressed to the bone.

"Kill dat bitch girl! Blood!! Make a muthafucka bleed Mayhem," he screamed.

It was there that the Gibson family responded with not only protest, it left the grandmother praying to herself, sitting behind the likes of the devil himself. Lela Mae Gibson, a retired teacher, knew exactly what Pedwell Jefferson represented. She knew that this was not the run of the mill ignorant Negro parent. No, her prayers were deep and thoughtful and served as a cry for an army of angels to watch over the poor child named Mayhem. That name, that man, a father? Her eyes closed that day in junior high; her prayers transcended the moment, the day and the year. Big Girl had been one of the girls mesmerized by Mayhem Jefferson. Despite the good home that Sarge and Lucille provided, the flash and glamour of street life had bitten Rene when she was very young. In fact, Rene loved the anointment of the name 'Big Girl'. She earned that name when she punched boys for pulling her ponytail and for knocking out a bitch for calling her "little Poco-hontas." That recognition by her peers was sweet.

Mayhem didn't go to school much. She was a sad child but an even sadder teenager. Something about the two young girls clicked. Zina liked both Rene and Mayhem, but her mother, Ramona, was closely monitoring her youngest daughter. Zina had an older sister who was also a super athlete in track, basketball and softball. Khand-ice Sarah Gibson and her younger sister seemed to share the same soul. Perhaps it was an intense desire to win, or the tough exterior to take on and defeat males or females in any sort of competition, but she never truly felt the name Khandice or Khandy, if one dared. In competition, she was known as Khan, like the ancient warriors from Mongolia. Despite Khan being away at the University of Northwest California playing power forward, she and Zina continuously talked to and motivated each other. Khan had watched over her younger sister like a coach and junior mother.

Khan had known the Jefferson clan a long time. She attended elementary school with Conquest and Assault. Not knowing that Mayhem was their sister, she was stunned that day at Dunbar, to see the same identical macabre behavior in one swoop of violence from young MJeff as she thrashed on an opposing player. It was a move so snake like and deadly that the whole gym couldn't believe that the skinny guard had hit another girl so hard, directly in her mouth and eye. It seemed, upon impact, that the girls' head exploded like a ripe tomato. What followed left the audience paralyzed and Zina and her teammates were rendered immobile. Pedwell jumped from his seat along with a crew of young men and stomped the bleeding player as she layed sprawled on the wooden court. When school security ran to rescue the girl, one of the crewmembers pulled out a gun.

Peddy screamed again, "beat yo bitch ass to death!"
Without ceasing, he grabbed Mayhem by the collar of her uniform and rebuked her weakness.

"Didn't I tell y'all to kill a muthfucka? Dis bitch dun ran over yaw. Dis is how we do it."

It was on that day that the Gibson Family decided that Mayhem could not be a part of Z's life. The father, Lloyd Gibson, was a Viet Nam veteran and former military police in the United States Marine Corps. Like a soldier, he instinctively covered his mother and wife the moment he saw the firearm. He thought of nothing but safety as he hollered at the top of his voice to call the police. As the melee disbursed, Peddy and the crew scrambled and fled before any of the authorities arrived. Zina cried tears of anger over witnessing such raw violence in the junior high gym.

"Khan" stood before her younger sister and without even realizing it, her words blurted out, "I know those guys. I went to school with some of them. Daddy, what was that? Why did they do that? That girl Mayhem Jefferson is one of them? I didn't know that she was one of them!!"

The gym is packed and the audience is made up of more than high school students. There are college scouts and media from all over in attendance too. Big Girl loved girls' basketball but Mayhem could care less. There was a time when she loved the game. The reality was Mayhem would have loved to be in Zinas' shoes. It was a big game. The Gibson family and friends were proud. Coming home from college to see the game was a bit of irony for Khan. The former Washington Carver star was a starting member of the University of Northern California's nationally ranked women's basketball team. Unfortunately, she had a major injury that put her out of play for the whole season. Her grandmother, in counsel, had pointed out that Zina needed that sisterly presence on this important day. The stands were jumping as the two teams warmed up. The music from the loudspeakers suddenly changed from old school rhythm and blues tunes to the deep beating hip hop sounds of Kurtis Blows', "We're playin Basketball." Zina led the warm up drills that erupted when she seemed to stop, in midair, leaving the basketball in a state of suspension. Before the ball can descend downward, the agile Kei Miller swoops into the basket. Eyes are still staring while everyone is in total disbelief.

"She dunked? That girl just slammed the ball!!!"

Kei Miller is the first cousin of Tyquan Miller. The cousins enter the gym with Xavier and Saul Long. They have just missed the commotion.

Someone tells Tyquan, who smiles and offered, "She been slamming since she was six!! That ain't nothing new to me!!!" Saul Long is not a basketball fan. He actually hates basketball. Xavier is a big fan of Zina and her sister. Dr Long "knows of" the Gibson family well. For him, the Gibson clan is old school African American. When people judge black men, or the lack of black men who spend TIME with their children and their families, Xavier thinks of the powerful image of men like Lloyd Gibson. While co-pilots run the clan, everyone knows it's the mother who is really the navigator. But no one is going to forget that Lloyd supports his girls with nothing but love. So, the dunk is cool and the smile on Kei Miller's face says it all. The six four center is all teeth while she can be seen giving Z one of those uniquely special gestures of her hands and elbows.

As she gives one of those low fives, she smiles again and laughs, "Zina, Z wo-man, got to orchestrate!! You got to con-duct this win to-day girl!"

The two are best friends and many colleges and universities are trying to sign them as a package. Kei Miller is an excellent student with one critical catch. The catch is that she wants to play for an African nation. "Z" wants to play basketball in Europe in the professional leagues. Kei speaks fluent Spanish and is good with Kiswahili and Hausa too. Marian Tubman is extremely proud of her special twosome. One wants to become a historian and the other, a linguist. Overall, the Washington Carver athletes are serious about college. Zina has narrowed her school list down to five. Miller, on the other hand, is making it difficult because she wants to go to a foreign place to speak authentic languages.

Tubman is not surprised by the lofty dreams of both of these girls. She coached them in track beginning in junior high. She knows their families and in Tubman's mind, their success affirms her lifelong belief that if you have advocates for smart kids, including solid faculty and strong parents, their success is made possible. The stands are crazed as the Sabres put on a display of ball handling evoking the spiritual memory of the old Harlem Globetrotters. Xavier is amazed, having been a young boy during the dark ages when all females in sports were considered "Les-boes," which was short for lesbians in the 60's.

Mayhem is quietly watching it all, showing little, if any emotion. In her mind, she thinks about the money on the table for the contract on Rickey Ricardo. She looks at Khan and Zina and wishes she had an older sister. For a moment, she stared at Mrs. Gibson, a grandmother and mother.

Mayhem imagined, "what if I had a father like Mr. Gibson?" Peddy, as a father, seemed to make her wish for anything but him. Basketball was something she loved when she was younger. She would sometimes talk with Con about what a nice life meant to her. Mayhem used to admire Zina because she was so smart in school. Teachers liked her, she treated Mayhem cool, and they genuinely liked each other. Mayhem knew she could have been a baller but nope, she belonged to a family of thugs and gangsters.

Mayhem laughed to herself when she remembered being brought before the court. She remembered the time when the stuck-up Judge Irene Ewing dismissed her when all she deeply wanted was to be reunited with her younger sister. Judge Ewing, a no- nonsense jurist, explained to the entire court what she felt about the likes of Pedwell Jefferson and his family. Mayhem could still see the elitist stare as if Judge Ewing smelled something spoiled. She glared at Pedwell and his children that dark day in court. Those cold eyes, the frown, her black robe with those big black framed glasses and her old- fashioned Negress hair were all a vivid memory.

Pointing at the Jefferson's, she lamented, "You are the types of Negroes that make me cry out for our leadership. I'm talking about folks like Reverend Dr. Martin Luther King, Jr, the NAACP, Rosa Parks, and A. Phillip Randolph. Do you think that Thurgood Marshall was fighting for the likes of you and your kind? Pedwell, you should have been castrated before you and your wife left a mark on society with these children. There is no way under the sun that I would allow this baby to be returned to the likes of you. All of these off spring are little miniature monsters. God help us if the one named Mayhem should give birth to more of your kind."

Mayhem's mind was not in the gym as she reflected on how she had fared in life. She could not help but to remember how the social worker, youth workers, teachers and counselors condemned her family, and her future before the Honorable Irene Ewing. She was looking at the community raving, and cheering for Zina and her way of life.

"Well, I am Mayhem Jefferson. I am a gangster. I am a thug and all these here muthafuckas got no love for me."

She is angry, pissed and agitated since the conversations are all about good students, good families, and happiness. Her fantasies are her nightmares and her reality is that she was watching a video that she could never star in. The cool coaches, the excited and supportive parents coming to see their children play; that was merely a fantasy if your name was Mayhem Jefferson.

Big Girl was still marveling at the slam-dunk and all the energy from the big game. While she didn't care about the game, she knew it was time to wear something fly. Big Girl wore her short mink jacket with the crazy badass tall leather boots.

"This is the time to let everybody see how you holding it down," she thought. Tyquan is greeting all the street fellas and notices a number of police who appeared, at least to him, to be undercover. Saul is near the concession booth with his Street Society Poets and Peace Project youth. Mayhem's girls, or as Sgt. Bannon claimed, her organized criminal gang looked hip hoppish and more like Mary J Blige and Wu Tang Clan than the threatening group of young people they really were. Tall, slim and extremely well dressed, there are nine girls showcasing their expensive attire. The girls look ghetto rich and damn good. The event is high energy like a concert with Kanye West and Jay Z performing, "No Church in the Wild." The detectives working on the dog fighting shooting had changed their attitude once the Feds got involved. Bannon and MacFarley were aware of Mayhem and despite the Feds being in charge of the investigation, they both took a more serious approach as a result of Mayhem Jefferson being labeled Public Enemy Number One. The Detroit Police were following several crews and underworld figures at the game. Mayhem grew more and more impatient while waiting for word from the Latina women.

"Wassup wit dis shit? I told'em that I had their backs and not to worry bout the big boys from the mob."
The game is a wipeout as Zina leads with a show that is worthy of college level competition. Washington Carver is a public school that works and Marian Tubman knows exactly why she is so successful.

"Our community and our school know what it takes to be successful. We work all the time."
On his way into the game, Xavier observed the parking lot. As he entered the gym, Xav saw a strange mix of the high school sports crowd and the many factions of folk from the city. Xavier thought about that term they used in the hood, "ghetto-fabulous." There were Range Rovers, Escalades, and brand-new cars everywhere. The basketball game was the drawing card that resulted in a social gathering of gangsters, working class, elite professionals and just good people.

Saul complained to Xavier how much high school had changed over the past several decades. Xavier Long loved the block he grew up on and loved the school system. School was always a joy. School was something that was special every day of his life and it remained so until right before he left for college in 1967.Now, drug dealers, murderers and all kinds of street types are co-mingling with innocent high school students at a sporting event. The school's colors are red and black, so it's a colorful crowd, to say the least. One could see letter jackets of school colors matched against the backdrop of outlaws with their expensively dressed young girlfriends. This is how high school looks in the "new day." Xavier has reminded himself to forget about old school. This is a new day and a new time and a new kind of air of madness. There was a great deal of thug watching by the authorities. The federal agencies were keeping track of the various underworld figures. High school sports competition in the third city was an experience that included much more than simply watching a high school basketball game. Tyquan is elated over the game and glows as he feels the love of a community that is proud of his progress. His relationship in public with Mayhem is always like the older brother she wished she had instead of the likes of Assault, Homicide and Rape.

Ironically, the game had become a secondary attention grabber for many in attendance. Two attendees were old associates from Mayhem's childhood. Black Mike and Murder Man were the boys on the monkey bars during her elementary school days. Black Mike was the leader of a small, unorganized collection of street gangsters. He and Murder Man were notorious for ambushing their prey. The twosome saw Mayhem and her crew and nodded in shallow respect since both men were devout women haters. Murder Man was aptly named for his record number of homicides. The reputation of the two included that few, if any, witnesses would live to report what they witnessed. Mayhem has never forgotten nor forgiven that day of humiliation on the monkey bars. That day she almost became a victim of the older boys.

Tyquan seemed to be greeted as if he was running for Mayor of Detroit. Saul Long looked at the different factions of hoodlums attending the game. The military training and resolve tempted his mind. Why not just eliminate all the troublemakers? There had been many family discussions about what to do with the thug community at the homestead of the Long family. The reality of what confronted Tyquan Miller was choice. It was his boys, including the Black Side Down crew he was once a member of that had pushed him away from street cosmos. Mayhem trusted Tyquan from earlier times. A handsome, urban rugged Tyquan had evolved from a straight up hip hop head to a more urban mix of hip hop and a touch of the conservative, streetwise, collegial type. Wearing his favorite reddish African print scarf, a black knit skullcap, with black Carhart coveralls with the Pelé leather jacket, his warm embrace of the gangster princess was genuine and spiritually strong. Love is the only word that Tyquan felt for Kilio, as he called her. That word means "warrior princess" in the small, rare, and dead language of the Furuanqi tribe. It was the study that Tyquan took up in the East African nation near Tanzania. The little gold earrings in each of his ears were made in Kenya.

One of his boys from Black Side Down told him upon his return from Africa, "Man, you been to Africa. Now niggah, nobody does dat shit here!! AFRICA! We be down in the D but Africa? Dat is sum shit only a niggah hangin wit Dr. X could do. Dr. Long is holding it down son."

Mayhem and Big Girl took a great deal of pride in their black leather string necklaces with the Maasi miniature arrowhead drop. Dr. Long had given them the necklaces while Tyquan had given Mayhem a beautiful shield scarf. The charms and the scarf were believed to possess the power to be able to return the warrior from battle without any harm as long as they wore the shield or the scarf. Mayhem wears the small, multicolored scarf loosely around her neck everyday. Watching Xavier as he was teaching Tyquan made Mayhem think about what it must be like to be able to trust someone so completely; someone like Xavier or maybe even Marian Tubman.

As Mayhem hugged Tyquan, he asked her about the latest, "So what's going on? Did you see Z and her girls do it big today? This time next year, Zina will be playing on some big-time college campus."

Her thoughts zoomed to another dimension placing her about a year from now. Mayhem could not stop thinking about the bounty on Rickey's head. One year from today she wondered, where will I be? The big rap to anyone who would listen was that T-Quan was going back to school. He had become an envoy and a human advertisement for higher education after years of hearing his mentor preach about the importance of education. Tyquan also remembered education was more than just a simple concern for Marian Tubman. Her non-stop personal mission was to help others embrace the value of education. Detroit youth had lost their way. Parents, government and worse, the youth themselves, had forsaken, for various reasons, the value of and respect for the subject of education. Tyquan had the fever. He believed in education and learned to respect the whole notion of education as a vehicle to better ones' self. Xavier, of course, had his mother, who was also a teacher, and an entire family demanding that all the lost and disconnected souls must re-enter the arena of the acquisition of knowledge. Judge Long and his wife knew that the language of what Xavier called "street-ease" would not take youth beyond the boundaries of the third city.

Mayhem Jefferson was on her way out of Washington Carver with crews from all over the city tailing her.

Tyquan had to keep telling Mayhem, "They are not Chinese." They ain't Chinese. They are Hmong. It's ignorant to call them China men. The word Asian covers all the people of Asia and that includes Hmong, Chinese, Japanese and Koreans and even more Asian people like that badass boxer Pac Man. He from the Philippines. Respect that and know that!! Its critical not to be ignorant about people."

Mayhem secretly admired how much Tyquan seemed to grow intellectually over the years she had known him. She wanted to go to school and regretted how she had allowed Peddy to dictate terms that never included high standards for education.

Contempt learned how to change. It was going to school under the ignorant dictate of his brothers and father that taught him the lesson of adaption. Contempt went to Detroit Community College. It is also the place where the perverted teacher, Mr. Locks, raped Mayhems' girl DaSheba. Mayhem was furious about what had happened to her girl especially since she had recently been encouraged to enroll in DCC by good folks like Mrs. Martha, an old woman from church.

She found the counselor, teachers, and other staff not helpful and worse, discouraging.

"Contempt could take care of himself," she thought.

Her experiences in school had not been good. Granted, Mayhem was not the easiest student to win over. One thing stood out in her mind, Peddy had beaten her mother Jerenda for enrolling in community college. Pedwell stood proud with his ignorant attitude that school, "was for people trying to be better than us." Education was de-valued by the likes of Pedwell. This was the case for many of the ill-gotten folks in America. Unfortunately, far too many in the third city sing the same song as if it is a third city anthem. Tyquan informed Xavier, momentarily numbed by the truth, that youth like Mayhem needed a way to realize the power of education. Young people needed more teachers like Marian Tubman.

Tyquan yelled, "Doc, Mayhem really wanted to learn. She was just caught up in how the haters from all the spots like her home, her hood, and even some teachers had discounted her and kids like her. Man, you showed me. Now, I'm trying to show her."

10

CONFLICT AND RESOLUTION

Tyquan was really concerned. He realized that the rape at DCC had deeper fallout than he had first realized. The incident that shook Mayhem's girl DaSheba was not yet settled. The rape by the perverted teacher, which had taken place in the instructor's office, had a sad but familiar outcome for Xavier. The problem was that the teacher had an excellent attorney. His lawyer got him off with a mere slap on the wrist. The news that Mr. Locks was charged with a lesser transgression had just been announced the week before. It was shocking to both the youth and the neighborhood. Worse, Tyquan had convinced many of the denizens that justice would surely prevail. After all, retired Judge Solomon Long, along with his daughter, federal judge Constance Long-McGuire, had reassured Tyquan that justice eventually works if you give it a chance.

DaSheba Moore was once a fast, but all-around girl. Due in part to poor parenting, she had become street smart and had more than her share of trips to a number of juvenile detention facilities over the years. While not the same warrior type as Mayhem, she was hardly a saint. During the trial, the seasoned attorney painted a picture of consenting adults.

"Yes. There was proof of sexual relations," stated the veteran attorney, "but it was hardly rape."
Calhoun is a middle aged, African American attorney that had little respect for the young ghetto houchee mamas. Clarence Calhoun is also an opportunist and a mercenary. Whoever has the most cash gets his first-class service front and center. As they left the courtroom that day, he whispered to John Locks.

"I told you, the judge could smell ghetto all over this case. So, just look sad. I will explain everything to this blood thirsty gang of reporters."

Chapter 10: Conflict and Resolution

Standing in front of the courthouse with his conservatively dressed client Mr. Locks, both seemed to bask in the spotlight of the television crews.

Calhoun had the case won on the fact he explained gleefully, "A confused young girl who mistakenly took my client John Locks for her lost father or something. That's what we are dealing with. My client tried in vain to bridge the gap for this young wayward girl. In fact, Mr. Locks is a church member and an outstanding faculty member of the Detroit Community College."

DaSheba was in total disbelief as she stood with the Assistant Prosecutor. Mayhem was livid. She had dressed as she had been told to dress by all of her friends and family; in dark clothing that looked like church. Xavier was worried the entire time he was on his way to court to lend support. He had not said much to anyone since he felt that Tyquan could assist the young girl with the support of his judicial father and sister. The talk began and Tyquan was trying to explain that sometimes things go awry. Mrs. Martha, senior citizen and strong advocate for Detroit youth, had her arms wrapped around DaShaba as she was comforting her.The assistant prosecutor was outworked and, in a personal way, he was not pleased. John Lock had openly bragged about the loose ghetto girls during many meetings in the faculty lounge at DCC. Mayhem left with Big Girl as she repeated her resentment of the system. Wearing a long black raincoat with a frown on her face, she declared to Tyquan and Xavier her unhappiness as they got into Dr. Long's black truck. Xavier was breaking the bad news to his father and sister as Mayhem's voice began to rise above every other sound in the truck.

"I know Doc. Dis here is justice. Really its JUST-US, poor niggahs, and we don't count. Bitch-ass Parks counts."
As he puts up his hand to signal he is talking, Mayhem turned to Tyquan.

Her voice begins to quiver and is now breaking with a stern warning to her boy, "Dun told y'all T-Quan. My way is the only way. Like BT Express and my no-good daddy always say, Do it til y'all satisfied!!!"

11

PRAYING IN THE HOUSE OF PREYER

Tyquan is sitting in the front seat texting on his Android Motorola phone. He is worried. Xavier is talking with Old Man River on his phone about the trial. River is adamant that this lopsided justice does little to help guide youth into constructive deeds.

"Doc, this girl was trying to go right. That fool Locks is a self-serving Negro. Time has run out for messing over that child. That damn Teachers Union knows he done screwed plenty of girls at that college."

Xavier is getting an ear full and its not good since River is literally yelling. Mayhem leaves in a fury and makes Xavier wish he were studying butterflies. What began as an inside joke between him and Tyquan soon turned into something gone horribly wrong. Tyquan tried, in vain, to contact Mayhem.

Mayhem heads over to her mothers house. Peddy is not home and Jerenda is stressed because she needs some money for her new-found interest in church. Big Girl is driving her brand-new Mustang. It is obvious that Big Girl loves at least three things: speed, fast cars, and motorcycles. Her car is her reward for the new business she and Mayhem have started. Like the days of John Dillinger, Ma Barker, and Al Capone, the most important word is protection, and paying for these here girls requires serious cash. Money is power and Big Girl is the shadow of Mayhem in her street business. The Mustang was old school ghetto news since Big Girl had the previous owner, who owned the business for only a few hours, sign both the car and the business over to her.

Julius, who was also known as JuJu, was a pimp on the southwest side of Detroit. He was in trouble for trying to pimp a half Mexican, half black girl named Angie Negro. Angie was cute and cool with everybody. Truth be told, she wasn't a promiscuous female. Silly JuJu was a fronting type guy who wanted everybody to think he was a badass pimp. The truth was he was a good distributer of dope for his family. Everybody in his family worked in the dope game. Their whole family sold trees. His father, mother, even his grandmother, were all in the business of selling big time marijuana. That is how he got with young Angie. This guy was a fake pimp and was strung out on that juicy, sexy, tight ass body that that young girl had. JuJu insulted some real serious Mexican gangsters because he was pimping out Angie. One thing led to another and Julius pulled his gun out on some Latin Counts. It was a bad move, especially considering all those present had been looking for his black ass. That is why he paid Big Girl to protect him and "pay big time," he surely did. It cost him his new white Mustang convertible.

All it took was for Mayhem and her girls to have a single conversation with the Counts. The Latin Counts were the real thang. Their leader was a tall, smooth looking pretty boy named Tony Ayala. He had the same name as this serious boxer who knew the great Tommy Hearns. Pretty Tony liked Big Girl and it didn't hurt that old girl spoke fluent Spanish. Everybody knew JuJu was just a street guy out fronting. He was showing off for the young girl and it was a mistake. Mayhem told JuJu that he would have to cut her in on all the business on the west side. It was that serious. Nobody wanted any kind of war with the Mexicans.

Big Girl and Mayhem were both smarter than Peddy. It is a brand new day, and Mayhem knew how to control violence. Old Pedwell had one way of taking care of his clients' wishes. He believed he should murder all of the opposition, while being careful not to leave any witnesses. Word was out on the street that Mayhem was independent. She had broken off from the Jefferson crew. As the all-female convoy followed Big Girl, a ring tone can be heard from inside Mayhems' tote bag. The Dolce-Gabanna bag was brand new and hot. The band of thieves who roam the third city had hit the prestigious and elite Somerset Mall. Earlier that day, Mayhem had put in a special order for her court outfit with Fat Shirley. What rich folks call a "personal shopper" is what Mayhem had in Fat Shirley. Fat Shirley was in the boosting business. She was fourth generation booster and one of many professional thieves in the city. Fat Shirley, like a trained shopper for Hollywood stars, personally selected the black raincoat, beautiful Escada pants and jacket, and the two thousand dollar black and white blouse for Mayhems' upcoming day in court.

Big Girl was looking at Mayhem as she began reading the text message. Without showing any emotion, Mayhem told Big Girl to pull over.

"Rene, that was Fat Shirley. She says dat niggah is clowning us. Drive over to White Castle. She is going to meet us there."
Mayhem is obviously agitated. It seems she believes everything is foul. The stereo is playing an old Temptation tune, 'I'll Be In Trouble'. Smiling in a wicked way, Mayhem thinks about her mother. She knows its time to move on from Peddy. It's really past time as she listens to the falsetto crooning of Eddie Kendricks. It's the one thing that makes her moms happy - the Temptations. While she is much too young to have ever heard the original group, she knew her mother and grandmother loved them some Temptations. Driving her Mustang, Big Girl speeds into the crowded parking lot on Gratiot. Fat Shirley arrives at the parking lot in her cream-colored Chrysler van. Driving for Fat Shirley is Black Charles, who is a notorious thief and good friend of the Jefferson Family. Black Charles is a light skinned, unassuming man around thirty something. His navy Kangol hat is tipped to the right side with his relaxed ponytail barely showing. Greeting the crew, he smiles at Mayhem and asserts he has good news. His teeth are white as snow except for the two front teeth that show two inserted diamonds.

As Mayhem gets into the van she comments, "Damn Shirley, you and Charles got this van filled with all these clothes."

Fat Shirley laughs, "Hey Charles, get me six White Castles, four cheeseburgers, a fish with cheese, large fries and a large red pop."
Black Charles is well built and he is disgusted with the order.

"Damn, Shirley. We just ate an hour ago. How in the world are you hungry?"

Before Black Charles leaves on the journey, he smiles again, and announces, "May-hem, we giving this van to Ms. Martha with all these clothes for her children at the church. We getting Book to give it to her cause that old woman won't take no hot shit. You need to know that." Mayhem is surprised and takes a defensive posture.

"Don't be silly. Y'all know muthafucking well dat old bitch ain't feeling no hot clothes or that van. Y'all been smoking. Dat old bitch been giving me dem talks. She is getting all kinds of niggahs up in dat church with dat young preacher."
Fat Shirley tells Mayhem to chill.

"Look, this money is clean. The van got real papers, and all the clothes got receipts dat Book can show her. Y'alls sweet ass brother Contempt gave us almost nine grand for the family. Dat is one sweet muthafucka."
Mayhem can't believe her ears. Everybody knows that it was Peddy that killed a young couple who were related to Otis Player. Otis was a little dope dealer who had cheated Keithland out of a few thousand dollars. It was the last job that Mayhem had worked with her clan. She and Contempt were deeply impacted when the young and innocent couple was savagely victimized when they lived downstairs from Otis Player.No one saw a thing, and fortunately the children were at a church event with Ms. Martha.

Ms. Martha was making a new life for the children. Contempt had given a great deal of money to the church for the kids. Ms. Martha scorned the senseless brutal world of the third city and while Mayhem had never felt the utter shame and deep pain, street actors were now contributing to the cause. Tyquan was one of the moving forces behind the movement toward making something good come out of a tragedy.Fat Shirley knew that the young boy called Book would make it work. Book, is a neighborhood ally, a loner from a family of holy rollers. Living in the hood meant little to Book whose real name was Paul Jacobs. Growing up in the same blocks near the Jefferson's, it was not common to find many kids who hated violence and all the gangster education. Book earned his name in elementary school due to his love of education and his thirst for books. Younger than Mayhem and a distant friend of Contempt, he knew a great deal about what was going on. He traveled the streets on a skateboard. His choice of transportation seemed out of place in the dangerous streets. An avid reader, his bond with Ms. Martha was connected to her late grandson. He fell victim to the dreaded illegal drug, also known as crack. Now Book serves as her other grandson and he has become an envoy for the third city. He knows the difference between the unholy, filthy, mammon and the likes of the grimy streets. He understands the worship and praying of Ms. Martha and he knows the preying of Mayhem Jefferson in the House of Preyers.

12

REMEMBRANCE OF RIGHTEOUSNESS

The charity work by the outlaws left Mayhem deep in thought. She hated that the innocent folks got smoked. Deep down in her heart, she was depressed over the ruthlessness of her brothers and father. It all connected to one "thing" as Ms. Martha would preach at her all the time. The Devil! Mayhem could hear that scolding, that preaching about Jesus, and about morality. She hears those warnings loud and clear.

"Lawd child, git away from the devil. This is sin. This here is the devils bidding. Y'all mother is a slave to Beelzebub, that Devil. The Evil One lives in y'alls house. Yaw names!!! Girl, who calls their children Homicide, Contempt, Rape, Felonious and You, you ba-by? Dis is the Devil living three doors down from me."
One can hear a deep sighing or a verbal pausing for a moment.

"I am down on my old knees, begging God to save this city. Beggin him to save you and to save yaw pitiful momma. Y'all need to get yo momma away from the Devil. Pray, May. I need you to pray. Just pray."
Fat Shirley told Big Girl some news that wasn't so good.

"Old boy sold you a bullshit deal. He just got that Mustang last week from a young white girl. The girl was straight. She went to the Black Party one of those guys from Party Down Detroit gave. She is cool wit Roc-ko but she got into that crack. Bitch was selling everything. So, JuJu got dat Mustang for some dope from dat little white girl. She ended up doing that shit for about 24 continuous hours."

Big Girl was looking at Mayhem and just shrugged her shoulders and said, "Big deal, the Mustang is brand new. I got the papers saying its mine. It ain't stolen, well not illegally. Anyway, we gittin' paid. JuJu is paying us 50% of everything over on Dexter all the way down to Davison and LaSalle. He knows dat shit is worth a bunch. Me and Mayhem scared that bitch ass niggah!"

Even Black Charles looked worried as he motioned to Shirley to explain more.

Clearing her throat, Shirley throws away the last cheeseburger commenting, "Charles, dem hoes didn't put mustard, ketchup or pickles on any of my burgers. Well, it's a little different fo real. JuJu is all about Peddy gitting y'all tied up in dat shit. Peddy says that if Mayhem is out here, she won't be in on the contract for Rickey Ricardo."

Looking hungry and still dry mouthed, like she hasn't had a bite to eat in days, Fat Shirley tells Black Charles, "Come on buddy. Let's head out to Sinbad's. I feel like some of dem big ass shrimps. Hey girls, If I were you, I would watch out fo old Peddy Dog. Dat niggah is playing y'all."

Black Charles shakes his head and screams, "Bet. Let's drop off dis van to Book. I can't be seen driving no van."

Laughing he yells, "Got me ridin' like I'm some sort of family man."

As Mayhem and Big Girl get out of the van, Black Charles whispered to Mayhem, "Julius ain't right bout dat bank. Dat niggah slicking yaw paper. Dey cheating on the paper. Dey giving yaw peanuts. Talkin' bout 5 percent and not 50 percent. Dat block is clocking big bank. Peddy is the one-gitting dat money. He owns JuJu."

Mayhem shook her head knowing that Charles was speaking truth. Pedwell is notorious for manipulating people and it is known that he does it well. Big Girl understood that Peddy Jefferson was doing his dirt. Besides being the Devil, he was first and foremost a woman hater. He hates that his daughter is out here being an outlaw. Both young women know that Pedwell and all of his sons, with the exception of Contempt, felt that Mayhem had gotten out of her place - big time. Peddy believes that all contracts AND all the money is his. Why would he let anyone, especially a fe-male, take what is rightfully his?

"My daughter, y'all sista, thinks she is going to compete wit us? Silly, young, fe-male. I won't have it. Naw, not dis time. Not ever."

Contempt didn't know about the plans to sidetrack his sister. Like Mayhem, he had decided that he wanted to leave the clan. His last straw was the murder of Otis Player and the innocent couple. Con was devastated to learn of the young couples' children. It mattered that these young folks were innocent and not in the street life. Contempt legally changed his name to Conquest Edward Jeffstone. Ms. Martha had been feeding him soul food, especially collard greens. She had fed and nurtured his lost soul. Mayhem, like her brother, found Ms. Martha unrelenting in telling her Bible stories. Conquest was an earned name selected after he began to actually keep company with Book and some younger members of the congregation from Gabriel Baptist. Martha Myers was a loyal member of Gabriel Baptist for over thirty-two years. Despite losing a husband to alcohol and her grandson to crack, she remained faithful.

For the past thirty-seven years, Gabriel Baptist Church was lead by the Reverend David Goodman. Goodman was a transplanted preacher from Georgia. A student from Morehouse under the influence of the iconic Dr. Benjamin Mays, he had fulfilled all of the requirements that instilled the tenets necessary to be recognized as a true Baptist preacher. Like the old prophets preaching in the wilderness, his journey needed only a blue suit and the word from God. Since arriving in Detroit, the good reverend has built a strong church with a congregation that quickly went from a few to a few hundred.

Sitting on the corner of 12th Street and Hazelwood, the dark burgundy brick edifice was the spiritual rock where the young pastor and his beautiful wife Hazel ministered to the flock for decades. Reverend Goodman knew the good sister Martha Mary Myers with her two boys and one daughter. The good Reverend was now in his twilight years, but he and Ms. Martha continued to preach the golden rule. A young Mayhem, along with her sensitive older brother Contempt, found peace and lots of love from everyone in the congregation at Gabriel. Martha prayed for Mayhem. She loved the children just as the word of Jesus taught folks to love children. She would sing the songs with Mahalia Jackson while she cried. While many in the community denounced anyone associated with Pedwell and Jerenda

Jefferson, she was the one who prayed for, at the very least, Jerenda. She believed both Mayhem and Contempt were deeply misguided.

Martha told both children, "God Bless all of y'all and that includes your poor mother." She would look towards the sky and explain, "Sorry, God forgive me, but I can't see anything good about that Pedwell Jefferson. I can't say he deserves anything. How can you pray to God and then pray for the Devil?"

Mayhem knew what she would do with JuJu and so did Big Girl. Suddenly, Marvin Gaye's "What's Going On" ringtone blasted indicating that DeShaba was calling.

Mayhem answered with a snappy, "Wassup?"

DeSheba was coming through the phone, "Where y'all be? I tried to tell y'all. Dat niggah just ripped my young ass off. Dirty dick muthafucka just called me and said he was ready foe sum moe young kitty. I can't believe dat niggah said dat shit, Mayhem!" Putting her speakerphone on, Mayhem responded strongly to DeShaba.

"Tell dat niggah you gonna suck his big dick. Tell dat old fool to meet you at the Motor City Casino Hotel in an hour."

DeShaba starts crying and shouts into the phone, "Iz you smoking? I want to kill dat old nasty mutha-fucka. He raped me!! Mayhem, dat muthafucka fucked me like I was nothing!! Dat bitch ass niggah fucked Little Lisa in her ass too. He dun fucked lots of girls jest cuz dey trying to git into college."

Mayhem explained to DeSheba again that she had to tell John Locks to meet her in the Motown Suite.

"Stop crying DeSheba. We are going to fix this shit tonight! I promise. I'm bout tired of dis shit. Trust me."

Mayhem tells Big Girl to call JuJu to meet her at the casino for a freak party. Asking Big Girl about procuring the Motown Suite for the evening brings a quick "Amen" from Big Girl.

"No problem. Kenny Boy got two suites comped for the whole year. He only uses one most of the time. He won't let Peddy have shit since they had it out."

Looking confused, Big Girl asked, "What is up with JuJu?"

Chapter 12: Remembrance of Righteousness

Mayhem is pissed about the double cross with Peddy. Big Girl is not surprised and she wants to get JuJu for the shakey deal on the Mustang.

"Mayhem, you think he will just come like that?"
In deep thought, she declared her intent to lure JuJu.

"Tell dat nigga you got him a bitch dat looks like Angie Negro. Remind him that dat nigga will come cuz his dick runs his silly ass."
The doorman knows the girls. Mayhem gives him a crisp, folded twenty-dollar bill. Looking him in the eye, she reminds him of her stature, her regal place.

"Don't tell nobody we here. Where is Kenny Boy?"

The doorman is quick to respond. "I aint seen a thang and Kenny Boy is at the table near the fountain."

Kenny Boy is Kennard Davis, a renowned hustler and gambler who lives at the casino. Once a high school basketball star, he was highly recruited by colleges all over America. The tall, six foot six, two time All-American went to the prestigious Braithwaite College.Destined for the professional league, it was a national scandal when he was caught shaving points. Kicked out of college, he returned to Detroit and took his title as the best gambler ever. Davis is loved by all, including the professional colored types. Kenny Boy is one of the few people who Pedwell loves and respects. He is famous for his beautiful women and fabulous parties. It is said that both the NBA and NFL warn their players not to take up company with Kenny Boy. That order is ignored and instead it becomes a mere wish. If you come to Detroit, you want to know Kenny Boy. Xavier was the person that encouraged Kenny Boy to give something constructive back to the community. Judge Long is not a fan, but Xavier reminds his father that whatever took the young star to the dark side does, in fact, matter. The ongoing debate within the Long clan has been that of Good vs. Evil.

Standing near the Motor City Room is Kenny Boy. He is with a fine, petite, mocha chocolate woman. Kenny is clever. His blue pinstripe suit lays perfect on his slim frame. Women and men admire Kenny and he knows it. The Motor City Room is the relaxing lounge for serious players. There are several political leaders attending a fundraiser for education. Dressed stylishly in an evening dress is Marian Tubman, who is sitting with social worker Carmel Embry, Ramona and Lloyd Gibson, and the school board president. There is a buzz at the fundraiser over the emergency financial manager appointed by the governor. While the financial manager is in attendance, its clear he is not welcome. Ramona Gibson is appalled that the very people who cut all sports and all the extra curricular programs and activities would show their face at this event. Talk about tension in the casino, there is enough energy to create a nuclear explosion. Kenny Boy is engaged in conversation when Big Girl greets him. She motions him towards the exit door trying to just blend in with the diverse crowd. The casino is a smoke-filled venue. The decorum is striking and opulent. Big Girl noticed Zina's parents and Marian Tubman. She doesn't want to see them or vice versa. Kenny hugs her as he gives her the security cards for the River Suite, which is on the far end from his Motor City Suite.

"Rene, I am living in the Motor City Suite this year. You got two bedrooms in the River Suite. Wassup with you women?"
Big Girl likes it when men flirt with her. She, like most women, find Kenny just good looking and sexy as hell. Dressed for work, she adorns an all black Carthartt with a smile that is beguiling. She is whispering while pulling him into the stairwell. It seems she has a few important questions for the superstar gambler.

"Kenny, is there a spa like the one in the Motor City suite? You know, one wit dat sweet ass big shower wit the open floor. One big enuff for lots of people?"

Grinning with suspicion, he laughs and then asks his own question, "Whoa, wassup Mayhem? Wanna have a freak party? Aiight". I'll invite some freaky niggahs, and some big muthafucka's.

Mayhem asks, "Can we make our music loud or will hotel security be on us?"

Looking at Big Girl, Kenny is laughing, "security ain't no problem. Dis Casino don't mess with big monay players like me. All of my suites is cool. Nobody gives a damn. Dis casino is all about fun and making money. Aint nobody looking at nothing else. Y'all can have that suite all week. It's slow in here."

Chapter 12: Remembrance of Righteousness

Mayhem is walking into the lounge with four of her girls. Like all the rest of the girls, she is in Carhartt attire. The slender figure cuts stylishly in her short dark brown jacket with a black corduroy collar. Her blue tinted glasses hide her watchful hawk eyes that are surveying the lounge. Suddenly, there is some kind of force pushing up on her.

Strong and expanding all around her, she sees two figures standing at the bar. The energy is definitely coming from that spot. The live music playing is a jazz composition by a trio led by Detroit's own Geoff Ryan. The two men are talking with Professor Long and Tyquan. Tyquan turns to catch Big Girl walking off the elevator. Excusing himself from Long, he rushes over to Big Girl.

"Hey. You okay? Where is May?"

No sooner than her name is spoken, Mayhem appeared in front of Tyquan. Without a word, she hugs Tyquan and walks to a nearby table. As they sit down, a waitress comes to the table and gets their orders. Big Girl tells the trio that Marian Tubman is on the other side of the room. Mayhem can't shake the feeling of being surrounded with this powerful vibe still emitting from the two men at the bar. She orders her gingle ale; carefully making sure the waitress understands the order.

"Canada Dry Ginger Ale, a twist of lemon, a half of lime with four cocktail cherries and crushed ice."

The young waitress didn't know who she was, but understood the tone.

As Mayhem waited, her feelings were moved by that same strong force. It was a deep thought about Tubman for Mayhem. Seeing Zina and Khan brought back memories of when they were all in middle school. Khan was holding it down in track and softball. Zina and Mayhem were on the relay team and Rene was doing the shot put. The team had won the AAU State Championship and Mayhem couldn't wait for the Junior Nationals. Tubman was her coach and the one person who really believed in her skills. It made her sad to think that Coach Tubman might believe she was just a twisted criminal like all of the Jefferson boys. Pedwell had made her get off the team after the authorities took little Des. Now, seeing Tubman didn't make her sad. It's true. She was not ashamed.

In an unconscious attempt to make sense of her feelings, Mayhem declared that, "a gangster does what a gangster got to do."

It was ironic. As tough as she was, Big Girl Rene was ducking from her old middle school coach.

Tyquan knew something was wrong. He knew that Locks getting off was seriously bad. Like most people in the lounge at that time, he was supporting the effort to raise money for the children. Yet, Tyquan knew that DeShaba was devastated. There was something bad in the air. Tyquan had been telling Xavier all day that something was going to happen.

Looking Mayhem in her eyes, he asked her point blank, "May, wassup with John Locks? I hope nobody gonna go medieval with him."

Ruby Redd is entering the lounge dressed in a beautiful red cashmere coat with a big red and white scarf wrapped around her neck. Ruby is smiling and greeting everyone by waving and blowing kisses but she almost immediately sits with Mayhem. As the waitress brings the drinks, Ruby tells the group the latest news.

"Mayhem, Murder Man is down with one of my dancers. Boyfriend says they gonna get paid. Black Mike is looking for Rickey Ricardo. I know that you and the girls are up for that contract."

Big Girl is surprised with this news, "Black Mike is a dog and Murder Man is just a twisted, freaky, killing kind of niggah."

As the talk continued with Ruby, Mayhem tells the waitress she wants a catfish sandwich.

Big Girl adds, "I want that red mayo on a shrimp sandwich. Y'all up on sweet potato fries?"

Mayhem looked at the men talking with Xavier. She asked Ruby who the two men were.

Xavier is greeting his brothers, Saul and one of the twins, Phillip. The two older men had just arrived at the function.

Ruby whispered as if the two men might have heard her say, "Girl, that is Black Hat Daddy and Adolph Gillespie. I'm talking about Black Hat Daddy from Black Bottom. Adolph "Yai" Gillespie ran all the games for the old chiefs."

Mayhem is curious about Black Hat Daddy and Mr. Gillespie.

Ruby laughed, "Neither of them is worried, concerned or scared of your daddy. Adolph Gillespie once whipped your daddy at the Chit Chat Lounge on 12th Street. When my father was running numbers, he worked for Adolph Gillespie."

Mayhem and Big Girl are looking at each other puzzled looks. Mayhem has never known anyone to do battle with her father and live if they beat him.

Big Girl was asked the question, "Wait, he whipped Peddy and he is still here?" The whole table stopped breathing. Ruby gave an account that deeply confused everyone. The pending business at hand seemed to fade as Mayhem listened intently.

"Look, Adolph was and still is the Original Gangster. He cleaned up a lot of the bullshit that made things difficult in Black Bottom. All the old heads depended on him and the big boss back then. Adolph has been in prison for almost eight years. He just got released on a technicality. They tried to put him away forever. Adolph is the man and even your daddy knows that. Keithland James and all that talk about Detroit's original gangster knows better. Anything you need to know about the real shit is standing at the bar with Doc."

13

ANCIENT HISTORY

Xavier treats Black Hat Daddy with the respect usually due street royalty. Tyquan is probing what is going on with Mayhem. Ruby notices that Black Hat Daddy has taken a table near their gathering. The tall, dark skinned, well-dressed man stands and greets Ruby as she leaves her table to pay her respects. Black Hat stands out because of his tailored navy suede suit, a matching navy shirt and navy chukka boots. His hair is snow white and he has a perfectly trimmed mustache. The atmosphere around Black Hat and Adolph is cool. It's an authentic coolness that is not obtained by mammon.

Adolph is dressed in an elegantly classic shirt and tie. There is an urban conservative tone to the dark gray suit, with the whitest white shirt and a contrasting red, black, and faint orange paisley tie. The pocket square is a purplish mixture of orange and slight slivers of silverfish gray. Adolph is what the Long boys call half-bald head. Like their jurist conservative father Judge Long, Adolph's hair is neatly cut around the bottom half of his head. Adolph looks no older than fifty years old. The look belies his eight decades plus an additional year or two. Both men know that they are special and that they stand above the lies and negative stereotypes assigned to black men.

After a pleasant exchange of greetings, Ruby turns to leave.

The deep baritone voice of Adolph asked, "Ms. Redd, is that lovely young woman with the ponytail Sarges' granddaughter?" Big Girl is astonished as she listens to the inquiring deep voice. Ruby motions for Big Girl.

"Come and meet greatness."

Ruby offered, "Doc, that is her and the girl with her is the daughter of Pedwell Jefferson."

A short Cuban waiter from the bar brought over a bottle of Glen Fiddich scotch for Adolph. Another waiter had a bottle of chilled Cabernet Sauvignon Reserve.

"As you requested sir. Here is the 1966 Robert Mondovi."
Without skipping a beat, Black Hat Daddy repeats that infamous name.

"Pedwell Jefferson - I knew he had boys but, a daughter?"

The two older men surveyed Mayhem, who was approaching the table slowly, with Big Girl. Staring at both men, she looked right into the eyes of the aged face of Adolph Gillespie.

"You know my daddy?"
Adolph, ever the gentleman, nodded with a poker face.

Without giving a sign of any emotion, he explained, "Pedwell Jefferson is acquainted with me and my associates."
Mayhem was mesmerized by how cool Adolph was. She noticed the firm hands, the manicured nails, and the beautiful yellow diamond ring. Big Girl is amazed that someone would recognize her or her grandfather. Black Hat Daddy offered them drinks.

"Would you ladies like anything? Ms. Redd, how is that father of yours? Your name is Rene, isn't it?" Ruby is accustomed to the two gentlemen of street legacy. Clearing her throat, she smiles and looks at the twenty-one-year-old scotch.

"We carry that at the club. I thought you would like it. Do you want something else Black Hat? Dad is in Florida for the winter. He is doing well. We have a nurse with him and my mother. They come back to the city in June and stay near the old house in a smaller condo. My sister has the old house."
Big Girl chimed in with a guarded and much thought about reply to the question of her birth name. She had never seen Mayhem so enamored. It seemed that the older men had a special spirit of some sort. The female gangsters have never been in the presence of grounded, aged patricians of the third city. Smiling with a conservative controlled vibration, Big Girl became the well-mannered Rene Mankiller. Mayhem is in disbelief. She looked at Big Girl like the court side scribes watching Moses' serpent swallowing Pharaoh's scribes serpents.

"Yes sir. I am Rene Mankiller. Well, my whole name is Rene "Morning River Mankiller.""

Black Hat smiled, "Ruby, this place of business claims to be first class. We had better back in the day with the Gotham Hotel."

Looking toward the bar, he asserts, "I am told that is the best scotch in the house."

Xavier sits down next to the twosome. He smiles at Mayhem as Tyquan is attempting to get his attention.

"Well, Mr. Ellington, are you coming to the lecture next Monday?"

Few knew that Black Hat Daddy is Wilton F. Ellington, a self-educated street scholar. Black Hat Daddy is a renowned hustler from the old school. Both of these men are concerned about the public schools. Looking at Xavier with an appreciation for his stance on public education, he acknowledged that he would indeed be in attendance.

"Of course I will be there. I am looking forward to hearing your keynote speech." Big Girl is always happy to see Dr. Long. Xavier has always encouraged her to return to community college. Like Mayhem, the whole educational experience has been tough. Her grandfather always held Marian Tubman in high esteem, so he couldn't understand why she didn't continue school.

The baritone began again, "Rene Mankiller is your mother's maiden name. She is a full Ojibwa or Chippewa. So that makes you part Ojibwa and African of some tribe."

Big Girl is puzzled as to the remark about Chippewas. Black Hat Daddy is part Cherokee and proud. While he never knew Big Girl's mother, he knew her grandfather well. Both he and Adolph are big boxing fans. Mayhem listened to the talk and thought about how these two men were very different from her father. Pedwell was so negative that one could feel his hatred. Evil thoughts seemed to consume his troubled soul. Black Hat Daddy sent a bottle of expensive wine to the table where Marian Tubman was sitting. Everything Black Hat Daddy did was cool and the way he sent the wine was oh so cool. The waiters and waitresses seemed to cater to every wish of the two old heads.

A young man dressed in a red Nike sweat suit with brand new white Nike Michael Jordan's, swept into the lounge. Heading straight to Big Girl, he bends over whispering into her ear. Along with him were three young girls. The girls were Mayhems' girls and each of them wore black hooded Carhartt sweatshirts pulled over their heads. Talking into cell phones, they hid their faces that were full of looks of damnation.

One of the girls says to Tyquan, "Heya T-Quan. Where are yawlls boys?"
As the girls move about quickly, Tyquan begins to sense a stronger wrongness in the air. Suddenly, JuJu is strutting down the hall towards the elevators. Tyquan sees JuJu and noticed his crew of four young boys following.

Mayhem whispered to Big Girl, "why all dese boys down wit dis niggah?"
JuJu is tall, lanky and arrogant to the tenth degree.

Seeing Mayhem, he loudly shouts, "Say yea to my bitch, Mayhem and Big Girl, we doing it."
Big Girl goes over to the elevator, abruptly leaving the company of Ruby, Black Hat Daddy, Xavier and Adolph.

"Nice meeting both of you. See you later Ms. Ruby."
Mayhem excuses herself with a polite nod. For reasons she didn't understand, she wanted to stay.

Tyquan tells the remaining parties at the table, "There goes trouble. Something is going on."

Sitting at the table as their meal is served, Black Hat Daddy comments to Adolph, "I can't believe how smart a lot of these young ones are. Sadly, they still don't know a damn thing about their people. That child, Rene, is smart as a whip and she don't even know the real deal about her grandfather."

Xavier, who is sipping a glass of iced tea with lots of lemons added, "Its complex. The public schools are dead and the charter schools are only for certain kids."
As the men talked, the big Sony monitors behind the bar and all around the lounge, all synchronized in audio and visual flash to a breaking news moment. The whole lounge appeared to be one big news flash.

The local reporter, who had been reporting from the hockey game on ESPN suddenly interrupted, "BREAKING NEWS. A VICTIM OF RAPE COMMITS SUICIDE IN FRONT OF THE DETROIT COMMUNITY COLLEGE.

DaShaba Moore, 20 years old, shot herself this evening in a classroom during a lecture. We are now live in front of the administration building of DCC. The reports begin to detail that the young woman was upset emotionally after the teacher, John Locks, was found not guilty of rape!!!" The entire crowd was frozen with disbelief from the dramatic breaking news. Tyquan mumbled something incoherently as he watched Mayhem on her cell phone from a distance. Big Girl and the other young women were all either talking or texting on their phones. JuJu was in his own world as he waited with his crew for the elevator.

With the precision of a combat leader, Mayhem commanded her troops, "Take JuJu up to the suite. Big Girl got dis down here."
Big Girl and the three other girls pushed JuJu's four young boys into the stairwell by the exit sign. The young man in the red Nike suit stood guard at the exit door as Big Girl instructed him.

"Nig. Nobody comes in or goes out of this door!"

Standing tall and relaxed with the red hood on his head, he quickly yanks out an AK-47 from a large white Nike duffel bag. The young boys face looked menacing as he peered all around while he guarded the door. Looking around, the hallway is empty with nearly everyone still in the lounge.

Meanwhile, as Mayhem is getting off the elevator, her crew is there to greet her. JuJu suddenly turns around and is puzzled when he doesn't see his crew. Inside the plush River Suite, there are two young girls working fast, laying large plastic sheets by the hallway leading into the white and grayish marble bathroom floor. The girls are moving quickly like busy bees and ants. The music is loud and it's drowning out the voices that are speaking. A young girl, who looked no older than twenty something, guides JuJu to the bar.

"Whatcha drinking?"

JuJu is completely confused and mumbled, "Cognac, Hennessey. What's going on?"

Chapter 13: Ancient History

The stairwell is completely quiet. One of the girls with Big Girl shoots out the stairwell lighting.

Suddenly, the lights come back on, and to the surprise of the young girl, Big Girl laughs, "Hit the back up lights. Git them and be sure to hit that camera on the top over there."

At this point, the other girls had already taken away the guns that were in the possession of JuJu's boys. One of them tried to jump bad, but he was met with the swiftness of a serious blow to the face with the butt of an AK-47. As the lights went out again, there is a blaze of gunfire bouncing off the bodies of JuJu's crew. Big Girl, who is standing at the top of the stairwell, directed the girls to pour gasoline over the stacked bodies. As the cans of gas are emptied, Big Girl knocks on the exit door. The boy guarding the door gets his next command.

"We gone! Make sure you take out that alarm box near the exit door by the men's bathroom. Put yo gat in the janitors' room and leave out that door. Blinky is in the lot near the guards' gate."

JuJu is aware that Mayhem is unhappy but he is not sure why. Walking into the front of the bar, she denounced Julius in no uncertain terms as his face registered his fate.

"Set me up cuz I'm a fe-male? You think I'm soft, not a gangsta?"

Before Mayhem can say another word, he offered, "May-hem, Peddy did it. He told me he would cool everything out."

Mayhem takes her Glock 9mm and, point blank, unloads into the skull of JuJu. His body shakes and he dies quickly. There was not another word. There was no emotional utterance. The body is dragged into the bathroom, placed into the plastic rugs and sheets that are lining the floor. As if it were an assembly line at the Pyramids in Egypt, JuJu is laid out and then sealed forever in thick plastic. Not a drop of blood exists anywhere in the River Suite. JuJu is signed, sealed and delivered as the crew rolls the body out as if it was King Tut himself on tour. Mayhem is on point but her girl is dead. Mayhem knows that DeSheba had not taken her own life, for real.

Mayhem thought, "Naw, her death is on the hands of many."

Mayhem is walking out into a waiting Denali with Big Girl following in her Mustang.

"Now, all these so-called men are gonna find out what a true gangster I really am!!"

14

DEADLY CONSEQUENCES

Robert McNamara Federal Building in downtown Detroit

The FBI office is the meeting place for the federal task force. The U.S. Attorney for the Eastern District of Michigan is a young African American woman. Anita Jones is a native of Washington D.C. and she has been appointed the first black female US Attorney in Michigan. She is listening as the task force is updated on their new witness, Rickey Bratten, also known as Rickey Ricardo. The prized catch for the feds is not Ricky but actually Walena Pope. Pope is a former adult entertainment dancer who is now a reformed drug addict. While her knowledge of Keithland James is deeper than many know, she is the link to Pedro Gomez known affectionately as Petey Gomez, the porno king. Pedro is the brain behind an international porno operation that makes millions. Gomez has strong ties to both South and Central American organized crime – crime that includes the peddling of pornography. Gomez worked with Rickey in Keithlands illicit commerce. He also worked for a South American drug cartel, in addition to an array of all kinds of underworld dealings. Anita Jones listened intently as the Detroit Police and Michigan State Police gave an intelligence report of the street operations of Keithland James. Detroit Mayor William Bracy was especially challenged to keep his remarks positive and encouraging since there was great reliance placed on street information. God only knows what Rickey would testify about. No one knew that Walena and Peter Gomez even existed. Walena and Peter Gomez had been undercover for over three years. The real breakpoint is the true religious conversion of Walena and Peter. Both have found Jesus. They are converts and the followers of a young street minister. The young United States Attorney for the Eastern District of Michigan thinks about how the old adage, "what you don't know won't hurt" cannot be applied in this case. The attorney understood that the success of this case was vital to rid the city of its thug population and the association with rampid corruption. The potentate Keithland James and D.O.G. had no real solid information about the trio of informants. The 'Holy Rollers' and Rickey Ricardo, who were very much in love with Walena, represented deadly information. An agent came into the meeting room and informed U.S. Attorney Jones of the four dead bodies that had been shot and burned at the casino. Jones was confounded, asking what, if anything, does this have to do with the pending investigations?

She then adds, "Or better yet, does this mean anything as it relates to Rickey?" The FBI agent begins to explain that the task force has intelligence that would result in the sorting out of a maze of problems. Another police agency attended the meeting on behalf of the Detroit Police Department.

Casino security detail is made up of several off-duty Detroit Police. Consequently, the casino incident would be difficult, if not impossible, to investigate. The video camera in the stairwell was destroyed before or during the shootings and fire. The director of Security is a retired Detroit Police inspector. Blake Duffey is a stout Irishman who is furious over the violence that has taken place in the casino. A short, robust man, who prefers Irish whiskey in his coffee, denounced the transgressors.

"Damn city is full of killers. They knocked out the monitors. Got the nerve to be smart like nothing you have ever seen before. Sons of bitches dressed in those got damned hoodies. When they move around the parking lot, all you see of those faceless bastards in dark hoodies."

Drinking his Irish coffee, he is accompanied by a group of security people from the casino. Reports are going around the FBI office about the existence of several hooded figures. There are also those pictures of Mayhem Jefferson and Rene Mankiller. Another agent has brought several casino employees to the office to look at pictures of casino personnel. One young Mexican-American male who worked maintenance makes a point that is well known to law enforcement officials.

"I can't help you. Nope, there was nothing going on when I was working. Nothing at all."

A doorman is telling how the crew of females arrived at the club looking for Kenny Boy. Anita Jones is curious about Kenny Boy.

"Kenny Boy is the celebrity gambler. Is he involved?"

One of the agents is asking the doorman, "What car did Mayhem drive?"

The young doorman looked worried. He slowly tells the cops he is not sure. His body language sends off a clear message. The message is that there will not be any true or accurate descriptions. Even the doorman developed a severe case of forgetfulness. Pictures of Mayhem and Rene revealed nothing of any evidentiary value. The Detroit Police department is embarrassed about coming up with nothing on four burned and murdered bodies. One detective summarized the ordeal.

"It's a wrap. Monkeys see nothing. Monkeys hear nothing and monkeys say nothing. That lounge area was filled with people and we got nothing."

The special task force is extremely pleased with the three potential witnesses for their case against Keithland James. While the two witnesses are secrets, there is no doubt that Keithland is acutely aware of Rickey Ricardo's' potential. Anita Jones is meeting with local, state and federal team members about their concerns. She is generally upbeat and hopeful about her team. While she is equally impressed with some members of the Detroit Police, she is suspect of some of DPD's major crime unit members. With a long history of navigating the good old boys network, the legacy of the radical 'Cowboys', and the strong racial undercurrents all work to give her strong reservations regarding issues of trust within the entire department. Judge Constance Long has been a reliable ally as much as possible. Connie, Anita, and all the other Long sisters are also sorority sisters. Police Chief Christine LeRocque is new as Chief but not as an experienced cop with a variety of key police assignments over the years. Finally, Lynette Long, a state prison warden, warns her tribe that their parents want a gathering not anchored with shoptalk.

"Daddy said no talk about anything remotely close to work. Mama seconded that point. We are to have a good time minus any talk of crime or death."

For Anita Jones, having dinner at the Long homestead was a treat. At least once a week, during the last several months of her heading up of the special task force, dinner invitations were given to several of the Long sibling's professional associates, and friends. The big house on the corner of Chicago Blvd. and Hamilton looks like a small mansion. All of the Long children grew up in the "Long Estate," as they called it. The dining room was prepared to serve thirty-three guests. Judge Long is a well-respected fundraiser for all the good and positive social causes in the city. Cooking the feast is left to Judge Long's old army comrade. Sgt. Major Cephus McDaniels and his wife Belda Lillian McDaniels are the cooks. McDaniels has lived in the coach house since his retirement from the army. Mrs. McDaniels is a professional chef and they live in Detroit during the summer and spend the winters in her native home in Belda, Barbados.

Anita Jones is pondering the cold reality of the casino shootings. The name of Mayhem Jefferson rings in her ears for the second time in recent reviews. The crime scene that included dead dogs had the eerie signature of this mysterious young girl. Mayhem? That name was so bizarre. Who in the world is named Mayhem? Who had requested her assistance to give all the data she could collect on this Mayhem Jefferson? Chief LeRocque had explained that in Detroit, when you talked about street crime, you were talking about Pedwell Jefferson. The more she read, the more she became confused about this Jefferson family. Those names. She was horrified, both by the criminal record of Pedwell, and the names he had bestowed upon his children. She didn't understand what it meant when parents gave their children such names: Homicide, Assault, Rape and Contempt. Why? What in the world is the whole story?

Frank Bruno is celebrating his 85th birthday at Morelli's on the Detroit River near downtown. Bruno, who still ran the family business, was known as an original silent partner of the Purple Gang. His birthday was an occasion that allowed all of the old mafia to meet and mingle with the new mafia. Bruno had taken a less visible role while he encouraged his sons and nephews to continue the legacy of criminal operations in Detroit and the surrounding suburbs. The small acreage between Grosse Pointe and Detroit was in Alexander County and, officially, this ex-urban community was exclusively the fiefdom of the Sicilian-Italian community known as Cardinal, Michigan. Bruno had a large Italian family made up of six boys and six girls. Bruno's reputation was connected to his days as the bodyguard and enforcer for the syndicate leader of the region's boss, Aldo Salvatore and to Joseph Corelli, the infamous Detroit Don that goes back to the days of the Purple Gang. Working his way up the ladder, Bruno became the Don after an accident took out the whole family of Salvatore. The mysterious disappearance of the entire Corelli family followed the accident of the Don, Salvatore and it left no doubt about the treacherous talent of the new powerbroker, Frank Bruno.

Bruno became the head of all criminal activities and controlled the crime enterprise in Detroit and has done such during the past fifty years. Thomas "Rocco" Bruno is the youngest son of James Bruno, and the grandson of Don Frank Bruno. Rocco is involved in the family business of produce supply. The youngest Bruno has a long history of troubles with the law. His grandfathers' birthday celebration is strained, to say the least. The angst is between the elder organized crime boss and his wayward grandson. As everyone is gathering in the large dining room, one of Bruno's men rushed in to announce the latest news to the old man. Bruno is a chubby, older looking gentleman. He is a throw back to the days when Italians ruled the crime scene. The birthday becomes bittersweet for Bruno, as he listened to the younger generation discussing Detroit. Old man Bruno, in his late years, hates the changes that show a disrespectful public. In Detroit, where his operations ran smoothly, the new generation of mafia soldiers has declined. His grandson is a sterling example of his confusion. He stares as young Rocco talks like a rapper, and as if that were not bad enough, he listened as Rocco declared himself a 'Wiggar.'

"A what?"

Bruno asked his son what the problem was with his grandsons' generation. James, known as Jimmy "Little Boss," is more concerned about the lost territories and the apparent invasion of the Mexican Cartels.

"Dad, look Rocco is just young. He is finding himself. He is straight, a full-blooded young boy!! He has that hot Puerto Rican girl. He is just kind of confused like most of these young guys."

Rocco is a young man who likes to brag about his sexual conquests and the list of hip-hop friends he personally has in Detroit. The fact that his girlfriend is a Puerto Rican cannot explain his rather feminine behavior. Old man Bruno is not satisfied at all. Acknowledging that, while the changes are serious, he still questions his grandson and all his "fruity" behavior.

"I don't like it. His hair is styled like a woman. What is he doing with all of those long-streaked curls, with all those colors? He likes the dark people. He's lazy. Your daughter is looney. She is always accusing me of some shit with a woman named Carmen. Since your mother's death, I have not had a woman. Hell, I am too old. My snake barely crawls. This daughter of yours, who I paid every red penny to send to law school, talks crazy. This girl cries about the work that paved the way for folks to be able to pay for a better life. She called me a Terrorist. She called me a Thug. Then she starts that crazy shit about my Carmen is going to come back on me. What is that Jimmy?"

Jimmy can't begin to explain the term karma to his ancient father. Like his father, Jimmy has been told, in no uncertain terms, that his gangster deeds are bad Karma. He does not have the patience, fortitude, or understanding to tell Bruno it is not a woman called Carmen. No. Its retribution of the metaphysical sense. It's something father and son knew nothing about.

As the two men are talking, one of the soldiers entered the den where they are engaged in deep conversation about the generation of today. The short, stocky man whispered to Jimmy. Looking puzzled, he turned to his father, who is sitting by the big fireplace. The fire is blazing as the music of Perry Como plays in the background. Jimmy is wearing an expensive Italian tailored suit with dark grey plaid. Unlike his father, he preferred the stylish tailoring like that of an entertainer. The truth is, Jimmy sees his image along the line of the late infamous New York Don, John Gotti.

Turning to his father, he speaks with a tinge of disgust, "Some mullee's killed four of their own and then set the casino on fire. Rumor has it that Keithland has a rat that could give us problems."

The phone rings in the den and another soldier answers and soon hands the phone to Bruno.

"Thanks, yes, what is the problem? Sure, come on I'm in the den."

The elder leader looked at his son, "Problems are worse. That was Lanza. He's on his way right now. It's that damn nigger. Like I said, they have taken over. For what we get out of that city, its not worth the time."

The dark blue Jaguar sedan pulled into the driveway. Vincent Lanza was the Bruno family attorney for the operations in Michigan. As he stepped out of the sedan, he moved swiftly into the side door off the garden side of the estate. A tall, rangy man dressed in a dark suit opened the door after the doorbell rang. Lanza walked over to the bar and poured from the large bottle of Johnny Walker Blue Label bottle. His long navy Vicuna coat hung on his body like it was a coat hanger. His aged face showed the stress of being one of the top mob lawyers over the past quarter century. Taking a deep breath, he opens the cigar humidor on the bar. Selecting a large dark cigar, he sniffed for a second then his gold lighter flashed as he lit up.

"Bruno, I am afraid we got to let Keithland know that there is possibly more than one witness. I got a call. The feds are sealing up everything. That damn U.S. Attorney Jones is a cunt ass, black bitch using a team we never heard of before. It's the same mode of operations they started to use on these damn international indictments."
Bruno is tired and therefore a bit confused.

He thought, "That black bitch. An attorney...a US Attorney, a nigger!"

Jimmy looked sheepish at his father and the old attorney. The litigator assured his clients that the information was reliable and could get even worse. As he departed from the house, Vincent explained that the new deals are on video, and that half of the indictments are divided between Keithland and some city officials including a few black businessmen. All Bruno can think of is how he allowed Jimmy to talk him into allowing the merger with Keithland James.

His last years have turned into a nightmare. There is a grandson who thinks he is a fruity nigger and a granddaughter who is an attorney for the legal neighborhood clinic. He can't help but to think that his dreams are gone forever. He thinks of his lovely wife Maria and how it might have been better if he had passed on with her. At least he wouldn't have to do business with the likes of Cubans, niggers, Arabs and Mexicans. He hated Detroit because, like it or not, the new gangsters in Detroit could give less than a damn about Don Joseph Corelli or his heir, Frank Bruno.

The plan to have John Lock at the casino had shifted. DeShaba's death has changed everything. Lock has fled and is in hiding. Mayhem is deeply disturbed by DeSheba's suicide. Without a great deal of discussion, Mayhem is feeling that she must avenge the death of DeShaba. The streets are filled with reports about how much Rickey Ricardo was snitching. The price on the head of Rickey has grown both within the street grapevine and with Keithland's disturbance in hearing from the Bruno people.

Black Mike is making inroads in finding where he and Murder Man can locate Rickey Ricardo. The city is buzzing after the deaths at the casino. While there is no evidence of who did what at the casino, the streets are screaming that Mayhem is the avenger. Big Girl learned from other members of the crew that John Locks was hiding out at the outreach program for the Good Sheppard church.

The realities of the third city are resonant in the larger picture. Mayhem is fighting with herself and she is deeply conflicted. She has difficulty comprehending all the praise and motivation about education that she had been exposed to and her connection to Tyquan was something unattainable in her thinking due to her rage. She feels that maybe sometimes Ms. Martha might be right about God. Does God know Mayhem?

Ms. Maratha always saying, "the devil will destroy itself."

Chapter 14: Deadly Consequences

Sometimes, all that spiritual connection makes Mayhem think that God does love her. The music from that old record player, or that crazy "big disc" as she called it, always played spiritual records, and, at the moment, she was pondering about the line between right and wrong. As she reflected on DeShaba's suicide, she can't and won't forget what John Lock said to DeSheba that made her end her life. DeShaba was distraught over having her attempt at completing college controlled by Lock especially since he constantly taunted her by reminding her that she really wasn't worthy. Mayhem always felt that it was her against the world. Her city, and her life were worth nothing. It was a concept she learned from listening to Xavier and Tyquan.

15

WICKED PIMP-WOMAN IN THE WORLD

A DIRECT DESCENDANT OF SLAVEOWNERS

The whereabouts of JuJu were unknown to everybody. No one had seen him since his trip to the casino. Pedwell was having a meeting of sorts with his crew at a little restaurant in Highland Park. Once the corporate headquarters of Chrysler, the city struggles now with the fact that almost everyone that could leave has abandoned the small city next to the Roman Empire. Pedwell is in good spirits. He chuckled about Black Mike, Murder Man, and all are his dogs. Peddy is enjoying his grits, bacon, sausage, pancakes and scrambled eggs with cheese. Contempt is texting Mayhem on his iPhone. The texting is a well-secured secret since the other Jefferson brothers are like their father, computer illiterates.

After their breakfast, the gangsters go to Smokes, the hangout and headquarters for Pedwell. The temperature is four below zero on this dark ugly February day. With the exception of Contempt and Homicide, everybody in the crew is wearing a fur coat. Contempt's personal constitution does not permit the eating of animals, nor the wearing of furs. Contempt still loves chicken, and truth be told, he favors the lifestyle of the less aggressive human beings.

Smokes' is really a hole in the wall for the miscreants in the underworld. It's an environment so ugly that there are few decent folks hanging at Smokes. It is a deep dark mood that is lingering as the pool table cloth becomes littered with ashes from men smoking both cigarettes and weed. Smokes is a small place. There is little decorum to the place. Big Black Dog posters and wall-size signs cover the entire club. The malt liquor sold in the club could never pass any legal evaluation that would allow it to be sold legally. It's a lethal concoction of high alcohol contents and a host of secret chemicals. Word on the street is that it is nothing but liquid crack. Peddy is its great pusher man. He and his crew are backing the young inventors of the malt. Black Dog Malt Liquor is made in Detroit and Detroit is its biggest market. It is a black market that is unknown to America.

Black Dog comes in a black bottle with the inscription, *Black Dog* written in blood red. There is an illustration of a big black dog pissing in bright yellow onto the Statue of Liberty. The young inventors of this drink are three students from the State University of Michigan. There is a growing market for the drink that seems to eventually drive its consumers literally mad. Dog drinkers are known to become psychotic, deranged, and more, in a short period of time. Homicide and his brothers have made great inroads in the suburban communities and rural places with their Black Dog product. The talent of young Rocco Bruno or Roc-ko, as he prefers, has become the linchpin for the illegal drink and its distribution.

A Detroit rap group has sampled 'Atomic Dog' from the infamous George Clinton led P-Funk and produced, 'Black Dog Down.' It's a big bass pulsating tune that all of the youth in Detroit and the surrounding region play on there little cell units. It is a multicultural tune with Arab chants and Hmong music incorporated with Spanish lyrics that forms a "We are the thug world" and "We rule" theme. As the music blared in Smokes, the owner and bartender come from the rear of the club. Ron 'Dog' Maxwell was a veteran of Viet Nam with a pension for motorcycles. He is also the main reason that the black and Latino motorcycle gangs started hanging out at Smokes.In a few words, Smokes is an illegal operating, grimy, after-hour establishment that is open twenty-four hours a day, and seven days a week. Suddenly, a short, stocky built man, who was once a football star at old Detroit Eastern High School, motions to Homicide to come over to the bar. Homicide is wearing a long black mink coat with a black mink baseball cap. The black Gucci sunglasses hide his eyes as he walked over to the bar.

Ron 'Dog' points to the backdoor, "Lookout in the parking lot. Somebody just dropped a package for Peddy."

Laying right at the backdoor is a large plastic wrapped package. It looked like some sort of frozen meat. Homicide pulled his glasses off in one hand. Pulling out his Gloc 9mm pistol, he walked slowly to-wards the package. There is a note on the big plastic item.

Felonious and Assault are walking behind Homicide as he hollered out to his father, "Man, its JuJu. He's frozen. Peddy, it's JuJu. He's dead. He's frozen with a note on him."

The large note is wrinkled and has large red letters that read, *"IT WAS A SET UP AND THE NIGGAH GOT FUCKED UP. THE DOUBLE CROSS GOT CROSSED OUT!"*

Contempt read the note out loud. Peddy was baffled. He looked at the bullet holes in the frozen head of JuJu. They were hard to see since the entire head was frozen. Contempt looked at his father with the unmistaken look of puzzlement.

Peddy lamented, "Muthafucking little bitch done went way too far this time."

The bar is quiet as Peddy goes berserk. He is really angry since, it seems, his whole plan has failed. Leaving the room for a moment, Contempt goes to the men's restroom in Smokes'. Contempt's ring tone was the song from Twista's, Death before Dishonor, and it was going off. It was Mayhem texting her favorite brother.

The text read, "I DID THE CLOWN, HOE, DOUBLE CROSS-ING FUCKA!! I GOT DIS NIGGAH DEAD!"

16

SOULFUL OASIS

Old Man River sits alone at the counter in Floyd Lee's, drinking coffee. It is almost eleven thirty-seven on Monday morning. Monday's menu features the chicken rice gumbo supreme. The aroma is striking and it's also the reason Old Man River stayed after breakfast beyond his usual nine o'clock departing time. Breakfast at Floyd Lee's is legendary. Chicken, waffles, Louisiana hot home fries with an almost perfect mix of clientele. There are police, teachers, lawyers, factory workers and retirees who ate at Floyd Lee's every morning. The air is frigid and Floyd Lee has a table full of old heads discussing the violence in the city. River just listens as he reads the newspaper. There is a new, shiny, silver Audi A8 parked in front of the restaurant. An older man gets out wearing a dark blue car coat and a multi-colored knit skullcap. As the man sets his alarm, the sound makes Old Man River smile.

The older man has a dark automatic pistol in his gloved hand. Black Hat Daddy walks slowly, like he doesn't have a care in the world.

As he entered, he looked at his old friend and smiled and said, "Good day Mister River. It's Gumbo Supreme since it's Monday, right? He goes on, "Floyd, is it too late for French toast, turkey bacon, and two eggs poached?"
Floyd just nods as he has already started to assemble Black Hat's breakfast. River is irritated with the constantly negative characterizations of Detroit and her citizens.

He is also tiring of the absence of old school journalists to get at the proverbial, "how did we get here?"

"You know Black, it really is a damn shame. The combined quality of these two lousy newspapers together, don't even add up to one decent paper. Now they charging one dollar for a thin newspaper with hardly no news."

Black Hat agrees and adds, "Indeed, then they let those opinionated fools, like that narrow-minded Finley, who attacks all the black politicians dating way back to Mayor Young."

It doesn't take long before Black Hat is hearing the old heads begin to debate about public safety. He is already tired of the rhetoric even though he just arrived.

Waving his hands at the gathering of old heads he offered, "Non-sense, all we need to do is let Death Squads loose! It's out of our hands at this point. There are way too many niggas out here. In South America, they just kill all those criminals. In China, they kill all the dope addicts. They kill all the suppliers and the dope pushers too."

Floyd Lee interrupts to ask the two if they had heard about the barbershop incident last week. Black Hat Daddy looked at Old Man River with a puzzled look.

River responded, "I went the other day and had a shave. I sensed something was wrong, Pops didn't say a word. That is not like him. What's going on?"

As Black Hat Daddy gets silent in prayer for his hot breakfast, River tried to get a piece of the turkey bacon before Black can open his eyes up again. Joseph River, like Black Hat Daddy, is always well dressed and well groomed. Black slapped River's hands off his turkey bacon while he calls out to Floyd Lee.

"Floyd, fix up Old Man a little taste since he didn't get enough this morning." Everybody laughs as Floyd is already walking over with a small plate filled with potatoes, turkey bacon and scrabbled eggs.

Old Man River complained, "I just wanted a piece of that turkey. I like pork bacon. Turkey bacon don't even sound right."

Floyd continued the barbershop story, "Well, ever since Pops put them hoodlums out of the shop, he and his grandson have been arguing. Things got bad last Wednesday when some of them hoodlum types were cursing in the shop. His grandson started talking back to Pops. Next thing we knew, we all hear shots going off."

Floyd Lee is both sad and happy with the big changing of the guard.

"Now, Pops and Cephus, the other old barber, were clearing out them hoodlums. Pops shot the Negro car up with his automatic shotgun. Cephus had his service revolver from when he was in the army. Those old guys meant business. Pops even put his own grandson out."

At noon, Judge Long and Xavier entered the restaurant. Retired Detroit Police Deputy Chief Ralph Freeman eventually joined them. Ralph Freeman was a serious law enforcer who was the first black Deputy Chief. Now, slowed down with partial blindness, he is a loyal friend of Judge Solomon Long. Sitting off the main room, their lunch is served in the small private room. Xavier is glued to his iPhone. There are flurries of texts coming in from Tyquan expressing concern about the murder of the four at the casino. Judge Long hates the distracting nature of text messaging and lets his son know that he believes it's just rude to text in his company.

"Xavier, can you put that damn toy down for a minute? We're here to eat. You remind me of that damn foolish, young ex-Mayor." Not one more word is exchanged. The King has spoken.

Rising with complete humility from his seat, he explained to his father, "Dad, please excuse me. Ralph, I mean no disrespect. We are involved with the shooting last night at the casino. I am going to be just a few minutes. You two, go ahead and start without me."

Ralph Freeman is visibly curious and asked Xavier, "Texting, do the police use texting? I know, on that show, The Wire, the cops were using all kinds of technology. I thought that was just something for television or make believe."

Excusing himself, Xavier tells Freeman that law enforcement frequently utilizes the latest technology if they can get it. Ralph Freeman is concerned and confused as he and the judge begin their lunch without Xavier.

Book is visibly and spiritually sad over the death of DeShaba Moore. He had tutored her over the past year. Going to college was a giant step for DeShaba. Her family was a mix of gangsters and members of the working class. It was DeShaba and Mayhem who had gotten the notoriously nerdy Book to help them with school. Tyquan had a great deal to do with a lot of youngsters from the neighborhood going back to school. Paul Jacobs was a high school senior taking courses at Detroit Community College for nearly two years. Marian Tubman had championed Paul Jacobs to be all that. Paul Jacobs actually liked the nickname 'Book.' Book came from a family that was the image of an oasis in the middle of a dry desert when it came to education. Book just took to helping Mayhem one summer at the church camp program. Ms. Martha's grandson was a nerd. He and Book were best friends. The two had reputations for leading special programs for kids who liked school. Mayhem admired the courage of Book and his family. Book's sisters were friends with Khan. In fact, Mayhem always thought Khandice was the coolest older sister. Book and Zina were tight at school despite the fact that Book hated sports. He had an added disdain for basketball, football and other familiar forms of combat that dominated their blocks. Book loved golf and tennis and had special admiration for Arthur Ashe, elevating him and his memory to the status of sainthood.

Book received a text from Tyquan about the death of their dear friend. It was the hard work of Tyquan that had almost successfully taken Mayhem to another world. Mayhem, like so many young girls in the hood, found Tyquan just plain old-fashioned fine and fiercely good looking. Tyquan had exposed Mayhem to college with a number of quick visits to Professor Xavier Long's lectures and a host of intellectuals from the colored side of the academy. It was also where Mayhem found whites and other cultures not judging her. Book was an envoy to the public schools. He rallied against the same old lame methods of teaching that he believed created the elitist charter schools. Book was fought over like a first-round draft pick when Detroit brought in an Emergency Financial Manager to take the brightest and best to these selected schools. Ms. Martha fought along side many in the community not to allow the dilution of public schools to some fast- moving quisling.

Mayhem never believed nor trusted the likes of John Lock or any of the other Detroit Community College people. Mayhem was furious with DeShaba the day she arrived early at the office of John Lock only to hear and see Lock's naked behind pumping up and down on top of DeShaba. The suicide of DMoore, as the streets called her, was like the death of Joan of Arc. It wasn't just the effort to go to college. DeSheba had entertained joining the church. She even contemplated getting baptized. Mayhem was on the edge of following her girl. Book had encouraged her and Tyquan. The church was part of the lure of shady John Lock who was a deacon at Good Shepard Church. Mayhem knew he wasn't true to any God except his Gods - pussy and money. Contempt had been going to Good Shepard since he loved the youth pastor, Rev. Stillwater. Both Mayhem and Contempt met the young pastor at summer camp when Ms. Martha secretly sponsored them without Pedwell finding out. The young pastor had something special, as he was always able to comfort Mayhem and Contempt, despite the fact that their daddy was the devil. The old pastor, Rev. Goodman, had a son, who loved to run with the likes of Keithland and others in the underworld.

While DeShaba Moore trusted John Lock, it was Tyquan who had warned Xavier that street knowledge had been reporting a shady, much darker, image of the good deacon. It was the likes of Julius Goodman that started the relationship with the street slick undertaker, Roy "Ro" Simpson.

Contempt told Mayhem of the partying, "Dem niggahs is shake. Goodman, Locks, and Ro Simpson be at all the freak parties drinking whiskey, smoking dope and fucking young girls."
DeShaba wanted to change. She wanted something different from the streets.

Mayhem remembered that it was a counselor at DCC who, years earlier in Roosevelt Elementary, told her that she smelled like piss. The exact words never left her "depository for negative words and phrases from the elite." That counselor was Ms. Jeanette Flakes, who had retired from the Detroit Public Schools, and then went to work at DCC. Mayhem thought she was just another black woman who hated the poor black children. Her words would sting poor DeShaba again, after more than a decade.

She heard Flakes yelling, "You and your girlfriend are some ghetto houchee mamas. DCC don't want your kind. College is NOT for ignorant people."

Flakes and John Lock destroyed any faith that life could be different for Mayhem. She started reflecting on who really killed DMoore.

Tyquan called Xavier because he knew texting was very frustrating for him.

"Man, she is mad. Crazy mad Doc! Something already jumped. I heard that a frozen dead body showed up over at Smokes'. It was JuJu!! He doubled crossed Mayhem." Mayhem. Xavier thought about how his relationship was always full of balancing the scales of her sharp mind and devious behavior that was a result, at least in part, by her rearing that was led by Peddy. He knew that she flirted with being a regular kid at different moments in her life. Sometimes she would take into consideration what he would tell her. For Mayhem, Tyquan's word was gold.

Xav understood that any unfortunate street clash could set off the rage of a young woman close to making positive change. Damn! If only he could stop what his head said was like, "the warning from Baldwin's The Fire Next Time." The night before his conversation with Black Hat Daddy, Adolph horrified him. Black Hat Daddy declared the dark truth about Pedwell Jefferson.

"Should just put him down with his whole damn brood. He's an evil niggah. Peddy is a dark demon, thrust upon the world. Imposed on black folks and their communities."
The conversation with Tyquan continued as they both tried in vain to head off Mayhem.

"Tyquan, is anyone dealing with John Lock? I'm worried she will hunt him down no matter what. She is not going to wait for my version of justice."

The U.S. Attorney's office is trying to bring in Walena Gomez and Ricky Ricardo. Detroit Police are working close with federal authorities to guard the whereabouts of Rickey and Walena. The mayor is worried about the potential ramifications of the image left by all the headlines about the casino shooting and how the feds are attempting to have a major witness protected. There is also a rumor about a Grand Jury convening about systemic corruption in the city of Detroit. While the mayor is clean, there is a member of the City

Council who is dirty. Its unknown how many more city officials will be charged with corruption.

Word in the street is that the Bruno Family is looking for some undercover informants. This point is disturbing for Anita Jones since she now realizes that there is a leak in her office. Mayhem gets a call from Ranita Wright, who is the sister of Rickey Ricardo. Ranita owns a beauty salon and has known Mayhem for years. She is all business and tells Mayhem, in no uncertain terms, she knows that Black Mike is aware of the location of her sister.

"Mayhem, I can pay you if you stop Black Mike. I know it's a million, but Keithland ain't gonna pay nobody. Dat niggah is foul. I got some money. Rickey got some bank hid away. You know me, him, and Walena are all trying to live correct now."

As she listened to the plea, Mayhem gets another call. It's from the Puerto Rican girl, Jamilia. She tells Ranita to hold for a second as she clicks back over to Jamilia.

"Hey Jamilia. Let me holla back in a second."
Jamilia tells her its critical to get right back with her. Mayhem goes back to Ranita, who informed her that Rickey is hiding over at the Christian Fellowship Center where homeless families eat and get aide. Black Mike and Murder Man are sitting on the front door of the center. They can't enter since the center has a tight security system with an armed guard in a security booth beside the electronic security gate.

Mayhem tells Ranita that she agrees to the deal as long as she gets paid. Ranita has one hundred thousand dollars cash for deposit. Mayhem makes arrangements to leave the money in the black Viper parked in front of her mothers' house on Hazelwood. Deep down inside, she knows that Keithland, and his fancy lawyers hate females who are in business. She instructs Ranita to talk to no one besides Walena. Hanging up from that call, Mayhem phones her mother to tell her to hide the money so that she can put it in her car in one half hour.

"Moms, use dat little code box when Ranita brings a duffel bag for me. Don't let nobody see you with that bag, especially Peddy."

Hanging up, another call comes in and it's Big Girl.

"Mayhem, we see dem niggahs. Its John Lock, dat bitch Jeanette and dat muthafucka Clarence Thoms from Channel 3."

Mayhem is livid.

She asked, "where dey at?"

Big Girl explained, "Dey at the church, Ms. Martha's church. Clarence Thoms is talking shit, saying how Locks tried to save the poor ghetto hoe. Locks and dat Jeanette bitch faking crying about how DaSheba Moore was just another ghetto hoe."

The press conference is with the DCC Trustees and in front of the Good Shepard Church. The Emergency School Manager is discussing the incident involving DeShaba's suicide and how difficult it is to reach the soulless families in the inner city of Detroit. John Locks is comforting Jeanette Flakes as she tells Clarence Thoms that DeShaba Moore came from a distressed family, a devastated neighborhood, and a poor school. To make matters worse, she never attended church. As the camera crew zeroes in on the do good-ers, there is a sudden flash of fury. A big black Hummer smashes into the TV 3 mobile van and drives it into the front walkway of the church.People were scrambling and screaming as Mayhem jumped out from the passenger side of the Hummer. A young girl driver continues to park the vehicle directly in front of the shaken cameraman.

Mayhem yells into the camera that is still filming, "Is this bitch still rolling? All y'all lying ass muthafuckas, stand the fuck up and look into the camera."

It's so cold that smoke comes out of Mayhem's mouth. It appears as if she could be a Komoda Dragon. She grabs Jeanette by the collar of her coat. With her wig in total disarray, Jeanette, like John Lock, recognizes her captor.

Mayhem is screaming at the top of her voice. She tells her crew to grab the judge and John Locks.

"Git dat bitch Judge. Hey, dat muchafucka is gitting away" pointing to the emergency manager who has managed to scale the fence in front of the Good Shepard church.

Looking at the camera, she warned the television crew, "dis here better be rolling live. Is it?"

The crew, shaking in their boots, tells Mayhem, "It's live and in living color." Looking red with rage, Mayhem is focused on Jeanette.

She tells the terrified counselor, "Remember me? Me and all my girls were students at Roosevelt Elementary when you embarrassed the fuck out of us. You said I smelled like piss. Called us the little nasty dirty girls. After dat, we wuz known as the PP Girls jest cuz you made us a joke. You said my hair was rough like squirrel titty hair. You called us out! You said DeShabas' name was ghetto and told the whole class dat our families were on welfare and used food stamps. You and dis here bitch ass niggah Locks, said my family was from hell. Yaw niggahs ain't so bad now huh?"

As Jeanette is trying to stand up straight, Mayhem rears back with her Glock and smashes Jeanette in the face. The judge gasps as the blood poured from Jeanette's face. Falling to the concrete, Jeanette is crying. Mayhem laughs as she pulled the trigger twice. There was a resounding, "BAM BAM." Mocking the crying captives, the shots ripped into Jeanette's right knee. The two shots literally picked her up and threw her back to the ground violently.

"Well, dis here is my homework. It's done. Now, Ghetto me got something better than my pencil. Member you said I couldn't rite cursive bit-ch? Ima riting dis Glock 45 and 9 straight into yo ass. Say MAYHEM JEFFERSON out loud like you made me repeat my wacked name when I wuz jest a little girl. You wuz always clowning me."
A faint sound, like that of soft running water, comes from where Clarence Thoms is frozen with fear as he holds his microphone or, as he attempts to hold his microphone.

One of the young girls in the crew laughed out, "Ole boy is pissing on himself." Looking at Judge Ewing, Mayhem declared, "Remember me Judge Irene Ewing? Yo old stiff, stuck up, bougie ass told me and my moms dat we were not the good black people Dr. Martin Luther King died for."

Mayhem continues her rant in the tone of a preacher, "Like Dr. Long said, the right people have to die for this here world to feel anything. Not niggahs, you said it. NOT niggahs like me!"

As a wounded Jeanette moaned in pain, John Locks seemed to know that something would eventually come his way.

Jeanette moaned, "Ms. Mayhem, I am so sorry. I did wrong by Ms. Moore. Please, forgive me."

Speaking with authority, Mayhem tells the world that the people responsible for DeShaba's death are present and that, "I am performing street justice!"

Looking at Judge Ewing, she told her to say that John Locks was guilty as was Jeanette Flakes. The veteran jurist was petrified.

Her voice trembled with a feeble, frail kind of fear, "I can't do that. He was acquitted in a court of law, young lady."

Mayhem was standing in front of the judge, turning towards Jeanette, who was lying in pain. Without a word, she points and fires three rounds from her nine-millimeter Glock into a stunned Jeanette. As the bullets ripped into Jeanette's' body and head, the act itself seemed to have killed the judge. She slumped to the ground.

John Locks was terrified and began to cry out, "Oh my God. You killed her. Oh, Jesus."

Mayhem retorted, "People always finding God when dey scared. Ms. Martha said that there really are Angels. I prayed about dis. Maybe, just maybe, a black Angel might come down here and save you, Mr. Locks."

Crying profusely with snot dripping from his nose, he seemed to be in unison with Clarence Thoms of TV 3. The cameraman was spooked.

Mayhem tells Clarence, "Bitch Nigga. Stop all that crying. Tell the world y'all are sorry for saying all that damn fucked up shit about Detroit. All dat kissing rich peoples' ass and saying my people is some animals. Tell dem dat dese here bitch ass niggahs killed my girl. Tell 'em if you wanna live. You bitch ass niggah!"

Clarence rose to the task quickly. He began looking into the camera as if he imagined he was Lester Holt from NBC.

He declared with vigor, "I am Clarence Thoms reporting from the Good Shepard church. This is the scene of the tragic and untimely death of a young woman, Ms. DeShaba Moore, whose suicide was caused by the wicked deeds of her trusted teacher, John Locks. The late Jeanette Flakes, a counselor who failed Ms. Moore miserably, is also to blame. We, at the TV 3 family, mourn her untimely departure and dedicate this show to her memory."

Mayhem is smiling. That was good. For real. Old Clarence did her good. The police arrived with a SWAT team and Ms. Martha and the original pastor, Rev. Goodman and the Rev. Dr. Stillwater, all gathered on the block as close as they could get. Mayhem knew that Judge Ewing was her ticket out. Putting the limp body of the judge into the Hummer, she told the police and the other authorities to back off. John Locks was literally twisting in the wind with fear. With the dead body of Jeanette laying in front of the gateway into the church, Ms. Martha was in trance a of sorts. Mayhem saw her and it made her think of all the time the dear Christian woman had loved and helped her.

The mayor and police chief had arrived. The SWAT team and all supporting police personnel had been given strict orders to stand down. Unfortunately, John Locks tried to make an escape. In the midst of the confusion, Locks made a sprinters dash towards the church edifice. His stylish Armani suit was soiled just like Clarence's urine-soaked suit. In his mad dash towards the church, Mayhem took aim at his left lower leg. Bam! He fell and she moved in for the kill. She seemed to be laughing as she glided past his disheveled body. As she moved, she emptied her Glock 45.

"Please Ms. Mayhem. I will pay you, anything. I never thought my actions would kill her. I was wrong. I am begging you." Those were his last words. She walked away, satisfied with her avenging moment. The Hummer had two hostages as it pulled out from the church. Mayhem had her Glock at Judge Ewing head and the young girls had two guns pointed on reporter Clarence Thoms. The police had no choice. The mayor demanded that no more blood be spilled in front of the church.

The media in Detroit went national and everyone was trying to figure out what was going on. Both the Governor and other politicians in Lansing and throughout the state capitol saw the live broadcast. The State of Michigan Police director and the State Attorney General are asking the question, why is it that the hostage kidnappers are allowed to leave the scene? Mayhem made an impression that

Mayor Bracey was not pleased about. Many members of the law enforcement community were angry that the mayor seemed to be over-ruling standard hostage operations for political reasons. The old guard is critical of more than just the taking out of the daughter of Pedwell Jefferson. There is little doubt, that letting the hostage takers leave the scene would be a great mistake led by, "a damn colored mayor."

The Detroit Police Incident Command van had units ranging from the Detectives unit, to the major crime division whose members were huddling to strategize. Detroit Police veteran Sgt. Bannon, and several detectives were commiserating over the failure to capture what they considered the daughter of Public Enemy number one.

"Having checked her out, she is definitely the daughter of Peddy. How in the world is it that we were left out of the information loop? We used to be the law in this city," murmured Bannon.

The State Police and Detroit Police helicopters overhead are in communication with the patrol and the other authorities that are following the Hummer. Suddenly, the Hummer speeds up and turns into an abandoned industrial complex. A large garage door opens with no sign of anyone or anything making it open. The helicopter radio explains that the Hummer has entered an unmarked abandoned garage. The orders, coming directly from field operations, were to stand down. The police do not enter the complex. All of the agencies were waiting for the next order.

Mayhem is on the phone with Rita regarding a new contract. Rita is adamant and, as always, to the point. Mayhem tells her that now is not the best time.

"Girlfriend, wassup? Make dis quick. Rita, We are here. My phone is cool. Is yours?"

The sound of a speaker coming from the police utility vehicle and a hovering helicopter is loud and pulsating. There was a stern voice of someone demanding to speak with Mayhem.

"Come to the front door. The phone is for you."

Mayhem laughed, "Dese clown niggahs. Look Rita, dis phone is straight. Get to it."

133

Chapter 16: Soulful Oasis

Getting out of the Hummer, Mayhem grabbed Clarence from the backseat. The news reporter was sweating profusely and his pants are visibly soaked. His white shirt was soiled, while the arctic air in the garage is mixed with the odor of staleness. Mayhem is cool. She instructs her girls to take Clarence to the front of the building. Her girls are moving the judge to another vehicle that is hidden in the garage. It's a Dodge Ram charger pick-up with a cab that is driven by a young white male. The young man talks with someone else who suddenly is assisting Mayhem with putting the limp body of the judge into the cab.

"We need to get Peter Gomez dead now. We got you, ok?" Mayhem is confused by the request. She thinks that something is crazy since Peter Gomez is the porn guy. Wassup wit dis?

As the young girls move towards the door, Mayhem tells Clarence, "Yaw bitch ass is dead if you say something wrong. Got it?" Clarence is beyond scared. He nodded like an obedient servant to his master, who at the moment was Mayhem Jefferson.

One of the young girls has retrieved the police cell phone. She immediately brings the phone to Mayhem, who is back in the garage directing her girls to take the Hummer to the front with Clarence.

"Let'em know that Judge Ewing is fine. Tell them we are ready to give up once I am done in that little tunnel over there." Mayhem is familiar with the complex. Unlike other folk, she knew that, many times over the last decade, her father would take his kidnapped victims to this same location. Unknown to authorities, the abandoned site is selected on purpose. Little does anyone know that police do not have the complex surrounded. There is a tunnel that runs from the garage to another exit, which is actually hidden by the building over a half acre. As the police waited for Mayhem to use the phone, she walked over to Clarence Thoms.

"I am letting y'all scared asses loose. Remember, if y'all tell dem anything about what is going on, you be dead real soon. Not a mutha-fucking clue of what happened here niggah!" As she walked away from Clarence, a shot rang out. Clarence falls to the ground, holding his buttocks.

Mayhem laughed loudly, "Aw, don't be no little bitch.   It's jest a little baby 22 in ya big fat ass. Dats fo talking shit bout us on television!!"

17

THE DAY THE EARTH STOOD STILL

The church is trying to regroup after the violent carnage is left on their grounds. Ms. Martha is devastated, as is Rev. Goodman, who is in deep debate with his son.

"This is our church. You cannot just get involved with hoodlums. We are not going to have a drive-in funeral parlor attached to our church."

Ms. Martha is feeling like she personally has failed to save Mayhem. Stillwater is calm. While not pleased with the events of the day, he remained detached from the whole ordeal in a manner hard to describe. Two lifeless bodies lay on the church ground. The mayor is overwhelmed with a feeling of disbelief. Chief LeRocque is embarrassed. Her sense of authority has been rattled.

One of the old detectives tells the old white resistant clique, "That girl is worse than anything I have ever seen in over twenty-three years of police work."

The old timers cannot help but to think of the years of Pedwell Jefferson and how their own sexism had left everybody in the city wondering, "where did this come from?"

As Bannon laughed with disgust, he blurted out, "Last month, I didn't even know that Peddy had a daughter. Hell. We been trying to close down his crazy gang that included his lunatic sons. Damn near every homicide in the city is linked to them in some kinda way. Hate. Homicide. Who even knew some damn girl named Mayhem even existed?"

Another detective offered, "Let's be honest. That son of a bitch is working for anyone with enough money. Truth be told, his sons are like some sort of Terminator. The damn dagos don't even really mean shit to them."

18

BLACK AND WHITE MEETING

The two attorneys meet in a small restaurant in Grosse Pointe near Lake St. Clair. Lanza is concerned about his client, Frank Bruno, being harmed by the loosely organized young gangsters in the Keithland James operation. Perry is an old conservative attorney who found working for the new hip-hop crowd complicated. Xavier thought about how they seemed to spend very little time attempting to evaluate or understand the severity of the threat. The restaurant is a quaint setting in a part of Grosse Pointe that does not see many blacks for lunch or any other meal. Both men are eating the Pate' de fish head that Pointe Blank is known for in the elite suburbs that don't seem to go out of its way to welcome Jewish brethren either.

Xavier had been told by reliable sources that, "The feds had three witnesses. Mr. James' connection to contracts with our people cannot come out."

James Perry is nattily dressed in his black cashmere sports coat with a purple and orange ascot. He looks insulted.

"Alright, I can handle the three Council people. The political people are not my concern. We know what is going on. Three is a new number though. I know about Walena. Who is the third?"

Laughing and adding salt to the wound, Lanza explained, "The Latin's have an operative that is really none of your business in one sense. The problem is if the Justice Department gets any of what these informants say, we could see a Grand Jury. That may be to the displeasure of everyone."

Perry finds Lanza simply an old conservative race hater. Thinking of how the young Latino's and blacks had reshaped the face of crime, it made the elitist posturing more difficult to swallow.

The facts were clear. Keithland James had spent over a decade assembling a machine that forced the old mob to make deals they simply hated. The young ones, those ignorant, money-spending crazies led by Pedwell Jefferson, made one thing crystal clear. This business was not the same business it had been. After lunch, the two men departed back to their organizations. James Perry got into his driver driven white Range Rover. The young driver is both his assistant and a law school student named Reginald Bolton. Bolton is a native of Detroit. He is attentively listening to the detailed radio accounts of the frenzied shooting at Good Shepard Church. As he puts on his seat belt, he can't quite make out what he thinks he is hearing.

The phone rings in the Rover and Perry answers, "I just got in the car. She did what? She has Judge Ewing? She killed John Lock and a counselor?"
The conversation continued as Reggie Bolton tried to listen to the breaking news.

The radio news report screamed, "AT THIS TIME, THE KIDNAPPED JUDGE AND OUR NEWS REPORTER ARE STILL BEING HELD HOSTAGE AT THE OLD AUTO INDUSTRIAL COMPLEX ON WOODWARD AND NAPLES. POLICE ARE AT THE GATE OF THE COMPLEX AND OUR SKY TEAM REPORTS THAT THE BLACK HUMMER DROVE INTO THE COMPLEX. WE ARE WAITING FOR FUTHER REPORTS. THIS IS BEING BROADCAST LIVE FROM CHANNEL 3 WFCK."

James Perry immediately called Keithland.

"Peddy's girl done gone berserk. She is gunning down people like they are flies. I don't like any of this. I told Peddy to pull this girl in. She has gone mad."

Keithland is furious and yelling at the top of his lungs, "So, what is we going to do?" Perry continued with more bad news.

"There are three informants. The two we know of are Walena and Rick. The other witness is not one of our people. It's the South Americans' people."

James Perry tells Keithland that something or someone has got to get rid of Walena and Rickey. Normally he would never tell any client something so bold. This is different and Keithland pays him quite well. Just thinking about losing his retainer if the James Kingdom is frozen by the Feds is sickening. Keithland has upped the bounty on both Rickey and Walena. The discussion about Mayhem is increasingly intense and heated.

"Look, dat bitch is fucking up things. Now dem muthfucking Dagos is mad. Peddy better make it right. Dis is his peeps."
Keithland is baffled. He tries, in vain, to get past the sexism of the hood. Keithland does not believe women should be doing anything that a man does not allow her to do. His younger sister is cool and she obeys his orders. His sons understand, as does everyone else in their thing, that women are hoes, bitches or babies mamma's. It's all about MOB, which is the underwritten theme, according to Keithland. MOB means 'Money Over Bitches'.
Pedwell is brooding over the misstep with JuJu.

"Dis here girl dun went crazy. She killing people dat ain't did shit to her. Why is she doing dis? Julius wuz a major player. Now what? We got trouble cuz she wants to swing her dick."
Contempt is texting Mayhem. Homicide walks away from the bar. His eyes are blazing with anger. He, like his father, is sickened by the deeds of his younger sister. Ron Dog is looking at the television and suddenly turns up the volume. The scheduled programming is interrupted and cameras are showing, instead, police at the industrial site.

"Daddy, look, dey at our joint. Daddy, Daddy, Daddy! Come here quick" cried Assault. He can see the police at the front entry of the industrial complex. As Peddy rushed to the bar, he could see the commotion at the front entry on the big screen.

There was much verbal chatter from the News 3 Live. There was also a scrolling flow of words moving across the bottom of the screen.

They read, "BREAKING NEWS ON NEWS 3. JUDGE IRENE EWING ALONG WITH NEWS 3 REPORTER CLARENCE THOMS CURRENTLY BEING HELD AS HOSTAGES."

Suddenly, Peddy's cell phone rings. He answers the phone with a detached sounding voice. He can see his many secrets at the hideaway unfolding on live television. Looking pale, both him and his sons sense the betrayal by their sister. In his full-length white mink coat with a big apple style white mink cap, Peddys' sense of invincibility has been pierced. The voice on the phone is Keithland James.

"Niggah, I need y'all to take care of dat business. Why am I hearing all dis shit bout yo young ass female daughter out here smoking niggahs Pedwell?"

Pedwell was silent and that was a rarity indeed.

When he finally began to speak, he spoke so low, Keithland screamed, "Niggah wassup? Are you dere cause I can't hear yo ass!!" Contempt was amused by his sister's plan to get rich.

Her text is funny and reads, "I am a mad bitch. Bitches killed my girl. So dem fake niggahs had to pay! Now I gotta collect on dese snitching ass bitches. See y'all later. Love, Mjeff dat girl."

The Detroit Police Chief LeRocque was coordinating with the feds on how to safely bring in the likes of Pedro Gomez, Walena and Rickey. U.S. Attorney Jones is concerned about leaks. The recent shootings at the casino have made her worries more real. The detectives resent the progress of the feds. Bannon and MacFarley are even more critical and are questioning the capability of the fed task force in keeping up with Peddy. Mayhem is the major concern of the mayor.

Bannon demands to know more from the feds, "Look, Pedwell Jefferson is a force like nothing you feds have seen. It's not just him. It's his sons and this Keithland has solid legal advice."

Looking bewildered is the lead Detroit police official Kelley Richards. She gets a glance from the Chief that she understands and sanctions her leadership.

Sitting in the squad room at DPD Headquarters, she scolds the detectives, "I told you guys. This is a federal operation. We are supporting their efforts. We are not at liberty to share, or even reveal, what we do know without their approval. I already told you. We now have international agencies participating. Everybody here is not just law enforcement. This is seriously beyond our jurisdiction."

Mayhem was finished giving directions for the scheduled exchange with authorities at the complex. Getting into a white Ford van, she makes certain that the judge is secured. One girl is sitting in the backseat making certain their valuable cargo is in custody. The tunnel is dark, dank, and long. Few knew of its existence. Mayhem is bothered because the cell phone cannot get a signal. She wondered if the police might be waiting at the end of the tunnel. There were several paths in a network of underground tunnels. The building, once a promising headquarters for a giant automobile dealership, has been the secretive meeting place for the third city potentates like Pedwell. The maze that Mayhem drove into demanded that one know exactly where they were going or they might just get lost forever. There are many signs of life beneath the industrial complex. Living underground was the ecological reality of a dirty, grimy, and dangerous landscape of an abandoned civilization beneath the streets of Detroit.

Judge Ewing is in a dazed trance and she seemed to have checked out of reality many hours earlier. Her hair looked like a birds' nest of twigs, leaves and something that could actually be alive. Her eyes were sunken in her face. Her skin was wrinkled and aged. The young girl sitting with her was a true assassin for Mayhem. She resented Judge Ewing because she was an enemy of the thug state. The runaway van was actually well commandeered by Mayhem.

Mayhem wanted to make the Judge suffer, yet she could feel Ms. Martha telling her that, "it was just wrong to kidnap a judge." There seemed to be lots of some kind of life below in the buildings. There were spooky looking homeless people walking around with little respect for anything or anyone. It was like a pseudo existence that dictated a lifestyle of anarchy and Darwinism. Mayhem entered a long, dark, dank tunnel. Finally reaching the end of the tunnel, she felt a sense of relief. The white van eased its way out into the street traffic. There was not much movement on the streets. Nearing the end of the ride, there was at least a quarter mile to the industrial complex. Mayhem entered the street slowly. On this Saturday, daylight was unusually bright.

Her cell phone rang twice. It was Big Girl sounding really bad. In fact, she could hardly speak.

"Mayhem, I went to git yo mother. I'm here now."

Her voice was quivering and she continued, "I just got here and Peddy was driving off. Jarenda was laying half naked out of yo car. They took the money and she is beaten really badly. I called for

141

help. Um, Contempt is shot too. He ain't moving. He is on the sidewalk next to yo moms. It looks bad Mayhem, real bad."

The whole world stopped at that moment for Mayhem. Silence. Everything went on pause. Nothing seemed real. All she could think of was her mother and her brother. The phone went silent. Big Girl is shaken by the violence but more revealing is the fact that, this is the work of Peddy Jefferson. Sitting in the van, Mayhem is feeling something she has rarely felt. She has an overwhelming fear that her mother might really be dead. Even worse, Contempt is wounded and she needs to go to both of them. Her phone rings again. This time, it is Tyquan. She ignores his call. Judge Ewing is crying and is scared out of her mind. Despite this, she asked the young girl to release her.

"Young lady, I am a judge, a grandmother, and a mother, and I don't want to die today."

The young girl is stoic. Ironically, she is the sum-total of the third city. Her family is made up of Mayhem and the crew, with Mayhem assuming the role of both the big sister and the momma. The young woman looks into the frightened eyes of Judge Ewing. Actually, she looks as if she is looking through the very soul of the judge. There is no empathy for the jurist or any kind of connection with another human being in this situation. This is the textbook case of what Professor Xavier Long termed, in his research, "Children of the Damned." Mayhem Jefferson is the surrogate mother of the streetwise young girl whose mother is probably one of the many former teenage mothers that were the subjects of Xavier Long's research. This is where Mayhem Jefferson's life collided within the third city socialization.

The Christian Center is secretively connected with the city designated River Sanctioned Safe House. Walena is a devout Christian follower, for real. Her connection is Ms. Martha, who has reached out and taken in many who have lost their way. The young, Reverend Dr. Nehemiah Jeremiah Stillwater is their shepherd. The safe house is unknown to few. It houses women and their children, all of whom are hiding from various threats. It was the ideal of Reverend Dr. Stillwater who was ministering to Ricky "Ricardo" Bratton and Walena Wright. The two had checkered backgrounds in the underworld segment of the third city. Over the years, Walena had been a prostitute, an adult dancer, and a dope addict. While she had a strong academic background in her high school studies at Detroit Cass Technical High School, her family was conservative and had raised her in the great black southern Christian tradition. She believed she had been tricked and bamboozled by the devil in the fast lane. She ended up running with Gwenny James, the younger sister of the kingpin of the urban jungle in Southeast Michigan. At first, it was all good. An ex-dope addict and tittie dancer who had simply fallen into the middle of making baller money along with the rest of the royal family of thugs, Walena knew her roots were all about that money or the proverbial golden calf.

Rickey Braddock was a hustler, since the early days of living in the Brewster Projects on the Eastside of Detroit. Gang membership was a normal and expected "rite of passage" in the lives of those being raised in the Brewsters. His young mother was simply overrun by the Social Services department. Hungry, cold, and lost in life, he and his brothers went to work early, when Keithland was just the dope man. Over a decade of on the job training culminated with his tuition paid state investment in Jackson Prison. Graduation included graduate work that led to the better paying jobs in the third city economies. School meant Rickey could observe a master teacher like Marian Tubman. The alternative experience meant he would meet a host of negative people and influences. Unfortunately for Rick, nothing ever materialized enough to provide the connection he really needed to break the cycle of poverty. Rick met Walena while they both were working in the James criminal organization. The streets employed young boys and crime was how they earned "their living." Organized crime has always been serious in Detroit. Rick Braddock was a pretty boy, who became one of the best collectors and distributors of illicit narcotics for Keithland. He could count money in his head. His memory was amazing. Valued most for his math skills, he had a business attitude that included the shunning of all narcotics. That stance made him move up quickly within the organization. He started working in the warehouses where they kept track of monies from all of Keithland's business endeavors. As a trusted aide, he worked closely with Gwen James, who was Keithland's sister. Family, friends and foes believed Rickey Ricardo Braddock was a baller. He was a baller who not only had learned math in the Detroit Public School District, but he also learned to speak Spanish fluently.The Spanish came in handy in his new job working with the outside criminal organizations. The Spanish speaking operations bothered Keithland a great deal.

Not having any such skill as speaking another language, or as James Perry would say when Keithland wasn't around, "These niggahs can't speak the King's English and now he wants to do business with the Columbians, Dominicans, Cubans, and the Mexican drug cartels. We need some real education up in here. These black niggahs can't read or write. Now Keithland wants to take over the damn Chinese, or those damn strange ass Hmong boys. How does he think he can communicate with them?"

Rickey met Walena and sparks were flying. They became tight since Gwen "Gwenny" James had selected Walena to run the adult entertainment inventory, responsible for keeping track of the Dancers fees and all. In the first year, Walena made things better. She made business good for the James. Secretly, Walena was wrestling with drug addiction and depression that intensified with the birth of her little girl. She almost died more than once. Seeking refuge and assistance, she went to Good Shepard Church trying to communicate with God. She began to pray. Her prayers were answered when she met Ms. Martha. Ms. Martha volunteered at the Interfaith Christian Center. Revered Dr. Stillwater worked with the religious coalition in the fight against child abuse. Ms. Martha asked the young pastor to assist her in finding refuge for the young children whose parents were incarcerated.

Marian Tubman ran a special afterschool program that initially had been funded by philanthropic organizations. Due to rampant budget cuts, Tubman's program was combined with other reduced city and school district projects. Over time, Walena had forged a new lifestyle that included getting all the way off all dope and alcohol. At first Rick found it a waste of time. He did not really believe in God and he didn't really practice any religion.

Walena found strength in prayer and she experienced a renewed faith in God that enabled her to better connect God to her young daughters healing. Few realized, or ever acknowledged, Walena's transformation even after her baby girl was healed. She totally rejected the wild street life and she was ashamed of her past life. Bible study with Ms. Martha was always deep. It included long hours of discussing how she could correct her wayward ways. Ms. Martha walked and prayed along the journey. During that time, she still worked with Gwenny and met Peter Gomez. Gomez was wrestling with his addiction to both cocaine and pornography. Rickey was the point man for all the porn businesses in and around Detroit. The public had no idea how Greater Detroit was one of the biggest consumers of pornography in the world. It was the suburbs, the exurban fiefdoms of expensive homes, and the elite citizens that spent unheard dollars on serious porn.

Xavier Long conducted research on the underground economy and always maintained that it was the most difficult work he had ever done. It was the discovery of how dark and devastating pornography was. And that didn't even include those Snuff movies, which the big gangs were now peddling. Gomez and Rickey became close, in part, because they were both employed by both the James organization and the Latino organizations. In Long's experience, Snuff movies were more deadly than pornography because of the numbers of young runaways, who believe they will become video and movie stars. During one year, a trio of young runaways were murdered. They were innocent, fame-seeking actors in a Snuff movie. Tyquan was in Miami with Xavier when the murdered teens were found. The impact on both Tyquan and Xavier became so strong that Xavier called home to talk with Saul about the atrocities. It was never palatable to Xavier when the victims were so young. Saul played an important part in making sense of the insanity. He had a great deal of experience with that in his life in the military. Xavier found relief from Ms. Martha when he thought about the bizarre death of the unknown teens. That same trip exposed Xavier to more information about the dark side of pornography, including the connection to international sex slaves and dog fighting.

Chapter 18: Black and White Meeting

Xavier was a guest at a Miami Heat basketball game when he and Tyquan observed Gomez, Walena and Rickey sitting courtside during the game. Rickey Ricardo and Peter Gomez were participating as guests of Keithland James and their treat was paid for with funds from James' growing empire. Tyquan wondered why a local gangster like Rickey was in Miami, and he wondered how he was able to sit in the most prestigious and expensive seats in the arena. Walena was wrestling, at that time, about the quality of her life in the underworld. Worse, Rickey Ricardo was in love with the perks that came with moving up in the James organization. Xavier was caught by the presence of the seriously higher ups in the illicit narcotics commerce.

The pictures she was exposed to by federal agents sparked Walena's transformation to a federal undercover agent. The FBI, ATF, DEA had the influence of one person connected to Walena and that person was Ms. Martha. Ms. Martha had a devout commitment to Detroit, her neighborhood, her family and the church but all of those came second to her personal determination to repay the underworld Lord of Destruction, Keithland James. Martha convinced the young woman to take her life back by participating in the destruction of the likes of that evil Keithland James, who had showered Detroit with untold violence over the past decade. The death of her beloved grandson, Michael Joseph Peters, was the real driving force behind the current motivation to fight against the devil. Martha had lost her only daughter Mary Martha Peters in an accident in Dayton, Ohio. On a rainy day, her daughter, who was a high school teacher, was killed along with her husband Michael Peters. The only child left was an orphan before his grandmother Martha Myers adopted him. The bond between Book and her grandson was an additional motivating factor on top of the fact that Rev. Stillwater was the youth minister at her church. Stillwater was a Godsend to her.

19

A DARK MOMENT FOR THE DARKIES

Mayhem is parked on a side street near the Christian Center. Her cell phone has a message, so it keeps vibrating and beeping. The van is dead quiet because there is no radio or cd playing. Judge Ewing is dizzy, hungry and confused. Mayhem is just sitting under the steering wheel feeling lower than low. She continues to think about the bad news and she either can't believe it or it is really difficult for her to accept the truth. Contempt is dead. Her mother is dead. Sadly, her father killed them both, and she couldn't accept it. The judge is nervous because the car is parked in an area unknown to anyone. Young girl doesn't say anything. She tightened the handcuffs on Judge Ewing.

"Young woman, why are you so angry? These handcuffs are cutting into my skin. Ms. Mayhem, what are you going to do with me?"
Mayhem opened her cell phone to read the message from Contempt.

"Moms is trying to run with the money. Peddy is nutso. He mad you smoked JuJu. I will take care of Mom. Git the job dun. Pops is freaking out! Shit ain't hanging right."
A ring tone goes off. She opened the cell phone. It's Tyquan again and the texting alert comes up.

The screen lights up with a new text, "I am at the hospital. MOMS and CONTEMPT are not Dead!"
Mayhem just laughed out loud as she stares at the screen. Suddenly, she just shuts the phone and dials a number. Mayhem needs to catch up with Murder Man and Black Mike.

She knows they are probably busy in their charge to kill Rickey. The phone rings twice and a deep baritone voice answers. On the other end is Black Mike, who is outside the Christian Center, attempting to enter. Black Mike is angry that he is having a challenge gaining entry. The security guard told Black Mike that no one was permitted to enter the private ground without a pass. Mayhem assures Black Mike that she can get 'em in on the grounds without a pass.

"Mike, I can get dem out. Walena got me down as a family member."

Black Mike is elated. He tells his partner, Murder Man, the good news. Black Mike gets loud as he tells Mayhem their plan.

"Bitch, we ain't waiting to git dem out. We coming wit you. We gotta smoke dem in dat place!"

Mayhem is pissed. She knows she has got to trick the two assassins. She is already driving to the Christian Center.

"Look Mike. Y'all need me. We gonna split the money."

Murder Man is yelling at the top of his lungs. He is high since he just consumed a six-pack of Black Dogg Malt. As if that weren't enough, he had also been smoking the street potent Red Weed the entire time he was drinking. Red Weed is notorious on the streets as the most lethal marijuana. With a view of the compound, it is hard to believe that four hours have passed.

"Yu's a bit-ch, a muthafucking ho. Fuck y'all daddy, and dem brothers. Fuck all of y'all niggahs." Murder Man has always been adamant about the role of women in life. Along with his partner in crime, Black Mike demands full obedience from Mayhem.

"Bitch, you might git a taste. Partners? A'aight, partner dese nuts. We going up in dat church and smoking everybody. We talkin like a million dollars? Bitch, you the ho. We is pimps. You work fo us. We doing the smoking! Got it bitch?"

Mayhem is pulling into a parking lot just across the street from the Church Center. She instructs her girl to gag Judge Ewing with a rag, and to make sure she is secured. While she is talking to Black Mike, she is walking to their car. The aroma of Red Weed and Black Dogg is strong. Mayhem thinks to herself that the two-some is simply dumb. Anybody could have smelled the weed and Black Dogg. Still walking, she wraps up her talk with Black Mike.

"Mike, I am here. I will get dem out onto the front entry and yaw can smoke'em."

Black Mike, again, tells Mayhem, "Fuck that. We is going in blazing. Smokin' everybody! Kids, preachers, anybody, long as we git dem rat ass snitches. Got it Bitch?" Mayhem entered the rear door of the 1991 Oldsmobile Cutlass Supreme. The rusty red hooptie is filthy. There were lots of plastic cups, beer bottles and decayed food with White Castle boxes and McDonald bags on the floor. Mayhem is disgusted with the nasty vehicle.

As she sits in the rear, she tells Murder Man and Black Mike, "Look, I'm not going to be no moe Bitches today. We ain't shooting in no church! I don't shoot kids. I don't do shit in no church!"

Black Mike turns around with a look of insanity in his eyes and yells, "You gonna be all the bitches we want."

He opens his mouth again and lets out a giant laugh, "HA-HAHAHAH. Now git yo hoe ass up to dat door."
Joining the hoe chorus, Murder Man takes both a swig of Black Dogg and a puff of Red Weed.

He belches and says, "May-hem, I smell yo pussy Bitch! Yo pussy stanks. Yo pussy is really stanking!"

Mayhem takes out two silencers and rapidly screwed them onto her guns. Her laser stare is fixed on the two miscreants in the front seats. As the music of Nicki Minaj's *Womp Womp* blared in the hooptie, Mayhem leaned forward and put each of her Glocks into the dirty, soiled backs of the front seats. Pfft! Pfft! Pfft! Pff! Her guns ripped into the bodies of the two gangster-thugs. No one notices the violently jerking bodies as they catch the wrath of, "one too many bitches." Reaching over the bloody driver side seat, where the corpse once known as Black Mike was, she pulled the key from the ignition. Mayhem took all the money from both bodies! She grabbed all of the identity information and their weapons. She took the liquor left in the bottles of Black Dogg and poured it over the entire front floor. Mayhem left out of the back door slowly. As she rose from the hooptie, she shot the back tire to a flat. Calling in the direction of the van, she tells her girl to start the engine. Mayhem, standing at the rear of the hooptie, opens the trunk, carefully placing all the weapons and ID's on the floor of the trunk. There is a gas can half filled. Mayhem grabs it and pours gas directly into some rags and newspapers.

Chapter 19: A Dark Moment for the Darkies

As the van pulls along side of the old hooptie, Mayhem thinks, "Dey don't count. Dey two nothing ass street niggahs. I dun put our competition to sleep. Dats right. I dun removed the competition. Dis fucks everything up real good!!!"

Phillip Hart FEDERAL BUILDING
DOWNTOWN DETROIT

U.S. Attorney Jones is meeting with her staff on the removal of Walena Pope, Richard Braddock and Peter Gomez from the Christian Center. It is late Saturday night. For the late evening work schedule, the choices include pizza or Coney Island hot dogs. Anita Jones has been sent a special operations unit comprised of some Homeland Security personnel headed by an outside contractor. Both Chief LeRocque and U.S. Attorney Jones have their suspicions about the contractor. Responding to their skepticism, Saul and Xavier informed the team that Pro-Tec was a private security company with a mercenary reputation. Saul Long had intelligence from some of his old operatives that informed him that this company was being considered as a replacement for both state and local police. Pro-Tec's perceived role as on loan to the government for peanuts "was really a Trojan Horse intended to rub out the unions."

The feds had several agencies working to relocate these important and highly sensitive informants. The team leader of the new escort operations was a slight built young man, who wore a brush cut that looked very military. He introduced himself to the group and explained how they were being taken over under direct orders issued from the Justice Department.

"I am ordered to deliver three individuals to the Justice Department's Relocation Program by Sunday, at 3 o'clock to Sullivan Airport in Northfield, Michigan. Our task is to protect and deliver the three witnesses unharmed."

The unit is comprised of six agents from the FBI Special Response Team, two Michigan State Troopers, four Detroit SWAT members, three Wayne County Sherriff SWAT members, and five Pro-Tec operatives who will work in the lead role. The team leader is the young spokesman, Dylan McMasters. There is mumbling in the meeting room as Jones underscores the importance of the mission.

"We must have Walena Pope and Richard "Rickey Ricardo" Braddock safely put on that plane. The third witness is equally important to a much larger investigation. He will have a bounty on his head, possibly from international sources."

McMasters gives the proposed meeting times for early Sunday morning. One of the Detroit team members asked if there was a reason for an early meeting, on a Sunday morning. McMasters looked more like a California surfer. His blond hair and blue eyes gave him an air of superiority in Detroit. His talk gave way to words like 'hostiles' and 'gangsters', 'thugs', and 'urban terrorists'. Anita Jones intervened to remind the contractors that Detroit Police knew the landscape better than anyone. A State Trooper seconded the notion, to warn the new team that they should listen well to those who knew Detroit best.

"We made that mistake early in our first joint efforts, while working with DPD. There is a lot to know. You guys might want to make sure you share everything with all of us."

One of the Pro-tec staff laughed, "Detroit is a small urban environ with ignorant natives. This is a practice exercise for us! It will go quick-one two three and out." The room is tense. McMasters tried to ease the tension by making a reference to his experience.

"These hostiles, including any serious mafia types, will never think that anyone would move out at seven thirty, on a Sunday morning. This Keithland James character could not be more dangerous than some of those Somalian pirates. We just extradited some of that type with very little fanfare."

DETROIT POLICE HEADQUARTERS

Chief LeRocque is watching the television when her cell phone rings. As if things couldn't get any worse, she finds out, at that moment, that a live television crew is reporting that Clarence Thoms has been freed. The report goes on to clarify that Judge Irene Ewing is still being held captive. Worse, the kidnappers escaped from the industrial complex without a trace. The red phone on the Chiefs desk rings. It is the mayor, who is upset over the latest newscast. Meanwhile the feds are ending their special unit meeting with the coalition known as, United for Operation Morning Dawn on Sunday, at six o'clock in the morning on February 24.

Mayor Bracey is stressed. The NAACP, Urban League, and a host of civic leaders are demanding to know, "where is Judge Irene Ewing?"

One radio show has reported that the kidnappers have already murdered her. The mayor does not have any solid answers on the kidnapping. Worse, Channel 3 reporter Clarence Thoms has been taken to the hospital suffering from exhaustion. The young girl with the Hummer is only sixteen years old. Chief LeRocque is embarrassed with the facts she has to share with the media.

"We are investigating where Judge Ewing has been taken. We have nothing to report at this time. Our best witness, Clarence Thoms, is under the care of doctors at Sinai Hospital."

The emergency response team leader is a young captain. He explained that the old industrial complex was much larger than they knew. The escape of the kidnapper was relatively easy, with an entire underground tunnel system that they knew nothing about.

"There are over three miles of tunnels underneath this city. We did not know anything was underground. That complex has been closed for a while. We thought it was sealed for, at least, the past decade."

The police chief and the mayor are worried about the elderly judge. Mayor Bracey responds to the question of Pedwell Jefferson's daughter.

"Hell, I thought, or perhaps had hoped, that bastard was dead along with his sons." As the chief and mayor huddled, an officer comes in. The Officer explains the fact that they must let the young girl go since she claimed she was a victim herself. The young girl had her young mother and extended family come to police headquarters with the tale of the young, 16-year-old, Brittany Bailey, being kidnapped by some unknown gang members.

Clarence Thoms was in agreement that the young girl was being held against her will, along with him and Judge Ewing. An older detective looked on in total disbelief.

Sgt. Bannon laughed in disgust, "The whole thing is a set up! Detroit cops are totally in the dark. Outsiders control everything and now this shit turns into some sort of reality show, like Dr. Phil. I'm gonna retire to Florida. Fuck Detroit and all its darkies."

20

INVISIBLE WOMAN

The whereabouts of Mayhem remain a mystery. The word on the street is that she took refuge deep in the underworld. She had the judge wrapped up and in hiding in an abandoned apartment building on the east side of Detroit. Her crew was waiting with her as she tried to get additional information about the condition of her mother and brother. Tyquan talked with Big Girl and the big news was now breaking news.

"There is an exploding vehicle with two unidentified bodies inside."

The street-side news was that Murder Man and Black Mike are dead by forces unknown. The dragnet for Mayhem intensified with the feds joining the search. Pedwell received the news about Black Mike as an omen, knowing it was his daughter.

"Dis bitch is ruining my life. Now what?"
For the first time in his life, Peddy felt troubled by his own blood. He was anxious and annoyed since his sons were wondering if Mayhem was strong enough to take on her father. The streets were silent. There was no trail. There were no voices that were telling her whereabouts.

Tyquan is talking with Xavier about the happenings.

"Doc, I know she is crazed. Big Girl knows that her moms is alive. Con is alive too. If they die, its gonna be hell. Losing DeShaba was messed up. But losing her moms and Contempt is beyond crazy."

Xavier is in touch with Rev. Dr. Stillwater and Ms. Martha. Both are already at the hospital. Stillwater is keeping vigil and is in deep prayer with Ms. Martha. Tyquan is waiting in the front of the hospital as he and Dr. Long have arrived on the scene. It is a sobering moment as the jazz music fills the air. Nibbling on fish tacos from Sadie's, the two men are puzzled as to what is going on with

Mayhem. Tyquans' cell phone rings the tones of samples of the late rapper, Proof.

Looking at Xavier with high energy, he leaps on the call, "May-hem, me and Doc are here. Moms, and Contempt are alive! We gonna talk with the doctor in a few minutes."
The other end of the call is silent.

Suddenly, Mayhem strongly orders, "Let me speak wit Doc."
Tyquan hands Xavier the phone. Xavier frowns. He had just started to chew a large bite of his taco. The voice sounds mono, cold, and defiant.

"You said important people count and poor people don't. Does dis here Judge Ewing count?"
Xavier swallowed slowly, choosing his words carefully.

"Mayhem, I said that, as it applied to the state of mind in America. Judge Ewing is a good woman. Don't harm her, please."

Xavier could feel Mayhem's pensive mood. Even on the phone, her deep darkness was penetrating. He thought of all the passionate talks and discussions of her world. Now, she was on track for something even Professor Long wanted nothing to do with. It was the truth of the streets or life in the third city. Death was a constant and insults were the norm. Mayhem was filled with anger, resentment, sadness, and deep pain having to do with her past, present and future. Professor Long was driving and, in the background of his truck played the saxophone of Joshua Redman. Xavier knew the tune well. As if an Angel requested Sweet Sorrow, the exactness of that moment was fitting. Mayhem, taking a long sigh, had waxed eloquently in her streetlese tone and tongue.

"Aight, my moms and my brothers don't count to y'all. DeShaba don't count. My no-good daddy don't count. My brothers don't count. A'aight! So who does count? Dat bitch niggah who is closing down all the schools? Folks like John Locks, a teacher wit his dick in his hand? Maybe dem big ole Preachers wit dem big rides, driving Benzo's, stealing from all dem dumb muthafucka's like moms, who want Jesus to make it all aight?"

Taking a slow pause, her rant continued, "like dat ho ass bitch Ms. Jeanette Flakes, who said me and DeShaba had fucked up names.

Bitch told me, when I was bout eight years old, dat my hair was ugly. She said it looked like squirrel titty hair. Doc, people hurt little kids like us. We didn't ask God to give us to Peddy. How is he a daddy if he is sticking his dick in his own child? My daddy sticking his dick in my brothers. My daddy beating my moms down like a dog."

Taking another breath of air, Mayhem sighs deeper and rants on.

"We got Peddy for a daddy; a muthafucka dat told me if another kid had better shoes than me, to go take dem off dat kid. Told me and my brothers to kill a muthafucka cuz dat was a'aight. I didn't git Zina Gibson's daddy. Naw, I got dat devil, mean ass killing Peddy."

Xavier is impressed with her meaningful and critical analysis. Before he can answer, she blasted the whole American Dream.

"All dat justice shit don't mean shit to people like me. DeShaba got fucked. She was buck-naked in dat muthafucking Locks office. He fucked all dese here students. Do you fuck yo students Doc? When we git fucked, nobody even cares. Nobody ever asked DeShaba if she was hurt. Not one muthfucka. Dis here bitch is the same bitch dat said my people was worse than roaches. Dis here Judge Ewing said I couldn't raise a dog. Dis bitch said Rev. King wasn't doing civil rights fo a family of Peddy Jefferson. She is a good person? She is one of dem people dat counts? Well, that bitch don't love me and I don't love her. You cool Doc. I appreciate you and T-QUAN. I got to do what I got to do." Xavier looked at Tyquan and without another word, he handed the cell phone back. As they proceeded to the hospital ward, Tyquan listened to Mayhem as she continued her indictment of society. As they approached the ward, Jerenda and Contempt were being worked on.

Tyquan tells his friend, "Mayhem, I am here. We're going into a meeting about their condition. I see Ms. Martha. Do you want to talk with her?"

The line goes completely silent and then Mayhem answered, "No, I will call back. Po-Po out looking fo us. Let me know bout Moms and Con."

Xavier walks over to Ms. Martha. His face is frowned and worried. Ms. Martha holds a Bible as her eyes look into Xavier with a beam of light that warms his inner self.

Without a word, she smiles, announcing in a whisper to the troubled man, "It is alright Dr. Long. An army of Angels is on this ground. The good reverend is over in the waiting room, deep in prayer. He is a special young man, but he wrestles with the devil everyday."

Tyquan is carrying a burden and is feeling confused. The tirade and charges by Mayhem have him in a whirlwind of doubt. His heart is torn and his belief in the wickedness of a man who beats his wife almost to death, is giving way to surrender. What in the world is this all about?

Xavier talks with the two doctors treating the Jeffersons. Contempt is in critical, but stable condition. Jerenda Jefferson is touch and go and her condition seemed to be complicated by the cumulative beatings she experienced, finally taking their toll. The young doctor looked at Xavier with a sense of, "death is upon us." Ms. Martha walked into the meeting with the doctors.

Without hearing the report, she tells Xavier, "It's all going to work out. Let me talk to that girl, Dr. Long."

Tyquan was near the meeting room, texting Big Girl. The hiding place was somewhere in Detroit. Big Girl's text is disturbing to Tyquan.

"T-Quan, how moms? Mayhem is busy. Get back later."

Xavier tells Ms. Martha that they have had some communications with Mayhem.

Tyquan shakes his head and tells Xavier, "I'm here. She is worried bout her moms and brother. What did the doctors say?"

Xavier is getting another call. It's his family, letting him know that everyone is at the homestead. The news is out about the two dead, burned out, bodies near the Christian Center.

Even though they both were looking at the television in the waiting room, the dead bodies near the center have not quite registered with Tyquan or Xavier. Another call comes to Tyquan, with news that the dead bodies are Murder Man and Black Mike. Street-side news is clear. Black Mike was working on behalf of Peddy. The bounty is seriously large. There are rumors of as much as a million dollars. In Detroit, that means that every gangster-thug is out for the pay. Xavier is now hearing the streets, and they are talking loud. Walena Pope and Rickey Ricardo are endangered species. Big Tiny calls Peddy to discuss the happenings of the dead twosome. Xavier gets a call to meet up at Sadie's for some vital information. Tyquan is remaining with Mayhem's mother and brother.

21

THE ROMAN AND HIS LEGIONS

In the hotel adjacent to the Federal Building, Dylan McMasters was having dinner in the dining room. His team from Pro-Tec had never been to Detroit before this Saturday evening. One of the agents said he had heard that Detroit evoked images like those in the movie, Blackhawk Down. McMasters has a muscular build. His blond hair and those blue-eyes belied his arrogance and military superiority. The young waitress took their orders and asked if they had attended the Red Wings hockey game at Joe Louis Arena. The five men are polite and order similar dinners. McMasters commented about how he would eat light since their mission was scheduled to begin early tomorrow.

The crew was surprised during the team briefing, when McMasters did not give any specific date, day or time.

Coyly smiling, he explained, "First, this is our mission. We don't need anybody besides you four. Second, and more important, who can trust these Detroit cops?"

A thick built, compact size agent replied, "I saw their SWAT team on television a lot last year."

Before the agent can finish, McMasters interrupted, "Exactly, what good operation uses their team for entertainment? This city is forgotten. This is ancient Africa. We will hit early in the morning since these so-called, dangerous thug-gang types, sleep all day. Detroit is backward. We will be on our way home by noon."

As the crew ate their dinner, the waitress was in the kitchen on the phone. Not everyone in the room knows that she is actually a Detroit Police Intelligence Officer.

"Sir, they are moving out at zero seven hundred hours. Only the Alpha unit sounds as if they think we are some sort of F-troop operation."

22

FISH AND OLD SCHOOL

Xavier is wearing his old high school letter jacket from Central High. Not having had time to change from his workout gear, his head is covered by a black knit Frederick Douglass College hat. As he entered Sadie's, he is met by the sounds of blaring hip-hop music from the likes of A Tribe Called Quest.

Sadie is waiting at the end of the counter laughing, "Doc, come on in the back. I know you are having a special guest."
Sadie is an old soul who has aged quite well. Her red hair swings with the sassy sway of her earlier days, when her parents established the Fish House. As Xavier moved towards the rear of the restaurant, the old heads intercepted him.

Old Man River and Black Hat Daddy are sitting in a booth over near the back room. Old Man River waves for Xavier to come over, as the two street scribes chuckled with Mona Mercer, a retired exotic dancer. Mercer is married to Sadie's husbands' brother, MacKenzie Mercer. Delighted to see the old timers, he exchanged lots of hugs, handshakes, and greetings. A positive vibe filled the air.

Mona was complaining about the times, "Hell, newspapers are filled with nothing but bad news. The fruit is growing with no seeds. Watermelon is being sold in February.
What watermelon is growing in the winter? Guess what? The damn watermelon and the green grapes got no seeds. How does it grow without seeds? These is some perilous times like the preacher says."

Despite her doomful messages, Xavier listened intently, as he said to himself, "she is a wise soul."

Getting up from the booth, walking over to Xavier, Old Man River whispered, "Professor, some strange things been occurring out in these here streets. Did you know those young lads killed in that burned out car earlier today?"

Acknowledging the information, Xavier tells Old Man River that Mayhem has become lethal.

River's eyes seemed to change colors as the old man lamented, "That little child is always respectful to me and my wife. Her brother is the one they call Contempt. Even he is a decent child like her. Pedwell Jefferson is a damaged, soul-less, miserable human being."

Black Hat Daddy is flirting with a young woman. The presence of Black Hat is enough to make any woman blush. While his gray hair is statesman like, his teasing about hip-hop music is meant jokingly, yet it's quite introspective.

As they hugged and bid farewell, Xavier's guest arrived at the table in the small dining room. It's a diminutive woman dressed in a Sable fur. Her dark glasses block a clear view of her face. The energy from her seemed to put a dark cloak on the entire room. Sitting regal, she wastes no time telling Xavier Long what she had to share.

"Professor Long, my name is Patrice Ewing-Powell. My grandmother is Irene Ewing. I am told that you know how to contact this Mayhem Jefferson. I have a message for Ms. Jefferson. Tell her if she lets my grandmother live, she will be paid handsomely. There will be no punitive actions as long as she is left unharmed." Xavier has many questions, beginning with, who gave this woman his name?

"I tracked you down with assistance from Old Man River. My grandmother is an elitist. She is a stubborn and mean-spirited woman. I am the only living relative that keeps an open line of communication with her. I flew in three hours ago. I want to get this done immediately. This girl is a gangster. My grandmother was in the wrong place at the wrong time. No questions will be asked. Just save her."

Rising from his seat, Dr. Long explained that he could not promise anything.

"I have already told her that hurting innocent people solves nothing. I will give her the message. We are waiting for her next move."

As the two talk, a call comes in. Tyquan is concerned about Peddy's whereabouts. Once again, Xavier has to leave Sadie's quickly.

Chapter 22: Fish and Old School

It is another failed attempt to enjoy Sadie's' great cuisine. As he prepared to rush off, Sadie was putting his doggy bag together.

"Man, you are getting skinny with all the half eating you do. Don't let me talk to Mrs. Long about your foolish ways."
Getting into his truck, his concerns become reality. Peddy is now hunting for the informants. Mayhem is determined to fulfill the contract.

Few knew that it was Mayhem that was responsible for the assassinations of Black Mike and Murder Man. In reality, the Detroit Police Homicide Unit is not at all saddened by the demise of the two homicidal predators.

One of the detectives offered, "Well, somebody did us a favor. These two have been on our list for years. Its strange that these two monsters would be anywhere near a church. Whoever cooked these dirty bastards, did a great job. The Coroner's report indicates that both of them had at least nine shots directly into their torsos. As if that weren't bad enough, both of the bodies were burned like some crispy critters. We should all be clapping and yelling, "Alleluia!"
Big Girl gets off her cell phone real happy.

"We cool, Mayhem follow me. Dat little Rocco hooked us up." Its 10:34 in the evening. Mayhem is tired and police are everywhere in the City of Detroit. State Police, local police including Southfield, Birmingham, Ferndale and the federal agencies are all looking for Mayhem. The white van is like a poster board with "thug" written on the side. Big Girl is in a hooptie with two more ragged vehicles heading towards the Grosse Pointe border. Mayhem warns the crying Judge Ewing to stop her moaning.

"Dun told you bitch; this is not your court. So shut the fuck up, whining and crying bout you sorry."

Rocco Bruno is waiting at the corner of Mack Avenue and Kercheval. A short blond haircut makes the young gangster look like the popular icon Eminem before he changed his hair color. Bruno is close to several black and Latino gangs. In many ways, his goodwill with ethnic crews is the future of the mafia. While his grandfather hates blacks, browns, white Anglo-Saxons and Chinese, Rocco is partners with Hmong gangs. He also sells bootlegged cigarettes and loves the crews of black female boosters. Popping pills while he waits, he gets a call from Homicide Jefferson.

"Hey white boy, you seen my little sister? Wassup wit yaw white niggahs?"

Rocco is aware of the manhunt for Mayhems crew.

"Naw, we jus chillin'. Y'all having a gambling party tonight at the house? You gon have some snuff movies and some naked dancers?"

Homicide usually dismissed Rocco because he didn't like the Italian boy's connection to the big-time bosses.

"Naw, we looking fo my sista. Holla if anybody sees her.

23

SHADOW WORLD

The garage of the Helton Hotel is empty, except for a number of federal task force vehicles. Nearby are two unmarked cars. One belongs to the Detroit Police and the other to the Michigan State Police. The basement floor is cold and somewhat hazy. The elevator door opens. Dylan McMasters leads a team of agents off the elevator.

McMasters, dressed in all black and olive camouflage assault attire, is telling a younger agent why Pro-Tec is the best organization, "I started out in Chicago with the police. My father, grandfather, lots of my uncles, cousins and two aunts are all on the force. I did my time in the Corp and was picked for Recon. Then I got lucky, and Pro got me."

As the team of five walked towards their vehicles, the two unmarked Detroit and Michigan State Police cars seemed to come alive. Each of the unmarked vehicles hemmed the group of agents into the corner near the elevator. The flashing overhead lights of their vehicles can be seen for blocks. Suddenly, a tall figure enters the garage from the door.

"Mr. McMasters, this is an effort that requires and demands the full cooperation of everyone associated with this operation. This is not a Pro-Tec project."

McMasters looks surprised and glares at the full team in front of him, led by the Detroit Police Emergency Response Team leader. Stepping back, Dylan McMasters regroups and admits his arrogance.

"I see my error. I wanted to take them by surprise with our early intervention. Sorry, I am not confident with multi-agencies in these matters. That is why I was brought in to coordinate this entire effort." Anita Jones is agitated with McMasters.

"No, you are mistaken. Coordination means just that. Your role is to spearhead the evacuation of our witnesses. First, Lt. Thaddeus Ervin is the leader."

Looking red in the face, McMasters yields to Chief LeRocque. Dressed in her black fatigues and wearing a futuristic flak jacket, she is fully supported by U.S. Attorney Jones and the Justice Department leadership team in D.C. The team huddled quickly in the garage. McMasters explained that the Christian Center has security that includes electronic gates.

"We are taking them out this morning since hostiles are more than likely not ready this early."

The Pro-Tec team is not pleased with the larger group being involved at all.

Ranita had talked with her sister, Walena Pope, in the early hours. Walena was aware that the feds were moving her, Ricky and Petey Gomez. Ranita assured her that Mayhem was ready to rescue her. Walena has strong reservations about anyone related to Peddy.

"Ranita, are you sure bout this? That girl is a full-time gangster. She is the daughter of Peddy Jefferson and the sister of those horrible brothers."

Ranita is visibly disturbed by the so-called "deals" being offered by the feds. The two sisters are not with the whole idea of being in the federal witness protection program.

"Walena, you have money. Running your mouth about Keithland's operations could get our whole family killed. The feds cannot be trusted. You and Rick can just go away. Keithland is dangerous and those Jefferson brothers and their horrible father will come after you. Mayhem will bring you out. I got some people and we got enough bank to just disappear forever - on our terms."

Rickey and Petey are nervous. They know they are marked men. Rick knows that Keithland can buy plenty of assassins, but his new relationship with God consoles his transformation.

The Christian Center is a place that is multi-denominational and not just for those that practice the Christian faith. All three of the witnesses are amazed by the peaceful environment and legions of different faiths together under one roof. There is a group of Buddhist monks, several priests from the Catholic faith, three Rabbis and many of the colored communities of Baptist, Pentecostal, AME and a few Asians such as the Buddhist monks, with a temple near downtown

Detroit. The good Reverend Dr. Nehemiah Stillwater is the key for all three fugitives. Javier Rivera is a young priest who has established a special bond with Stillwater while working with him and the troubled youth in the barrio of Southwestern Detroit. The center has changed its name in recent months to the Prayer Center for Humanity. Even Peter Gomez is feeling peaceful at the Humanity Center. Petey has asked for special prayers, and wants to be forgiven for his long life in the streets and the many terrible deeds he participated in. Stillwater has worked along with Father Rivera in convincing the gangster, from South America, that redemption is the cornerstone to healing.

Walena Pope believes that she is in God's hands, as long as she is following the new street ministry of Stillwater. Nehemiah is a cut from the old Southern religious tradition. Like the iconic Reverend Dr. Martin Luther King, Jr., he is an orator and he is a black preacher. Nehemiah has spoken the word, translated it, and understood it for what it was – naked, raw truth. Ironically, the connection to both Xavier Long and Nehemiah Stillwater was the gospel loving Ms. Martha. Ms. Martha has the whole center listening to gospel music of the legendary Mahalia Jackson. The prayer center is a fortress, mainly because of the maintenance manager Joe Robinson, a retired Wayne County Sheriff Deputy. Robinson, an ex-Army Ranger, was nearly killed twenty-five years ago in a shootout near Good Shepard church. If it were not for the church members who prayed for him during the seemingly forever wait for the ambulance, he is convinced he would have died that day. Retired and having lost his wife of thirty-three years, Robinson makes sure the loving atmosphere of the center is well protected. He trained the security force of eight for twenty-four hours, seven days a week. Joe Robinson has been alerted that the feds were coming to pick up the trio. Walena, Petey and Rickey are all in prayer in the beautiful atrium. Walena's phone rings and she steps outside in the cold prayer garden near the atrium to answer the call.

"Walena, Mayhem just called. Get your things. She is coming in as your cousin. Its on time," said Ranita.

The police chief is not comfortable with the aloof Dylan McMasters.

"Anita, what is with this Pro-Tec guy?"

Looking disgruntled, she speaks in a low mono voice, "Who knows. They came from higher ups. Feels like that creepy ass Rumsfeld-Cheney thing. That guy is really dark. He is typical of what we get whenever there are foreign connections. The Asian, Latino and African interest will have something private always these days."

Chief LeRocque laughs, "Right here in the ghetto where schools are being attacked by Uncle Tom ass financial managers, here comes the damn CIA."

Meanwhile, McMasters lectures the group, "we know that the witnesses are connected to the local hostiles. The Mexican hostile is from Columbia and that means we must take special precautions."

One of the Pro-Tec agents interrupted, "He is not Mexican. You just said Columbia! Which is it?"

McMasters is pissed, "Mexican, Dominican, Brazil, Puerto Rico, or Cuban. Does it matter?"

Back at the hospital, Ms. Martha is on the phone with Xavier who is trying to find the whereabouts of Mayhem as he talks with both Ms. Martha and Tyquan.

"Dr. Long, her brother is dead. Jeranda is fighting for her life. We are here, praying. Are you praying?"

Xavier is on his phone in the truck, while holding an additional conversation on his iPhone with his sister, the judge.

"Look, what are the feds doing? Constance, you are playing judge. You have friends in the Justice Department. What is really going on?"

It is now seven forty-five, Sunday morning and everything is slow motion. Entering the Prayer Center compound is Big Girl. In another car is Mayhem, with three confederates of her crew. The loud ringtone of Mayhem's phone can be heard as she looks to see who is calling. It's Tyquan. He is coming through the phone.

"Mayhem, Contempt is going to make it. Jeranda needs you. Do you hear me girl? Yo moms needs to hear you. Ms. Martha is here. Please, don't do nothing crazy. Not now."

Ms. Martha takes the phone away from Tyquan.

She lays it out to Mayhem, "Jesus, May. Jesus, your story is with Jesus. JESUS is standing with you baby. All that the devil done did is nothing. JESUS, hear me at this moment!! LAWD!! Have mercy on this child!"

While Ms. Martha continues to pray aloud, a voice speaks to Mayhem beyond the physical phone. Usually stoic, inside and out, Mayhem is feeling the words. As only a God could do, Mayhem seems grabbed up by the Holy Spirit. She is frozen in her seat. The young girl who is driving is puzzled by Mayhems behavior. The car just stops as Ms. Martha hands the phone over to Nehemiah. At this moment, the spirit world is in charge. Reverend Dr. Nehemiah Stillwater is in the car without Mayhem understanding how he entered. Stillwater is speaking in the ancient lingo of an African tongue for a second only to transform to the Native American tongue of the black Seminole. Voices are speaking loud to Mayhem in her vehicle. A dazed and subdued Judge Ewing is hearing what she can't believe in the trunk. It sounds like gospel music if she could hear better it might be the old traditional gospel of Mahalia Jackson. The judge feels something is happening, as there is some sort of brightness in the dark trunk. She begins to feel her body being lifted out of the trunk that had started to feel like her grave. Mayhem is still caught in this sense of something very powerful is upon her. She hears a voice from afar. She recognizes the voice. She recognizes that crying sound. It's Ms. Martha.

She is crying and Mayhem can hear voice faintly begging, "Baby come to Jesus. Let go and let God."
Suddenly, thunder erupted and the sky turns blackish blue. The morning is standing still.

A voice speaks to Mayhem with distinction and direct commands, "YOU MAY DEFEND YOURSELF ONLY. YOU ARE NOT ANYONE'S CHILD BUT MINE AND YOU CANNOT LOSE IF YOU ARE OBEDIENT. PEDDY IS NOT YOUR FATHER. I AM YOUR MOTHER-FATHER ALWAYS."

Mayhem is sitting while the inside of the truck is lit in some sort of bluish lighting. The young girl is confused, thinking to herself that she needed to cut back on that green tree dope. Gathering herself, she looks at the cell phone. Its ring tones are loud. Mayhem doesn't remember hanging up during the talk with Ms. Martha. As she clicks her phone, she hears the faint voice of Jeranda.

"Baby, baby it's me. Come git me. He took your monay."
In the backseat crying was Judge Ewing. Her voice is heard pleading with her captors.

"Lord, something is going on in here."

Tyquan is on the phone telling Mayhem, "Doc says we can help. Don't do anything crazy."

Tyquan clicks back to Xavier, "Tyquan, tell Mayhem that Judge Ewing's family is offering a reward if she doesn't hurt her."

Tyquan tells Xavier that he is talking to Mayhem at that moment.

24

BATTLEFIELD GHETTO

Pedwell and his sons are at Smokes' having breakfast. Peddy is open-ly angry about losing the dynamic duality of Black Mike and Murder Man.

"They were my connection for getting dat rat ass niggah. Now dey fucked everything up. Homicide, you and Assault git a line on y'all sister."

Smokes' is the spot for early breakfast for street bikers, especially if you were the nasty, dirty and unclean type. There is the smell of ba-con and mesquite salmon patties. The strong scents of buttered bis-cuits, grits, and scrambled eggs with cheese add to the smoke house flavor one got as soon as they entered the establishment. Smokes' morning Cook is an older Haitian woman. Her hatred of Pedwell is not known to anyone. In preparing his plate, the short dark skinned Haitian hacked and softly spat into his buttered grits. Muttering in French, her eyes glared a hatred filled look directly at Pedwell.

The table with the Jefferson clan was both talkative and loud. A couple of young girls are sitting at another table near the clan.

Rape Jefferson hollered to the two, "Y'all bitches work at the Body Rock?"

Peddy is still fuming over the shooting of his son, Contempt. The music is loud, as always, with Junior Walker's 'SHOTGUN' in the background. Nobody is listening to anyone. Sunday is always slow with a bar full of miscreants, misfits and murderers.

"Dat niggah and Mayhem always siding with their hoe ass Mammy. Dis here lots of bank fo dat young bitch ass Mayhem."

Mayhem is back on the pathway to the Prayer Center when her phone rings. The ringtones indicate that it's Big Girl.

"We here. We already passed the guard and showed dem passes. So, we takin' who? How far are you from here? WHOA! Mayhem, some bad ass police niggahs is here."

Three hummer type vehicles have pulled directly in front of the Prayer Center. Suddenly, Dylan McMasters walks in leading a squad of eight. Big Girl looked around the lot. There are more police and at least two more police cars waiting.

"Mayhem, dis the army and the heat. Dese muthafuckas is serious. Dey went inside. How y'all gonna git dese here niggahs wit all dis army shit out here?"

Mayhem tells her driver to hurry. They are just up the block from the Prayer Center. As she hits another button, she calls F-U.

"F, need a hook-up and new cars. Can you git me outta of the D? Need it bad. B coming dat way soon."

F-U tells Mayhem to meet him at the car wash he has over on Keller Street in Grosse Pointe. Mayhem tells the driver to take Judge Ewing there, and to gag her real good. Driving into the Prayer Center, Mayhem tells the security guard that she must go inside immediately. Judge Ewing is making too much noise with her repeatedly kicking the inside of the truck. Mayhem jumps to the back of the truck placing the Glock against Judge Ewings temple.

"Wanna be dead?" Judge Ewing immediately freezes her body. Mayhem takes more rope and tied Judge Ewing tighter. Another girl gets in the van after Big Girl tells her to assist Mayhem.

Big Girl called Mayhem to report, "They got all of them. There are four soldiers surrounding them. They got a bitch in front wearing a suit, with walkie-talkie shit all in her ear. Dis big muthafucka that looks like Robocop is leading."

Hearing the advice of Tyquan, and knowing Ms. Martha is praying, she decides that she wants to get out of the courtyard. She tells Big Girl her plan and then signals to her driver. There is another girl who has been instructed to hold Judge Ewing down in the rear of the van.

As if she is reminding herself, Mayhem silently thinks, "no shooting in the Prayer Center."

Suddenly, she can see the plan come clear. She tells Big Girl to have two vehicles ready. Out of nowhere, a security guard called out to

Mayhem as she walked into the front door. The guard waited, as one of the plainclothes officials stopped all traffic.

The feds approached the main entrance. With a stun gun hidden on her side, the petite young girl jammed the stun gun into the guard, who fell immediately. As the plain clothed agent walked towards the door, another young girl stopped him. There was another young assassin, jamming the stun gun into his neck and chest.

Mayhem is now looking directly at the crew led by Dylan McMasters, who is relaxed and arrogantly telling his team, "See, not one hostile in sight. These kind don't know what morning looks like. Detroit is still sleeping, lazy, and useless. Church? Hey look over there at that group of Buddhist Monks."

Her eyes talked to Big Girl. She steered over to the side where an agent was discussing the transfer of the trio to safer ground. The agent is telling Walena, Peter, and Ricardo that they will have the team with them until McMasters gives the green light.

"Ms. Pope, we will leave very soon. Don't worry. This crew is the best protection we could ask for."

Walena sees Mayhem and Big Girl as they are coming in the entrance of the center. Walking over to the reception area, Big Girl acts like she is on the pay phone. Mayhem calls the waiting car to tell the driver that the plans have changed.

"Look, make sure dat old bitch is tight. When we come out, y'all take out anybody in our way. The hook will be out and we moving fast wit dis shit. Watch out for John Law. Dey got super gats. Some of em' are wearing dat SWAT shit."

One of Mayhem's crew is talking with a young priest and Rabbi Stein. Both men are friends of Reverend Dr. Stillwater.

Mayhem is wondering, "what is dis girl doing?"

Big Girl smiles at the vigilance of the security team as they scope the room.

Walking over to Big Girl she whispered, "what the fuck? Is dis bitch crazy talking to those church people?"

The two talked briefly before Mayhem made things clear, "Dat Petey Gomez got to go. Nobody is shooting round all dese people.

Dese muthafucking China men, wit der red robes, is what? I got dis big muthafucka wit all dis here killing gear."

The feds move out with Walena and Rick. It is a chess game with the Fed team moving about without realizing that Mayhem is on their playing field. It is crowded and Walena is anxious and worried about the two groups colliding. Mayhem and Walena are watching each other. Mayhem is waiting for the chance to grab her bounty. Walena is watching Mayhems eyes looking at the cars parked to the right side of the circular drive. Suddenly, one of Mayhems girls intercepts, pushing Walena and Rickey towards their crews' cars with another Mayhem gangster girl making certain Peter Gomez is not lost in the sudden commotion. Gunshots begin in the street entry as the small crowd gets frenzied with the sound and sight of rapid gunfire. Mayhem can see Dylan McMasters moving towards the fleeing witness. McMasters and the Pro-Tec crew were caught completely off guard. The screams of women and children could be heard from the front of the building. McMasters returned fired from his M-16 as Mayhems crew jets away in their getaway cars. The Pro-Tec crew was firing at will. One of the plainclothes feds had been shot and was being picked up by Mayhems crew. Mayhem is yelling to her crew to leave as she looks for Gomez. A young member of the crew was talking to the clergymen and suddenly ripped out her automatic weapon from her Vuitton bag. She was making certain that the holy men were covered as she walked, without fear, into the path of federal agents. She fired rapidly into the tires of the parked cars belonging to the feds and Detroit Police. One of the younger members of Mayhems crew was busy pinning the police down by constantly firing her weapon. She turned towards Mayhem, who was within reaching distance of Peter Gomez. McMasters was in total disbelief as he watched the witnesses being snatched away, in front of his eyes.

"God, almighty. Please forgive me for all my sins," cried Gomez.

Still pleading for his life, Gomez was thrown into the Hummer by two of Mayhems' young girls. McMasters runs into the street, firing at Mayhems' back. He doesn't see Big Girl, who is driving slowly behind him. She used the black Ram Charger with the black brush

grille to run over the camouflage dressed McMasters. Blood poured from under the truck as it picked up speed. Mayhem looked around the grounds. While there were a number of people wounded, none of the wounded were kids. She laughed as she jumped into the backseat of the white Ford Excursion. The outlaw convoy is moving like its NASCAR. As the convoy speeds away, Mayhem noticed that one of the bodies in the truck was that of a wounded federal agent. She put her phone down and screamed, "What the fuck is dis? Y'all crazy? Who in the fuck pulled dis wounded John Law in here?"
At the rear of the truck was a crying Petey Gomez. He was confused and scared.

He was so scared that he was mumbling in Spanish, "¡Dios mio! Ayudame por favor. ¿Quienes son estas chicas y por que es esa chica Mayhem esta tan enojada y deprimida? ¡¡¡Ella es como el Diablo!!!

The phones were ringing back and forth and all three vehicles were taking orders from Mayhem. She was wondering why she didn't smoke Gomez. Why didn't she kill the hook with all that killing gear? She was wrestling with what Martha and Rev. Dr. Stillwater said to her. One thing was for sure. She had a million dollars coming her way. No, she wouldn't double cross Ranita, but one million dollars for a contract was real. The only person she was certain she wanted to kill was her father, Pedwell Jefferson.

25

OUTLAW AND HIDEAWAYS IN THE SNOW

It's 11:40 in the morning and the big screen flashed with BREAKING NEWS, A SHOOTOUT WITH FEDERAL OFFICIALS AND UN-KNOWN PARTIES HAS RESULTED IN FEDERAL WITNESSES BE-ING KIDNAPPED. TV3 WILL CONTINUE COVERAGE ON THIS NEWS BREAKING STORY. Pedwell stops dead in his seat at Smokes'.

He shouts, "Bitch dun did our contract. Dis bitch is fucking up our name and my rep on the block."

Homicides' cell phone rings. He answers with his usual bad attitude. "Wassup, who? Yeah, Big Tiny, we looking. Naw, we didn't know shit."

Peddy grabbed the phone from his son.

"Well, we got it. See, we got dis down. Tell Keithland, we meeting wit her and not to worry."

Peddy was fuming, "Homi don't know shit? Dis is our con-tract. Young bitch got dem contracts. We gonna smoke her peeps. Mayhem does what I say. Is you stupid niggah? We ain't letting dat Keithland give dat bitch our bank. Mayhem is my hoe. I tell my hoes what to do. Trust me!"

Word travels on the streets, and the word was that Mayhem and her Female crew fucked everybody up. In recent hours, Attor-neys Lanza and James Perry have talked. Back at Keithland's club, Keithland feels elated and is celebrating.

"I told ya. Cut out muthafucka's snitching."

James Perry is reserved in his reaction. He is not comfortable enough to celebrate.

"We don't want no surprises. The Bruno family is still con-cerned. The old man is concerned about the official report, an FBI agent kidnapped? Police officials are wounded? The stories are crossing and jumping all over the streets. Lanza is not certain that the witnesses are neutralized. Frank Bruno wants a body count. The old man actually said, "Do any of those darkies have actual proof of anybody being dead?"

James Perry gets a call. It's Mayhem. She wants assurance about payment.

"Ok, let me talk to Keithland. I did the contract. I need my payment in full. I got your witnesses silenced. Pay me now. My people will come in the next hour."

James Perry had a feeling that was not good. He tells Keithland, who says immediately, "I 'm not paying dat little bitch no million. Is her daddy playing us, or what? Get Tiny to handle this." James Perry is not in accord.

He yells, "Keithland, you need to pay her something, seriously."

Keithland James shows his true colors. His rants are loud, vulgar, and arrogant.

"Fuck that whole family. As long as that business is done, fuck'em. Tiny, give dat bitch sum fake dollars and kill dat bitch." James Perry tried, in vain, to change the new course of action.

"This is not good. She could cause lots of trouble. Even a half million would work. Walena, alone, could bury us. She had books and contracts. You know about all our contacts in South America and Mexico."

Back at Smokes', Peddy was ready to meet his daughter, Mayhem.

"Homi, you Assault, Hate, and Rape, get things cool with her." The cell phone rings.

"It's Mayhem."

Looking surprised, Peddy puts on his best gangster daddy voice, "You dun did well girl. I'm proud of you."
Mayhem is settling into a hidden building in Grosse Pointe. All her valuable cargo is under one roof. F-U is more than willing to assist Mayhem, as he makes sure that the building is secure. Mayhem lets Big Girl handle the hostages, as she makes arrangements to meet her father.

The building is large, with living quarters that are comfortable. F-U keeps the building for his personal work on motorcycles, and for storing his snowmobile and old racecars. Big Girl directs her crew to set up a perimeter in order to watch and make sure everything is as it should be. The order makes F-U laugh.

"Big Girl, I got my closed-circuit hook-up all over this place. There are electronic doors and alarms everywhere. Nobody is gonna see her, anyway, we right across the street from the police department."

Mayhem tells her father that the million is his to divide. He tells her that Big Tiny is sending someone to pay her the money at Smokes. Mayhem was happy. She tells her father that his plan is a good plan. She will meet them in about an hour.

"See, Mayhem is a good ho. She did it all fo me. Her Mammy really didn't understand dat my dick and fist make it work, every time."

U.S. Attorney Jones stands in front of the Prayer Center. The police command is discussing the events of Sunday morning.

A Detroit Police commander explained to the mayoral aide, "Nobody was injured except three government agents. Our scout cars were shot up badly and the tires were blown out. Everybody said the assailants were fast and that the hit was planned with precision. The crew appeared to be excited. The only injuries were to the police agencies, since the assailants only shot the vehicles."
Jones is dismayed and is looking for McMasters who was coordinating the evacuation.

"Chief LeRocque, this guy was shot by his own people. He was the expert. He was the badass terminator. He told us to take his lead and now, we got zero, zilch, nothing to show. I've lost my valuable witnesses."

As the two officials commiserate, a tall rangy man, with long gray and black hair is loudly preaching. Carrying a long wooden staff, his ragged clothes are muted colors of red and black. He has on a dingy, white plaid jacket with a long green scarf. His shoes are worn, brownish New Balance snow boots. His voice booms. His eyes are clear and intense. He denounced the City of Detroit's Common Council, the Governor of Michigan and last, what he called the false Mahatma's and their golden churches of greed.

"THE WORKS OF GOD HAVE SPOKEN. ON SUNDAY, RIGHT IN THIS CITY, THE DEVIL WORKS WITH COUNCILMEN AND THAT WHORE COUNCIL WOMAN WITH HER FILTHY MAMMON. DRAGONS WITH FIRE WERE HERE THIS MORNING. I WARN YOU TO WARN THE FALSE PROPHETS IN YOUR CHURCHES OF GREED. GUNS, DOPE, LIES, DECEIT, SECRETS, WARS, DETROIT, WARS, PEOPLE, POVERTY, LIES, CITY COUN-CIL, STATE, PRESIDENT, CONGRESS, SENATE, WHORES, MAM-MOTH GREED."

The EMS team was treating McMasters for injuries he received after being run over by the Ramcharger.

The Latina attendant said, "This attack suit and helmet saved your life man!"

Another attendant asked the question, "What kind of material is this suit made out of? My emergency scissors can cut anything but I can't cut anything here!"

McMasters is in a fog. His face is smashed since it landed first when he was knocked, literally, off his block. The preaching man walked over to the emergency truck and looked directly into the disoriented face of Dylan McMasters. He began pointing his long finger into the face of the EMS Techs, as they tried, in vain, to move him back.

"Doing the devil's work. See, you have been warned and re-buked by the Spirit on the Sabbath. YOU devil disciple, with all your fancy war clothes. There is nothing in your heart but blackness. Like Caesar's Legions, you Roman thugs are trying to ignore the Sabbath. This is your last warning. God and his angels have asked me to tell you to drop your weapons and change that ugly black thought in your heart, NOW!"

The EMS Tech's supervisor asked one of the police officers who the tall preacher was.

The officer, standing with another Detroit Police and a Michigan State Trooper offered, "That is Gerald the Prophet. Some call him Prophet Gerald."

The supervisor laughed, "Is he real? Why don't you guys arrest him?"

The cops laughed.

The Detroit cop clearly stated, "Right, Gerald the Prophet is real. When I was a rookie, I saw him stop a murderer with his words. If you arrest an agent of God dude, what is going to happen to you?"

McMasters is embarrassed and humiliated. He muttered, "Where is my team? The hostiles fired on us. There are too many. How many?"

As Anita Jones sits on the EMS truck, she informed the agent, "It was friendly fire. It seems that it took three of your fellow Pro-Tec agents. All three are in the other EMS trucks. There was nothing life threatening. But they were all shot by your guns. The assailants were guilty of shooting up our vehicles during their daring escape with all of our witness. Oh, and one FBI agent was wounded and taken by your hostiles."

In the background, the team leader from Detroit Police, along with other multi-agency units, were livid and riled by the cowboy type leadership of Dylan McMasters.

One of his fellow Pro-Tec officers offered, "McMasters always claimed that the streets of Detroit were like Somalia, and he was right. Somalians kicked the asses of the Rangers, Recon Army, Seals and those damn Marines. The skinny is that Dylan called them just this morning on our way over here. The problem here in Detroit was that this was a 100% Skinny girl crew that kicked our ass. Thanks Dylan McMasters. Guess that was the international skinny on the Detroit Skinny."

In the evening, F-U brought in some pizza for Mayhems' crew. The pizza is from Sal's Pizza. Sal is connected to the community of made men. The girls were laughing and listening to Lil Wayne cd's while they played video games. Big Girl was worried. For the first time in her long relationship with Mayhem, she was confused by the actions and moods of her comrade. Mayhem was entangled with a great burden. Over the past few hours since the kidnapping, Mayhem had talked with Tyquan and Xavier in small increments. She is concerned that her contract business is not the same as it is for males. Her fathers' voice began clashing with Keithlands' voice. She felt like all of them were playing her for a fool. The phone rang. Rita sounded elated that Gomez has been snuffed. Mayhem did not confirm his assumptions, nor did she deny them. She was openly hostile as she continued to hurl questions about her payment.

"My bank ain't here, wassup?" Rita is surprised.

She retorted, "Hey Mayhem. We are doing business like always. We'll bring you the cash. Where do you want to meet?"
Another beep was heard coming from Mayhems' phone. It was Ranita. Mayhem told Rita that she would call her back. Clicking over, she could hear the fear in Ranita's voice.

"Mayhem, is Walena safe? We heard on all the news channels that they were kidnapped. I got the rest of your money. It wasn't easy, but I told you. You are paid in full."

The phone goes silent. Mayhem is thinking about honoring the contract. She thinks about all the negatives - the messed-up things that Rickey had done for Keithland. She also knows that making Walena talk will put Keithland away, and that will shut his entire kingdom down. Mayhem remained silent and Ranita was troubled by the silence.

"Mayhem, I need my sister alive and you promised. Yo brothers and yo daddy are scary. None of them are worthy of trust. I came to you as a woman, a black woman, begging for my sister's life. Walena has changed. She got kids. I am giving you every dime my whole family has to its name."

Mayhems' phone rings again. It's the ringtone for her mother. It was Tupac's, "Dear Mamma." When she answered, to her surprise she heard Tyquan's voice. He was attempting to blow up the phone lines.

Mayhem said, "Wassup, moms good?"

Her other line rang again. The beep this time, registered a name, Martha Myers.

"Mayhem, Christ has filled this hospital. There is no room for non-believers. As I speak, the doctors just said your mother is doing much better. When she heard your voice baby, her connection to the only force in this universe was the almighty Creator of all, and it all poured into her heart and her mind. Baby, she is doing so much better right now. We need you to come to her bedside."

Mayhem could rarely stop the things that happened in her life. She began to cry.

She whispered back into the phone, "Ms. Martha, I am at her bedside right now. I love you. Thank you. Thank God. I can see now." Mayhem hung up and then called Big Girl. Her look had changed significantly. She was relaxed and refreshed.

She tells her girl, "Lookee here, I got bank over at Smokes'. My daddy took my bank that my moms was holding. I'm going to git it. We ain't smoking nobody on Sunday, ever again. It's the Sabbath. We doing something new, something different, so don't worry bout it, ok?"

Mayhem took her phone and called Book. "Heya, Book, I need a favor. We cool, a'aight?"

Keithland is happy and has sent out a death squad for Mayhem. The plan is to erase the whole Jefferson Clan. James Perry has shared with Keithland that Contempt is near death as is, Jerenda Jefferson. The plan was to kill Mayhem first then finish off Peddy and his sons. Keithland has bequeathed the bounty for Rickey and Walena to his personal terminator, Big Tiny. All of the information that Keithland knows is not exactly accurate. James Perry is not in favor of the dastardly plan. Perry is deeply concerned about how ignorant and poorly skilled everyone thinks Mayhem is; yet, no one can find any information as to her whereabouts since the incident at the Prayer Center. If she is so ignorant and lacks skill, how and why is she the one with the witnesses' fate in her hands? Dismissive, sexist and arrogantly, Keithland proclaims that his organization is his baby and he is the true Mack Daddy of all times.

Laughing he declared, "After all, I am the Niggah of all Niggahs, forever."

26

A CHANGE IS GONNA COME

Mayhems' proposal to Book is surprising for the young man.

"I will pay you for setting up dat video thing in your computer. Ok?"

Book is not really a fan of Mayhem. His relationship with Tyquan is good. Ms. Martha is someone that he respects. Since the request doesn't include violence, he agrees to assist Mayhem. She wants him to simply do some video work and then put it on Facebook. Mayhem is worried about Judge Ewing and the FBI agent who is wounded.

Big Girl says, "The FBI agent needs medical attention and Judge Ewing is refusing to eat."
One of the young girls tells Mayhem that Judge Ewing may be in shock.

"My moms is a nurse. I know about shit, anyway dat ole judge is breathing hard." Mayhem tells Big Girl that F-U can get a doctor.

"F-U can help us wit dat Judge Bitch. I should smoke dat bitch. I could just kill the FBI."
Big Girl nods in agreement. She is wide open since that is what gangsters do. They smoke people.

Mayhem goes into her Sabbath talk since its still Sunday. There is also the lingering problem of Peter Gomez.

"Why smoke Petey? We can make some money off him wit Rita and dem."
Big Girl has heard enough. She is tired of the mood swings from her girl.

"We gangsters. We got a contract to smoke'em - all of dem. Fuck the FBI. Fuck dat judge. Gomez is just another dead guy. We agreed to smoke'em so what's the problem Mayhem?"
Mayhem thinks for a second and then agrees to the G talk. She tells the girls to hold down the fort. F-U tells Mayhem his doctor people

can take care of the FBI. The toll on Judge Ewing is clearly turning for the worse. Mayhem can't shake the voice of Ms. Martha. To make matters worse, she keeps hearing Stillwater. She can't tell Big Girl or anybody else. She really missed Contempt. She could ask him what was wrong. F-U walks over to Mayhem in a positive, brotherly way. Looking in her eyes, he sensed the turbulence in her being.

"My guy is a real doctor. We can fix the FBI and your judge. He dun fixed a lot of gun shots for my family."

The eyes of Judge Ewing are saddened and weak. She feels woozy. The pizza aroma makes her sick to her stomach. As Mayhems phone rings, her feelings of uncertainty are interrupted.

"MAYHEM SHE'S GONE. YOUR MOTHER HAS PASSED ON. BABY I AM SO SORRY," sighed Ms. Martha.

Mayhems' vision becomes blurred. She feels dizzy. She begins to vomit. Everyone in the big room is looking and wondering what is taking place. Mayhem is crying louder and louder. She grows angrier by the moment. F-U doesn't know what to do nor does Big Girl. Suddenly, like a sweeping tornado, the room is filled with rage and darkness. Peter Gomez begins to pray out loud. Walena hides in the corner as she quickly moves into the bathroom. All of the girls in the crew are puzzled. Seeing Mayhem like this is a brand-new experience. As Gomez recites the Lord's Prayer, Mayhem walks over, and without a word, blasts the praying Gomez.

As the fury rises in the room, Mayhem, walking faster towards the wounded federal agent, yells in a loud, profaned filled voice, "Y'all never saved her. John Law hunted us. Y'all never cared about her."

After completely unloading the Glock nine into the body of the agent, she proceeded to reload her gun. Her glare was tempered only by her brutal handling of Judge Ewing. Judge Ewing was terrified.

Mayhem yells, "I am dat roach. I am dat ugly squirrel titty hair no reading niggah. I am dat dumb, no nothing, pissy smelling, ugly black bitch. Like you said, me and my kind ain't worth the time of all dose important, smart, educated people. Reverend Doctor Martin Luther King did not march fo me! You so a'aight, you know I ain't shit! No, I didn't go to college and NO I didn't go to church. No,

Chapter 26: A Change is Gonna Come

John Locks didn't respect DeShaba. No, you said, No way could I SEE my little sista. No, you said I was not human. I AM NUTHING AND NUTHING KILLED YOU! BAM BAM BAM the whole building is dead quiet and dead black.

27

REVELATIONS AT THE SCENE OF THE CRIME

The room seems frozen as F-U tells his people, "Got to get those dead bodies wrapped. Got to move them out of here right now."
Walena, hugged up with Rickey Ricardo, is screaming in fear, horror, and disbelief. The phones are ringing off the hook but no one is answering anything. Big Girl is satisfied.

She looked at Mayhem and gently asserted, "Sorry bout Moms. I am really sorry. My moms been gone a long time but dat shit still hurts. It hurts all the time."

Walena asked Mayhem, "You, you just killed that old judge and you killed Peter? Why you killing us?"
Mayhem is still cursing and turning her head like a spirited Hawk.

With her eyes beaming a red glare, she tells Walena, "Bitch, best shut the fuck up. People like Judge Ewing hate black people if dey ain't just exactly like dem. Dat old bitch hated my very life. Dat bitch was constantly hatin' on my young black ass. She dogged my moms. She hated us more den white people hate us."

Walena continued her questions, "Why you so damn cold-blooded Mayhem? You just kill and murder motherfuckers with no feelings? Petey Gomez accepted his savior, Jesus Christ. He didn't do anything to deserve what you just did. You murdered that FBI guy and you didn't even know him." Mayhem looked at F-U. He was moving the bloody clothing and furniture out of his building. She laughed out loud and opened her phone to call her father.

"Daddy, did y'all hear? Moms is dead. I'll be dere. On my way now. You just be sure to have all my bank, ok? We'll split dat bank. Naw, I'm cool. I just accept that Moms is gone."

F-U doesn't say a word. Deep down inside, his gut knows not to say anything. He knows Peddy and his progeny very well. One of his people is petrified with fear.

Chapter 27: Revelations at the Scene of the Crime

As he moves the lifeless body of the three dead victims, he whispered to another helper, "Man, we were smoking and drinking in the basement when all the shooting started. I heard some scary shit, but when you out here with F-U, shit happens. This girl, I mean, that woman is a show nuff full time gangster. She blazed three people without coming up for air."

Walena is sobbing uncontrollably. Rickey is worried and, as a result, doesn't trust anyone. He tried to get Walena to quiet down but it did not work. His understanding and first-hand knowledge of Peddy, Tiny and even his marginalized knowledge of Mayhem, is more than enough. Walena cannot accept the death of Peter Gomez.

"Pete had changed. That was why he was willing to witness against Keithland and those Columbians. You didn't have to do that Mayhem!"

Mayhem stops dead in the middle of her tirade and moves within inches of Walena's face. Mayhem's face seems contoured and her body appears enlarged with her eyes focusing on nothing but Walena's whole presence.

"I killed dat niggah cuz he couldn't take dat shit back. You is a shallow hoe. I know you wit Jesus. Hell, God's voice and presence spoke to me. Ms. Martha prayed that the Angels would help my moms."

Mayhem swallowed slowly like her saliva was thick with blood. She struggled but was able to capture her rage and hold it at level three out of ten. As she continued, she looked more impassioned and her tenor became luculent.

"Y'all boy was a pervert. Dat muthafucka played wit children sexually. Like dat low life Peddy, Petey boy was filming babies getting sexed for perverted dirty dick muthafucka's all over the world. He sold dat shit for his mob and I found out from Lil' Bit wit Ruby. He told her dat it was some good pictures of little baby girls and young females jest like the pictures my no-good daddy used to take. Everybody better off wit PGomez dead!"

Big Girl laughed, "A'aight, we gonna git paid fo dat hit. Dem big guys made dat happen. Fuck'em, cause dat perverted freak niggah deserved to die."

Rickey was really scared now. If Mayhem smoked Gomez, she must have known he was the one running all the pornography for Keithland's organization. F-U asked Mayhem if she needed anything else since his cleanup crew was almost finished removing the bodies. Mayhem's phone rings again. This time, its Tyquan trying to tell her about the judges' family offer again. Mayhem won't answer the call. She looked at Rickey and barks an order at him.

"Rick, if you want to live you best understand you going to talk on television about dat Keithland niggah."

Rickey can't believe his ears. He is wondering which would be worse; getting killed right this moment or a slow death while waiting for Keithlands' bounty to any street denizen in the third city. Walena is now hysterical. She tells Mayhem they won't do it.

Mayhem laughed, "bitch yaw ain't running dis thing, ok? All of the information you stole is on some computer shit, a'aight?" Walena hedges trying to stall until Mayhem and two of her young girls place guns to the head and groin area of Rickey Ricardo.

"Alright Mayhem, I understand. I will give you all the info on a flash drive. The feds need all of this material and that deal means we are not going public."

Big Girl nodded in agreement, "Dat works, Mayhem. Those files will end Keithland's world."

Mayhem decides that Big Girl can do what is needed between Walena and Rick. Without much fanfare, she takes a new stolen Toyota Camry from the building of F-U's hideaway.

"Big Girl, git our dough from dem girls Rita, for smoking sorry ass Gomez. Take care of dese snitches as long as dey do it right. I need Keithland out of business forever." The sound of a text message comes from Tyquan's phone. It's Xavier. Mayhem just stared at the text.

"Mayhem, need to talk. It's not the end of world. Sorry about Jeranda. She wants you to be well and happy."

The news cycle had yet to include any information regarding Jeranda Jefferson's death. The death of the judge and the FBI, or Pete Gomez has not yet been uncovered. The mission now, for Mayhem, is to get paid for taking the rats for Keithland.

Chapter 27: Revelations at the Scene of the Crime

Another call comes in and its Big Tiny for Keithland, "Mayhem got all of yo bank girl. My man Greg will meet you right now over at China House."

Mayhem takes a small cadre of her loyal crew. Two of the girls are just out of the army. Both girls did three-year stints with all sorts of special training. The two are twins, Reese and Nicki Jackson. Their specialty, over the past year, is robbing armored trucks. They have toys like grenades and AK-47s and lots of other military equipment, stolen from a nearby National Guard Armory. Reese, the younger of the twins, is well built with noticeable biceps. The other twin is the training partner of Big Girl. Nicki is the proverbial tomboy. She is always willing to engage in combat. They have two stops. The first is a meeting with Keithlands' rep and then it's off to see Peddy Jefferson. Mayhem knows that the streets will be filled with law enforcement once they realize that there is no more talk about Judge Ewing or the FBI agent. She instructs her driver to speed it up.

"Git it on. Our monay is waiting."

Greg is a key enforcer and a hitman for Tiny. His job is to pay Mayhem with more than just cash. Greg has a reputation for ruthlessness. His approach is straightforward and unrelenting.
As the white Navigator pulled into the parking lot next to China House, Greg signals to his comrades to get ready. Mayhem gets out of the Navigator with a new gun; a Sig 45 in one hand, hidden under her coat. In her boots is a pearl handled blade. As Greg greets her, she walks right into his space, hitting his massive chest. Greg is outdone with this young females' boldness.

"Damn big boy. You need a bra. Yo male titties is sagging." Greg is not amused with the young Mayhem.

"Whoa young girl. Back the fuck up. Yo monay is in the Denali. What is that you got in my chest?"

To his disbelief, Mayhem has her compact 45 in the center of his chest. The bulky gray and red sweatshirt reveal a heavy-duty bulletproof vest. To her surprise, like a powerful bull, he pushes Mayhem back and grabs her by the throat. In one swoop, her long legs pulled back with her pointed toe wicked witch of the east boots and she connects with his testicles. He dropped her. Suddenly, another black Denali pulled in front of Mayhem's Navigator. Its pure chaos, looking like, despite her great field goal kick, Greg and his boys got the drop on Mayhem. The driver in the Navigator is helpless. Greg is moaning as he tries to straighten up. He is pissed.

"Heard you was a little fighting bitch. I got something fo your ass."

Mayhem is staggering and is about to fall to the ground. Greg throws a large, dirty brown duffel bag in front of her.

"Dats yo monay bitch. Too bad you ain't gonna live to spend it."

While their Navigator is blocked by the Denali, there is one man with a large caliber rifle standing behind Greg. The other man is sitting behind the wheel of the Denali. Both men are turning to begin the end of Mayhem and her girls. Swoosh, swoosh and swoosh sounds can be heard in the air. Greg's face is locked with a look of disbelief. Both of his boys heads are opened up like honey dew melons. Each man has a single bullet hole directly between the eyes. Greg's bullet hole leaves him speechless. All three fall over where they had been standing.

Mayhem smiles and appears pleased by the carnage, "Dat girl Nicki is a shooting ass bitch, thanks to that Recon Sniping School."

Using a small walkie-talkie that her sister is holding in her hand in the Navigator, she corrects Mayhem, "Naw, dat be Sniper School for Recon Team One, U.S. Army. I'm a bad bitch."
As the Navigator makes another quick getaway, Mayhem calls Big Girl.

"We out, Nicki was across the street. Just like you said, Keithland and Tiny played me like a weak ass hoe female."
The final scheduled destination was to go and meet Peddy.

Mayhem called her brother Homicide telling everybody that, "Boy got our bank on da way."

She told Homi to, "Tell Daddy dat Keithland tried to smoke my black ass."

While she gloated about the loot, she found more Keithland trickery. Reese taps her on the shoulder with a face full of trepidation.

Chapter 27: Revelations at the Scene of the Crime

"I know this ain't a million. Not even close to a million. I dun counted maybe $25,000 and ain't much more in here."

Mayhem goes ballistic and begins yelling, "See, Big Girl said dis muthafucka ain't no big Willie. I did the contract and dis niggah is cheating me?"

Whipping out her phone she rings up Keithland.

"Hey, is dis Keithland? Well, yo boys fucked up and so did you. Greg is dead, fucking wit dis female. Now git my full pay right away or I'm up dat ass like a Gerbel BITCH!!"

Keithland is dumbfounded. He can't believe his ears. Tiny? He repeats Tiny's name, over and over.

His phone rings and Tiny is livid, "Dat little crazy ho bitch dun smoked my boys. We out here and dey in there dead. Not just dead but shot between the damn eyes. What the fuck is going on?"

Attorney Perry is shaking his head and says, "Keithland, I had a bad feeling. I told you. A complete maniac raised that girl. You cannot have this girl running around. The truth is, we have absolutely no proof she did the job. Suppose Walena and Rick are just her hostages?"

Keithland is even more puzzled. It is clear by the look on his face that he doesn't understand how this could have happened. He begins to wonder what kinds of effects being raised by the devil could have on his, now grown, progeny. James Perry is worried. His feelings included the fact that loose ends with the mafia, politicians, and Peddy were not good.

It's midnight and Mayhem gets a call from Ms. Martha. She takes the call as the crew drives to Smokes'. Ms. Martha gingerly begins to discuss her mothers' funeral. Mayhem is not really talkative. She listened to Ms. Martha discuss her mothers transition and showed little, if any, emotion.

"Your mother is resting in a good place May. You need to get some rest. This is a good time to reflect. Let's meet at my house. I can fix up the spare room for you. We can pray, talk, and think this thing out. Its time to re-think your life."

Mayhem breaks down and begins to share all of the bad news with Ms. Martha. The news is earth shattering; even for the devout and faithful Christian activist. She admits to Martha that when her mother died, she went crazy.

"I killed dat old judge and I killed dat FBI agent. Nobody cared bout us and my moms is dead. All dose important people think they are so damn important and they think we ain't nothing if they even think about us at all. Xavier Long told me dat poor people's deaths are not important to society. So, I figure that dat damn Judge Ewing ain't important to us. I smoked all dose people who are important to y'all. DC College didn't think bout my moms. DeShaba is dead and my Moms is dead. Do you hear me Ms. Martha?"

Ms. Martha is in deep prayer. She can feel the presence of another being within the sphere of Mayhem.

Mayhem, unaware of what Ms. Martha can feel, continues to talk to her, "Face it Ms. Martha. My daddy is from the devil. He is evil. You are good and I am no good. Me and my brothers are killers and my daddy killed my mother. Oops!! Ms. Martha, I got to go. I'm going to pay my daddy back."

The phone hung up and Ms. Martha fell to her knees. Her prayers intensified and became deeper. Her prayers were abashed with humility and forgiveness.

She whispered as if an angel might be eavesdropping, "Jesus, this child is misguided. She needs us more than ever."

Except for the music blaring, as always, in the dimly lit atmosphere, Smokes' is quiet. Standing at the pool table were Homicide, Assault, Rape and Felonious. They looked sad but not sad enough for their sister Mayhem. Carrying the duffel bag into the front bar, she threw the money filled bag onto the pool table.

Smiling like a happy being she announced, "Well my brothas, here is our pay. Split it up wit yo daddy. Homi, did you hit yo moms wit Peddy?"

The brothers are tearing the duffel bag apart. Homicide doesn't hear his sisters' question.A dark figure in the rear of the bar is standing at the door. Peddy comes out of the Men's' room laughing. He opens another cold beer. He looked at his sons scuffling over the duffle bag of money on the pool table. His eyes are large and almost dilated with a yellow tint.

Chapter 27: Revelations at the Scene of the Crime

Looking at Mayhem, he laughed and said, "Sorry bout your mother. It was an accident."

Mayhem is staring at him.

She asked, "Where is dat monay? The monay you beat her for!"

Pedwell doesn't like the tone or the question. He takes a sip of beer and released a nasty look.

"Watch yo mouth girl. Monay is right here where it belongs. Don't get it twisted Mayhem. I am your daddy. You is my hoe. Yo mammy WAS my hoe. A pimp can do whatever he wants wit his hoes!!"

As Peddy continues his rebuke of his daughter, Mayhem walks up real close and fires her 45 directly into his penis. The music was turned up so loud that it acted as a silencer. The shot was barely audible. Falling to his knees in anguish and excruciating pain, he looks at Mayhem in disbelief. Another plunked sound emits from the pool table.

It's Homicide falling on the pool table with a single bullet hole between his eyes. With identical exactness of a bullet between the eyes, like sitting ducks, the other brothers dropped dead. A dark, female figure walks from the rear door with her rifle in hand. Pedwell Jefferson is looking at his malcontent brood stacked near the pool table. His knees are smashed and his breathing is labored.

With an air of calmness, she looks directly into Pedwell's eyes and says, "You ain't my father. God told me that. An Angel told me to kill yo ass. It was the Death Angel."

Peddy begs, and cries, "I DIDN'T MEAN TO KILL YO MAMMA. PLEASE MAYHEM!!"

The bass laden sound of a hip-hop track pulsated around the room while Tupac could be heard in the background proclaiming, "I see death around the corner." The next sound was an audible BOOM! When the sound subsided, EVIL WAS DEAD and the evil was Peddy Jefferson.

She took out her cell phone and, using the camera feature, she began flicking pictures, one after the other. She looked around for the owner and finally saw him hiding behind the bar.

Made in the USA
Coppell, TX
21 March 2023

14540905R00201